Mr Pussy

Mr Pussy

Before I Forget to Remember

Alan Amsby
with David Kenny

NEW ISLAND

MR PUSSY
First published in 2016 by
New Island Books
16 Priory Hall Office Park
Stillorgan
Co. Dublin
Republic of Ireland

www.newisland.ie

PRINT ISBN: 978-1-84840-567-7
EPUB ISBN: 978-1-84840-568-4
MOBI ISBN: 978-1-84840-569-1

Typeset by POLAND, PUP Introkar, www.introkar.com
Cover design by Kate Gaughran

10 9 8 7 6 5 4 3 2 1

In memory of my boyhood chum, Derek Banks, who died far too young. I wish we could have grown old together.

Contents

Foreword

by Rory O'Neill (aka Panti Bliss)

As a popular T-shirt says, 'It takes balls to be a fairy', but to be a fairy in full drag in 1970s' Ireland (and with an English accent to boot!) took more than mere balls. It took nerves of steel, a mischievous sense of humour, a delight in the ridiculous, a steely determination, a quick wit, a brazen disrespect for authority, and a fabulous wardrobe. And luckily Alan Amsby had all that and more. He may have started out as a 'mod' in the 1960s, but 'Ireland's leading misleading lady' was, and remains, a true punk.

The first time I became aware of Mr Pussy was some time in the 1970s when, as a boy who felt awkward and different in a small town in Co. Mayo, a glamorous and exotic gal with an equally exotic name shimmied onto our family's black-and-white television screen. I have long since forgotten what the show was and by whom she was being interviewed, but I never forgot her. I couldn't have told you then what it was about this glamorous creature that captured me, nor why I immediately felt an exciting frisson of recognition—as if a small part of me was being reflected back at me for maybe the first time, the same part of me that usually made me feel awkward and different, but here was being reflected back at me as something exciting and fun and (despite the monochrome screen) colourful. This gorgeous creature wasn't ashamed of that part of her—she had thrown glitter on it and celebrated it. I was intrigued and impressed, and have remained intrigued and impressed by my 'Aunty Pussy' ever since.

One night many years later, having just returned to Dublin in the mid 1990s after a few years living abroad, I nervously approached her at the bar of the Kitchen nightclub in the basement of the Clarence Hotel. At the time, Pussy was the reigning doyenne of late-night Dublin, her Mr Pussy's Café De Luxe the epicentre of Dublin's new early Celtic Tiger nightlife scene. As always, she looked gorgeous: sequins spilling to the floor and blonde curls falling onto her shoulders, from which a fur coat slid languidly. I mumbled something about how much I admired her, and she looked me up and down—a skinny 'baby drag' wearing God-knows-what and a cheap wig—and like an imperious queen, she dismissed me gracefully. And I loved her even more for that!

But over time (I guess after she had decided I had paid my dues and wasn't going anywhere!) Pussy decided to take me in. She became 'Aunty Pussy', always encouraging me and following my career with interest. Always ready with words of advice or a gentle admonishment. She was kind and generous to me, which she didn't need to be, because whether she knew it or not she'd already given me and people like me a lot. By the simple but courageous act of being her glorious unapologetic self at a time when being herself (and himself) wasn't easy or always welcome, she opened a door and made space for people like me in the country she adopted. And for that I will always be entirely grateful.

And it's about time Alan finally wrote this book! He has enough stories for ten books, and I've been lucky enough to hear plenty of them over a drink. Or ten.

Chapter One

The Kitten in the Pram

'Move your arse, Bill. I need to take a wee, and Alan needs to be changed.'

My father ran his fingers through his Brylcreemed hair in mock exasperation and looked at my mother, who was almost cross-eyed with gin and a full bladder.

'Change him? Change him? We've only just bleedin' got him.'

Mum threw her head back and gurgled like a freshly plunged sink. I laughed too, not understanding the joke, but absorbing their good humour like a terry nappy.

'Oh, Bill. Get us a taxi, will you? I'll never make it home.'

Dad protested.

'Taxi? After what we've just spent in the battle cruiser [boozer]? No way, love. Shanks's mare.'

'Okay then, you tight old git, I've a better idea…' Mum hoisted me out of the buggy and squeezed herself into the small, rickety frame. The wheels creaked, which said more about the state of the pram than her weight. My mum was a lovely looking woman with a petite, slim figure.

'Go on, then. Get pushing.' Dad laughed, gave the pram an almighty shove and set off at full tilt down Peckham High Street. The G-force (or whatever it's called) sent my mum and me into the

1

back of the pram. She hooted, and I wet myself. (Just a little. I was a very polite two-year-old.)

'Ro-o-o-o-oll out the barrel …' Dad sang the old music-hall song in the style of Hank Williams as he shoved us down the road.

'Shut up about barrels, will you? I drank at least two of them. And mind the bumps. Oh, me waterworks!'

This is my earliest memory: Mum, Dad and me returning from a pub through south London, the sound of laughter ricocheting off the bombed-out buildings. We were a tight, happy little unit. Well, Mum was tight with gin, at any rate. I still recall how much they loved each other. If anyone looked at Mum sideways, backways or whatever, Dad would roll up his sleeves and there would be a dust-up.

I remember him flooring a fellow for giving him cheek on the way back from a night out. He was huge, my dad. A lorry driver who looked like John Wayne, without the mincing walk. I always thought John Wayne walked like a man with piles and the trots. Whenever I attempted to mimic him as a kid, I ended up walking like a bar-room tart. I was never cut out to be butch. Or a bitch. My parents saw to that. They raised me well: by example, being kind and loving. While Dad was tough and rough-edged, and Mum was a tartar when crossed, they were never cruel or nasty. As the cliché says, they hadn't a bad bone in their bodies.

Mum and Dad met when she was sixteen and working in a tobacconist's shop. He fell for her immediately. Well, she was a cracker. They went out on a couple of dates, but then she broke it off. 'I'll get you in the end,' he vowed. A few months later, Mum was passing Elephant and Castle on the bus with her friend Eva, and got off to see if he was hanging around with his mates. He was. They took up where they had left off, got engaged and tied the knot. Then a short-arsed Austrian painter decided to pick a fight with

Europe. Dad was never one to miss out on a good scrap, so he threw his lot in with old Montgomery and headed off to Africa to stick it to the Hun. He was gone for six years.

I don't know how many German arses he kicked. He never spoke about the war in all the years I knew him. I can only suppose he saw some dreadful things. Eventually, Hitler did the decent thing and topped himself, and Dad came home. He quickly made up for lost time, and little Alan was born.

Mum was in her thirties when she had me, and she used to parade me around as she thought that having a baby made her look younger. But she *did* look young. She was a gorgeous woman, very glamorous, and so smart, acerbic and witty. I once asked her why I didn't have any brothers or sisters. She said, 'Oh, I did the sex thing once and didn't like it.' We had that kind of banter.

I don't recall anything about my early, early, early years, except that before the 1960s everything was in black and white. The streets, the sky, the people. And there was a touch of grey and yellow too. I remember the fog. In 1952 a particularly nasty cloud of it shrouded London, causing the deaths of around 12,000 people. I remember the fog of my childhood as being straight out of a Sherlock Holmes film, and when it was a pea-souper a man would walk ahead of the bus carrying a lamp. He was there to prevent stupid gits from walking under London's famous red double-deckers. He was an eerie sight in a halo of yellow light.

'Oooooooooooh, there's the bogeyman coming up from the river to snatch us,' Dad would say. 'But don't worry, son; I'll give him a smack in his chops if he comes near us.' I would then snuggle in under his arm, all safe and happy to have this lovely, hard, decent lump of a man there to protect me.

When he wasn't off driving his lorry or protecting me from ghoulies, Dad would take me to Clapham Common to play soccer and cricket, both of which I was very bad at. 'On your head, son,' he would call, lobbing the ball in my direction, intending me to head it.

'What's on my head, Dad?' I would reply, feeling my hair for insects while the ball was making a perfect arc towards my face … THWACK.

'You all right, our Alan?' He would try not to laugh. And he always let me bowl at cricket for this reason. Dad never showed any sign of disappointment in my lack of male sporting prowess. He just used to smile a smile that said: he is who he is, and I love him.

Dad was a character and popular with his mates down the pub. If they were ever in trouble, physical or financial, he would help out with a closed fist or one full of money. We lived in Peckham, which everybody knows is the fictional home of Del Boy and Rodney Trotter. There was actually a Mandela House—Winnie Mandela— and it was a blind school, not a block of flats. I knew all the places John Sullivan references in *Only Fools and Horses*. He and I went to the same school, although I didn't know him personally.

There were plenty of Del Boys and spivs knocking about at that time, still selling black-market luxury items. Anything you wanted, they could get off the back of a lorry—even guns. This was post-war London, and as kids we used to play on the bomb sites. For us it was a playground; for my parents it was a tragic landscape because of all the neighbours who were killed during the Blitz. Next door to my school there was a church. It was bombed out, and I used to climb through the rubble to get to classes. In the afternoons we used to play there—with real revolvers and army uniforms. Tin hats were prized as there was a lot of stone-throwing. To us, the sites were battlefields with trenches. Our guns were not loaded of course, and had been brought back from Europe by demobbed servicemen. Most of these were sold on to the wide boys, but some were kept as souvenirs, and we would borrow them to play with.

It wasn't all soldiers and guns, though. We would also play knock-down ginger and all the traditional games. (I was 'ginger', but wasn't easy to knock down.) We used to tie a string from one doorknob to another and run away. When the occupants tried to open the door, their neighbour's knocker would rattle and they would try to answer their door. A tug-of-war would then ensue between the two houses, one door half-opening, the other banging shut. It was hilarious to watch. Try it sometime.

Only three million British homes had a TV by 1954. We were one of the few families in Peckham to have one. Not that I spent all day glued to it like today's kids. We were outdoor children. The streets were safe back then (if you avoided the collapsing bomb ruins). Parents didn't worry themselves sick like they do now about marauding gangs of paedophiles or traffic. In 1950 there were two million cars in Britain. The odds of getting knocked down were a lot less than they are today. Mum was so confident of my safety that, when I was little, she would send me around to the landlady to pay the rent. The woman used to give me an old penny with Queen Vic on it to buy sweets. The rent was a pound a week. It doesn't sound like much, but in the 1940s a pound could buy you twelve pints of beer and ninety-six first-class stamps. I wasn't around in the 1940s and had to look that up. In the 1950s it would get you twenty-six pints of milk. I can't remember anyone ever actually buying twenty-six pints of milk all at once. It's called 'context', dear.

I know all old geezers say this, but it really was a more law-abiding time. There were police boxes everywhere, like the one in *Dr Who*. You could see the reassuring blue light through the fog. Or if you were walking home late you always knew there would be a night watchman around the next corner, sitting in his hut beside a coke fire, protecting his roadworks and watching out for trouble.

Old ladies didn't get mugged, and telephone boxes were fully glazed with intact directories and a paybox full of coins. We would never have dared to vandalise anything. We feared people in authority such as policemen and teachers. Even park keepers. We all knew that we would get a smack around the ear for misbehaving, and then another when we were brought home in disgrace.

That said, my parents never hit me when I misbehaved. Mum, who was the disciplinarian, had a 'special look' that she deployed when she wanted to terrify me—along with the other kids in the house we lived in. There were three families living there with two children upstairs, me in the middle, and a young fellow called Reggie downstairs. We were a little gang, scraping our knees, scrapping among ourselves and sharing sweets. We were popular with the grown-ups as we were good kids. We used to mess about, but were never *too* annoying. Neighbours used to look out for each others' children then. They even bathed us. One thing we loved doing was climbing up on the old air-raid shelter in our yard while 'Uncle' Joe from upstairs would run a hose out of his window and shower us on sunny days.

'Enjoying the hose-down, kids?'

'Yessss,' we'd shout back.

'That's not a hose I'm using …'

He had a filthy sense of humour did Uncle Joe.

Aside from outdoor showers, we kids all shared the same bath. Not at the same time, it has to be said. It was a galvanised metal tub that was kept in the yard and brought in at bathtime. We bathed on different days to the adults: grown-ups were always first. I can still see the fire blazing away in the grate and the front room full of steam, and hear the sound of my mum yodelling away as I did my ablutions, while Colin from upstairs awaited his turn. By the time I'd finished splashing suds all over the lino there was no water left for him.

After I'd been towel-dried before the fire, we'd have our tea, which was nearly always stew. Mum loved her stew, just like her mum before her. I still have the plates she used. They're hanging on my wall here in Dublin. They're late Georgian and probably worth a few bob, but I'd never sell them. Meat was scarce back then due to rationing, so everything went into the pot: dumplings, small pieces of lamb's neck, carrots, toenails.... Okay, that last bit's made up, although there was the occasional varnished fingernail. Mum used to say that her stew improved with age. Maybe it did, or maybe it was just wishful thinking. (I think I once spotted one of Sir Walter Raleigh's original spuds at the bottom of the pot.)

'It improves with age, just like you, Mum,' I would coo angelically, hoping to score some points.

'Are you saying your mother looks like a shrivelled up old lamb's neck?' Dad would lean across the table and pretend-glare at me.

'No, no … I meant that she …' I would stammer.

'Ah, leave him alone, Bill. You've a head like a dried-up old dumpling yourself.'

We'd all laugh, and I'd spatter gravy down my napkin. God, I loved my gravy. The thought of it still makes me hanker for London's pie and mash shops, where you could devour minced beef pies, spuds and parsley sauce (which we called 'liquor'), with salt and pepper and vinegar. I also miss jellied eels. If you think that sounds like the most disgusting meal imaginable, then remember that the Irish invented coddle—a foul concoction of milk and boiled bangers and other assorted muck. Someone should open a pie and mash or a jellied eels shop in Dublin. They would make a fortune out of English stag parties: it's great soakage grub.

As I've said, this was the age of rationing. The queues for basic food items began in 1940 (earlier in Germany, would you believe?) and British mums used to have to make ends meet as best they could. Less than a third of the food available in the UK at the start of the war was produced at home. Enemy ships targeted merchant vessels, preventing supplies from reaching us. The swine.

The first foods to be rationed were sugar, bacon, tea, meat and butter. Soap was rationed to one bar a month, and up until 1941 you could have only one egg a week. People used dried egg powder instead (to cook with, not to wash with, obviously). One packet of that horrible stuff was equal to a dozen eggs. This was fine if you liked them scrambled, but they were impossible to boil or fry.

Paper, petrol, washing powder and loads of things we take for granted these days were rationed. Spuds weren't though. You could have any number of potatoes. You just couldn't have chips, as oil was hard to get. Then there was Spam, which everyone has heard about, and the snoek, a fish from South Africa, which nobody has seen or heard of since. One person's weekly allowance of the basics would be:

1 fresh egg
4oz margarine
4oz bacon
2oz butter
2oz tea
1oz cheese
8oz sugar

Meat was rationed by price, so cheaper cuts were popular. Points could be saved up to buy cereals, tinned foods, biscuits, jam and dried fruit.

There was no Lidl or Tesco; you went to different shops for different items. Greengrocers did fruit and veg; ordinary grocers did jam and tea and cheese; butchers did meat; fishmongers fish, etc. There was no wandering around with a basket or trolley; you were served by the shopkeeper from behind his/her counter. It was always a good idea to 'keep in' with the local grocer, who might hold extras for favoured customers.

Many people grew vegetables at home, and kept chickens, ducks and rabbits to eat. The rabbits loved their carrots, and so did the kids. There was a poster character called 'Doctor Carrot' which was used to encourage children to eat more of them. Here's a fact you may not know: carrots don't actually help you to see in the dark. That was a myth dreamed up by the Ministry of Propaganda to explain why the RAF was having such great success shooting down German planes at night. The truth was that the air force had introduced top secret on-board radar, which was giving the Bosch fliers hell. Whether Hitler believed this rubbish is unknown, but the mothers of England did, and carrots became a staple in most meals. They were sold as 'treats', and it wasn't unusual to see children eating carrots on sticks instead of ice cream or lollies. We were an ingenious bunch back then. So ingenious that women used to paint gravy browning on their bare legs as a replacement for silk stockings.

Although I wasn't born at the time to hear her, Marguerite Patten's cooking tips on the Home Service drew six million listeners daily. Housewives were taught how to be creative, using 'mock' recipes which included 'cream' (margarine, milk and cornflour) and 'goose' (lentils and breadcrumbs).

You'd think that with all this rationing the health of the poor would have been a problem, but it actually improved as people were encouraged to eat more protein, pulses and fruit and veg. Babies, expectant mums and the sick got extra nutrients like milk, orange juice and cod liver oil (yuck).

Despite the hardship and the queues, nobody complained about rationing. It continued right up until 1954 as a large number of our dads were still in the armed forces—and, of course, the economy was buggered.

Anyway, this young kitten had to be different to all the other sturdy post-war kids. I got very ill when I was six and nearly died.

Mum had done everything she could to keep my health up to scratch, but sometimes kids are just susceptible to illness, despite the best efforts of their parents. One of those best efforts was my mum's advice always to wear a scarf and a hat to stop my hair getting wet. 'You'll catch your death,' she'd say. Mums are great at giving mad advice like that. When did a child last get its arm broken as a result of upsetting a swan? When did someone last suffocate on account of swallowing chewing gum? And that is before you consider how difficult it would actually be to have someone's eye out with a ladder, etc. Becoming an adult largely consists of coming to terms with the fact that most of what your parents have told you is utter crap. I don't know if anyone has ever actually died after getting their hair wet, unless they stuck their damp head up against an electricity pylon. Or fell overboard. You'd definitely get your hair wet and die if you fell overboard. Well, I did get my hair wet, and I did nearly die, so she was almost right. I didn't just come down with pneumonia; I was struck by DOUBLE pneumonia … and whooping cough … and jaundice … and all at the same time. It was horrible, fighting for air and burning up with a fever. I remember Mum and Dad standing beside the bed and me looking up and saying, 'I'm Jesus. Mum, you're Mary, and Dad, you're Joseph.' I was delirious. Dad went into the toilet and cried so hard that the neighbours came to see what the matter was.

My parents weren't religious, and didn't send for a priest like folk do in Ireland. I don't know where I got the Jesus, Mary and Joseph stuff from either. Mum was hardly a virgin (as she had given birth to me), and I'm no Jesus—although I've been crucified with a hangover on more than one occasion. Dad came closest to sanctity as, like Jesus's stepdad, he was very good with wood. (He built me a shed around the back of the house once, and also made me the most gorgeous US cavalry fort. Wasn't Jesus crucified on Mount Cavalry? Or am I just bad at spelling?)

Anyway, the good news is that I pulled through (obviously), and lived to tell the tale here. The other good news was that all my aunts and uncles came to visit me and brought presents. I swear that the eighty gallons of Lucozade I drank over that period saved me. I even held on to my cough for longer than I should have to squeeze all I could out of my sickness. Eventually, Dad kicked my arse out of bed and shunted me off to school, just in time for the Christmas break.

That was the first Christmas I recall clearly. I woke up at about 6 a.m., and there was a pillowcase at the end of my bed, stuffed with gifts. Well, maybe not stuffed, but to a six-year-old it was Santa's grotto. Before sweet rationing ended in 1953, the most treasured thing in your Christmas stocking—or pillow case—was a small two-ounce bar of chocolate. I got one of those and ate half, putting the rest under my blanket for safe keeping. Later, when I went down for breakfast, Dad nearly threw up: 'For Christ's sake, love, I thought we'd potty trained the child.' The chocolate was stuck to the seat of my pyjama bottoms. He nearly fainted when I picked a lump off and stuck it in my mouth.

The rest of my gifts were unmemorable, except for one that looked like an odd-shaped bicycle pump. Great, there's a bike waiting for me downstairs, I thought, ripping off the wrapping. It was a plastic trumpet. Despite what you may think, I was delighted, and woke the house up playing what I reckoned was *Colonel Bogey*, but in reality sounded like a bogie being blown.

'Shut up, you little bastard.'

Uncle Joe upstairs was in that purgatorial stage between drunkenness and hangover.

'Sorry, Uncle Joe.'

I blew a raspberry through the trumpet.

Later, we went around to Gran's for Christmas lunch, and I was told I could bring my favourite present. I took the trumpet and tooted along with my extended family as they belted out 'My Old Man (Said Follow the Van)' on her rickety piano. My mum's family were all musical and theatrical. Her aunt, Florrie Felden, who owned a pub in Vauxhall, had been a former music-hall artist. That's where I get it from. Blame her.

Everyone would stand around the piano, drinking beer and doing their 'turn'. All the wartime camaraderie was still there among the grown-ups. They were proud of their country and its part in Hitler's downfall. They knew everybody on their street, and felt that they 'belonged'.

After the singing, the oldies would play cards. That was a serious business, and the children would all be sent out to the parlour to play. Or fight. Or both. Despite all the rationing and hardship, Londoners liked to party. Uncle Joe used to have parties all the time. He had a wig and would dress up as a woman to entertain the guests.

'Hey Joe, as a woman you look pretty ...'

'Oh, yes?'

'... pretty fucking horrendous.'

Everybody loved a good drag act back then, and they still do. I used to watch him getting ready. Joe was gay, but nobody knew it. Not even his wife or kids. I think he was probably the one who initially set me on the road to drag superstardom. He played a fairly big role in my upbringing after Dad left us. The last memory I have of my father is of him waving to me.

'You all right, son?'

'I'm fine, Dad,' I shouted back. He was a good nine yards away. The man next to him groaned a 'shut yer gob' in my direction. Dad, in turn, growled back at him. It wasn't his usual growl though. It sounded like it was struggling to climb out of his mouth.

The sister on duty patted me on the head and gently led me back out into the corridor. The smell of disinfectant still clings to my memory's hooter. Years later, whenever I arrived in a freshly cleaned and disinfected dressing room (which was rare), I would think of my dad in that hospital bed and ten-year-old me waving at him across the ward floor, my voice echoing among the bedpans and kidney dishes. They didn't allow kids on the wards back then, and he was right at the end, in more ways than one. He had been taken in with a burst appendix. Mum had sent me to stay with my cousins while he convalesced.

The convalescence didn't last long. 'Peritonitis,' I heard my auntie whisper to one of her friends when I returned to her house. 'Blood poisoning.'

Two days later, I was brought home. I sat in my chair and saw Dad's ring on Mum's finger. I knew that something was wrong.

'What's up, Mum? Why did Dad give you his ring?'

She kneeled down beside my chair. 'I have something to tell you, son …'

Seven little words have never hurt so much.

Dad, my hero and playmate, was dead. Mum and I were on our own. I cried for days. There were times when I felt like I was drowning. Eventually, the torrent became a trickle. Mum knew that life had to go on. I think I knew it too. What else was there for me to do? The kitten had to start growing up.

Years later, when I was visiting Peckham, I popped upstairs to see Joe, who was an elderly man by then.

'Did your mum ever tell you that we have a ghost in the house?' She hadn't.

'It's your dad, Alan. I've seen him.' I felt a chill.

'He's still here. He never left you.'

Chapter Two

The Cat-O'-Nine-Tails

'Roger Green, stand up.'

The assembly hall stank of stale breath, wax polish, rotten apples, wet dog and sweat. The latter aroma emanated from just one pupil—Roger Green. He was sweating like a piggy in a sausage factory. You could literally smell his fear. The rest of us were giddy with nervous excitement at the prospect of what was about to happen to him.

Roger was a small boy for his age, with large jug ears and a dray horse's fringe. He also had a stammer and rolled his R's, which was very unfortunate. To look the way he did and have a speech impediment was bad enough in a school where you could be wedgied just for wearing polished shoes (this was considered 'lah-di-dah' and pretentious). To have TWO speech impediments was considered plain inflammatory. Roger spoke like a cross between an anti-aircraft gun and Jonathan Ross, and might as well have had a sign pinned to his arse saying 'Kick Here'. Whenever the big lads saw him crossing the yard they would shout, 'Wedgie Wodjah!' Thinking back, I can't understand why his folks didn't change his name from Roger to, say, 'John', when he started to speak. Cruel bastards.

Roger had been caught stealing conkers from a display cabinet in the school. Most schools had trophy cabinets; we had conker cabinets.

Actually, it was probably a science display or something. Who cares? Theft of any kind—even one as pathetic as this—was punishable by caning or expulsion. Even our school, which was as strict as they came, couldn't throw a boy out for stealing conkers. It would have been a hard one to explain. And so Roger was brought before the whole school to be caned. The poor chap shuffled down the length of the hall towards the raised stage and climbed the stairs with his head bowed as if he were about to be crucified. I wasn't brought up to be religious, but one wag, who had obviously been to Sunday school, picked up on the Jesus, Barabbas and Pontius Pilate theme. As Roger reached the top of the stairs, the smart-arse shouted: 'Welease Wodjah!' It made the entire assembly corpse for at least two minutes. This actually happened, and I have to point out that it was a couple of decades before Monty Python had even dreamed of *The Life of Brian*.

The punishment was horrible. I can still see the headmistress, Miss McGregor, standing in the assembly hall, waiting to give the order to begin the flogging—like Captain Bligh from *Mutiny on the Bounty*. She treated Roger like he was a sailor who had stolen water from the ship's barrel. To her right stood our sullen form master, Mr Tizer. He looked miserable, as usual. We had nicknamed him 'Tizer' because of his sparkling personality. If it were raining champagne, sad old Tizer would have left the house with an umbrella. But he was far from the worst of them. I liked him, and he seemed to have a soft spot for me.

Miss McGregor, on the other hand, was only ever interested in finding pupils' soft spots—and applying a cane to them. She was a complete psychopath; a sour old sow who suffered from chronic piles. We knew this because she kept an inflatable ring covered with a headscarf under her desk, and would slip it onto her chair whenever she had to sit down (she suffered from varicose veins too). She was a real horror when the veins and piles were flaring up. She must have been having a bad day on this occasion. 'Begin the caning,' she said through gritted teeth. Roger screamed and screamed as the bamboo thwacked off his backside. He was eight. Then, when we thought he'd had enough, she said, 'More.' I lost count of the blows he received. As I said, my mum never hit me; she just gave me her look. Her dad did the same to her. You don't need to beat kids up to punish them.

Once McGregor had deemed his punishment sufficient, she dismissed the assembly, and Roger shuffled painfully off to class, snot and tears streaking the front of his jumper. Mr Tizer looked as though he was about to cry too. I still get angry when I think of the state Roger was in over bloody conkers.

He got his own back eventually, though. Months later, Old Sow McGregor sat down on her pile cushion at the start of assembly and leaped four feet in the air, howling like a banshee with nettles in her knickers. Roger had smuggled in five large conkers and gently deposited them in the centre hole of her inflatable ring. I say 'gently' because, unlike the conkers he had stolen, these were still in their green husk with their spikes on. McGregor had to take a week off sick, and never found out who had spiked her bottom.

Actually, that last bit isn't true. I just made it up. Life went on as normal. There was no payback, although we pupils shared scenarios like the above to make us feel better. Roger's punishment, and McGregor's lack of answerability, was an early lesson in the unfairness of life.

With such happy memories, would you be surprised to learn that I hated school? I disliked everything about it. The lessons in maths and Latin that I would never use, the defeated air of the teachers trying to fill young heads with facts, the frequent violence in the yard and the class … And the school dinners. My God they were disgusting. All I can recall is green slop, probably cabbage, and pink meat, probably bacon. Form master Tizer used to sit at the top of the table near the food counter as we queued for our meal.

Some of the poorer kids would sit near him because occasionally the dinner ladies would call 'seconds', and those at the top of the table always ate twice (if they had the stomach for it). They must have been hard up, those kids, to eat that muck. The only thing that was almost palatable was the spotted dick, and naturally I gravitated towards that.

When I wasn't in school I was very much a free agent. Mum was always working. After Dad died, she held down three jobs to support us. She would rise at 5 a.m. to go office cleaning, come home to get me ready for school, then head to the BHS to work as a cook, and at night she worked as a barmaid. Incredibly, she never looked worn out or frazzled. She had good genes, my mum.

She didn't remarry after Dad died, but she had boyfriends. I especially liked the ones who gave me ten bob when they came around—to bugger off.

At night, the neighbours took turns to look after me. Mum had a wonderful support network, and I had a wonderful childhood. I wanted for nothing. At weekends, when she wasn't working, Mum brought me out shopping, and I was always well dressed. I gravitated towards the more flamboyant clothes, but Mum wouldn't let me dress like a spiv in pinstripes.

A friend of hers brought me to get my hair done once as a treat. They tonged it (as opposed to tongued it), and I felt like a billion dollars. The next day I went to school with more waves than the English Channel, and loved all the attention I got. Unfortunately, it started to snow at lunchtime, and we had a snowball fight. My hairdo was ruined, and I was distraught. Mum spent half an hour re-rolling it with her fingers and pinning it up when I got home. My hair was naturally straight. Probably the only thing about me that was straight. I was the least boyish boy in Peckham, and I loathed sport. I've always been naturally thin and fit, and have never needed to run around fields chasing balls to keep my figure trim. It's all a load of macho nonsense. On Wednesdays, the other boys would pile into a bus to go and play a match somewhere. I'd slip away and head to the pie and mash shop. Nobody gave me any grief for that. Mind you, nobody wanted me on their team. You might think that I was picked on as a result of my lack of machismo, but I wasn't. I was a popular kid, and used to make my mates—and the school bullies—laugh.

Even the milkman knew 'Young Master Amsby', and enjoyed giving me a lift on his carthorse in the mornings on the way to school. I used to clown about for him doing Roy Rogers impressions. I suppose I was what you might call a 'character'. I had a lot of friends, and my two best mates were Clifford Inso and Roy Farrington. Roy was one of the toughest boys in school, but he used to look out for me. I think he may have had a bit of a crush on me, but nothing ever happened. We bunked off together every Friday afternoon and would go to each other's houses to listen to Elvis, Lonnie Donegan and Cliff Richard records, or go for pie and mash. I don't know how I kept my gorgeous figure eating all those pies.

I went away to scout camp when I was thirteen, and I think Roy was a bit lonely at the thought of me leaving. He came up to the back of the lorry where I was sitting and said, 'You have a good time.' He reached out to shake my hand, and I could feel something small and disc-shaped between my fingers. He had slipped me a half-crown—a small fortune. It was a very sweet gesture, both paternal and fraternal. I still don't know where he got the half-crown. Probably half-inched it.

On Saturdays, Roy and I would go to the cinema with a gang of other kids. One person would pay to get in, and then open the side door for the rest of us. Those mornings were pure bedlam. You could barely hear the films … *Zorro, Hopalong Cassidy* … with all the screaming and shouting. The ushers would go around with armbands and torches, and must have felt like clobbering us, but they didn't. We were their bread and butter, after all. I loved the idea of wearing an armband, like the usherettes and the prefects and monitors at school. Any excuse to dress up. The nearest I got was 'ink monitor', filling up the wells and giving out nibs. I'm not sure when exactly this desire to dress up actually started, but I think the seed was sown when I saw Uncle Joe upstairs pull on his wig for the first time. I thought: *I'll have some of that.* I wanted to be noticed from an early age. Being an only child, I would spend hours in front of the mirror pretending to be different characters from the movies. My granny used to give me old costumes and wigs, which I used to dress up in. I always wanted to be someone special. I even used to parade up and down through Peckham in my scout's uniform. I had an enormous bayonet. No half measures for Alan.

I was thirteen when I tried out drag for the first time. Mum had bought herself a pair of new shoes. This was rare enough, as most of her money was spent on rent and me. I went to her room, pulled down the box containing the new red suede kitten heels, and placed her mirror at floor level to see myself. I put on her coat and clumped about and posed, but after a few minutes I felt the urge to try them on concrete. I think this was me subconsciously wanting to be seen wearing them.

I sneaked out the back door and walked around the muddy yard. I felt fabulous, and suddenly very adventurous, so I sashayed out onto the road and up and down a few times. I spotted a neighbour, Old Geranium Face (we called her that because she was always at her window, peering through the flowerbox), gawking at me. Mortified, I pegged it back home, stopping to run back and pick up the shoes every few yards as they kept falling off.

Two weeks later, Mum was going on a date, and took them down to wear them. She went mental when she saw that the soles and heels were already scuffed. 'Who the hell has been wearing my shoes?' she shouted, loudly enough for the neighbours to hear. I gulped, anticipating a good earful from her. I slowly walked to her room, and thought of Roger Green ascending his Calvary.

'Mum, I have to tell you something….' She was busily brushing the nap back into the suede.

'Give me a minute, Alan. That bloody Janet from upstairs has been wearing my new shoes. I'll bloody kill her!'

I legged it. She came out of her room ten minutes later, dressed like a movie star.

'How do I look, darling?'

'You look gorgeous, darling,' I chirped.

'What did you want to tell me?'

'Oh, nothing.'

Thirty years later, I admitted it was me. Poor Janet. She got pregnant at sixteen. When Mum heard this she saw it as a chance to open up a discussion about the facts of life.

'Alan, I have something to tell you. Janet is expecting a baby.'

I was horrified.

'It wasn't bloody me!'

She wet herself laughing, and that was the closest we ever came to talking about the birds and the bees. Or 'birds and blokes' as we used to say in Peckham. I knew from about the age of thirteen that girls weren't for me. My mates would be talking about boobs, and I would be thinking: *what's all the fuss about?* I wasn't particularly interested in men either. Mum did try once to set me up on a date, though. She was the daughter of one of her friends. I can't recall her name. I was ordered to take her to the pictures. I think Mum was trying to see if I would get a taste for females. She may as well have been trying to refloat the *Titanic*.

I was brushed and ironed and washed, and given a splash of Uncle Joe's ancient and rotten-smelling aftershave. (He had only ever owned the one bottle.) Mum stuffed a few bob into my pocket and walked me, with a few of the neighbours, to the bus stop at the end of the road. I'm not sure if she waved me off with a hanky, but there was definitely a tear in her eye. The kind of tear that mothers shed for their virgin daughters as they head off on honeymoon. There was no danger of me losing my virginity that night. Or, indeed, any danger of the girl losing hers either. She was frightening, with thick milk-bottle glasses and buck teeth—the kind you could open beer bottles with. I bought her an orange ice lolly, and we watched *King Solomon's Mines* in total silence, sitting on our hands. Our own hands, not each other's. I couldn't wait to put her on the bus afterwards. Or under it. I heard she got married ten years later and had six kids. Poor cow.

I left school at the age of fifteen. I couldn't wait. I threw my cap in the air, and it stuck on a railing. I thought: *I'm free now to do what I like.* I had a fairly clear sense of who I was and what I wanted to be. The latter can be summed up in one word: 'fabulous'. I just wanted to be a star. I had already started to pay visits to the West End, and had been in a couple of gay clubs while at school. The die was cast. The following year I would meet an Italian named Bernard who would change my outlook on the world.

As I said earlier, I always wanted to be noticed. I was unusual in that sense as most gay people back then were forced to keep a low profile. One man in particular was very keen not to be seen on the scene. That didn't stop him saying 'hello' when I bumped into him in a West End gay bar two weeks before I left school. I had never seen him look so happy and comfortable as he sat and drank among like-minded men. He was positively sparkling when I went over to his table to shake his hand.

'Why, Mr Tizer,' I purred to my form master, 'what a lovely smile you have.'

Chapter Three

Bernard

'Come in, you flash cunt. Tea is being served.'

Uncle Joe from upstairs was holding his weekly 'afternoon tea'. China cups, saucers and plates full of Eccles cake and cucumber (and Marmite) sandwiches were laid out neatly on the table in his sitting room. I was starving, but knew better than to tuck in before all the guests had arrived. I admired my sixteen-year-old face in his Gran's gleaming cutlery and looked up to see who the new arrival was.

I knew he must have been a good friend if Joe was calling him a cunt. If you said that to someone who was only a slight acquaintance around the East End back then, claret ('blood', dear) would have been spilled. The cunt in question was a tall, handsome young man in a black velvet suit, stiff white collar and a red knitted tie. He was in his mid twenties and a dead ringer for the actor Alan Bates. Years later, when I was working in a theatrical wigmaker's, Bates came in, and I nearly fell over, thinking I had seen a ghost. They looked so alike it was frightening. This velvet-clad geezer was the kind of man you noticed, and I could see that he had noticed me. Joe ushered him to the table, and he plonked his neat little bottom down beside me.

'I hear you're a cunt. So am I. We should get along famously,' I said, thinking I was being urbane and debonair and witty.

22

'I beg your pardon?' He looked at me from under a raised eyebrow. I suddenly didn't feel so smart any more.

'Joe ...' I stammered, '... you know ... what he said to you at the door... the C-word....'

The young man was silent for a moment, and then laughed wonderfully; the same posh way you might hear Leslie Howard or Noël Coward laugh.

'I think you misheard Joe. My name is Bernard Salvi. Count Bernard Salvi. I am a *count*. I am also a cunt as well, and very pleased to make your acquaintance.'

Everyone at the table was laughing now. I didn't know whether to be mortified or impressed that I was speaking to a member of the upper classes. And, better still, he was interested in talking to me. For the next two hours we chatted about life, his family, art, Italy ... my head was like a sponge, taking in everything this exotic creature had to say. Count Bernard Victor Salvo Salvi was an artist and writer. I loved art at school. It was the only thing I loved, and I was good at drawing. One of my pics was published in the local paper—I was famous at twelve. I still keep it up, and did one for Noelle Campbell Sharpe recently. It sold immediately. I'm not half bad with brushes, at least with the painting and make-up variety. Back then, the closest I had come to hearing anyone talking about painting was my mum nagging Dad to redecorate the front room.

Bernard painted in oils and watercolours, and was a fantastic cartoonist. He had a brilliant, mischievous sense of humour, and I was immediately in awe of him. He also wrote books. One was called *Boy Minus*. I don't know if it was ever published, but he later showed me letters he had received from Macmillan publishers. I was very impressed by this as the company was run by the former prime minister, Harold Macmillan.

Bernard was used to dealing with toffs like Macmillan; he came from aristocratic Italian stock. His family were from Lucca, a beautiful walled medieval city in Tuscany, which had at one stage been ruled by Napoleon's sister, and was home to Puccini (end of history lesson). The 'Salvo Salvi' family's castle and lands had been taken off them when Mussolini came to power in the 1930s, and they had fled to London, where they lived in a nice semi-detached house in the suburbs. It was a far cry from the old walls, rolling countryside, terraced olive groves and vineyards, but still very upmarket by my standards.

'You are a very good listener, Alan,' he said. 'Would you like to learn more about art? Shall I take you under my wing?' He raised his velvet arms and flapped them.

'That would be lovely,' I replied.

That evening, he asked my mum if it would be okay to take me around a few galleries and museums. She was delighted that such a fine young man was taking an interest in my intellectual development, although she would never have put it like that. Mum was a plain speaker, and would have given me an earful if I got too uppity, using words like 'intellectual'. One of her friends once very grandly dropped the word 'ethics' into a conversation they were having about the etiquette involved in queueing for rations. 'Ethics?' my mum replied. 'I've got a friend who lives there.' She was taking the piss, but her pretentious friend got the message. (She was an Essex girl herself.)

The ethics of allowing a sixteen-year-old boy to be squired around town by an older man were not discussed that day. My mum liked him, but never mentioned the pachyderm in the living space. She must have suspected how I was inclined, but never said anything. Bernard's friends, on the other hand, were in no doubt. One day we bumped into one of his mates in Piccadilly. Some time later Bernard asked him if he thought I was gay. The friend said, 'My dear, he's the campest thing I've seen in years.'

All that aside, Mum was just glad I wasn't running around the streets getting into trouble. Actually, she was delighted; Bernard took me to places that none of my friends would ever have gone to. I went to my first museum with him: the Victoria and Albert, where I was really taken with the Roman stuff and the Egyptian mummies.

'Dare I say that you are a mummy's boy?' he quipped.

'You dare not, count. Because that is the worst joke I'm ever likely to hear.'

Bernard loved this kind of back chat. He was incredibly funny himself.

Naturally, when we went to the Horniman Museum, double entendres were dropped faster than a West End prozzy's drawers. I loved the Horny Man Museum. It had been open since Victorian times, when Frederick John Horniman first opened his house and collection of objects to visitors. (I've looked all this up, so pay attention.) The collection included anthropological material and musical instruments. It also had an aquarium, and loads of natural history stuff. It was a magical place for me. Here, you could pick the displays up, try them on and even play some of the instruments (badly). I later learned that Horniman's daughter, Annie, had been the financial benefactor behind the setting up of the Abbey Theatre. I often think of my trips to that museum when I'm watching a play there. And I thank Bernard for fostering my love of drama. The first play I ever saw was *Romeo and Juliet* at the Old Vic with the count.

Now you may think that the sight of a south London teenager and a dandified count attending *Romeo and Juliet* would have raised a few eyebrows, but it didn't. This was, in part, down to the fact that we both looked fabulous. Bernard paid for me to get my first suit made. I designed it myself, and Burton's tailored it for me. It was a light grey check, with a double-breasted waistcoat. It looked very mod with my winkle-picker boots. I was so excited getting fitted for it, with the assistants beavering away, measuring my inside leg like Mr Humphries in *Are You Being Served?*

Burton's was where most mods got their suits made. Back then, older men wore boring navy or brown double-breasted jobs that were made out of the kind of material you could patch up circus tents with. The Mods used to tear pages out of Italian fashion magazines and bring them into Burton's to get them made up in lightweight mohair.

I'm presuming you're familiar with the term 'Mod'. If you're not, then here's a quick overview. The Mod movement was a fashion- and dance-obsessed (and terribly cool) subculture that sprung up in London and some southern English towns in the late 1950s. The word comes from 'modernist', as these hip young things were all into modern jazz and everything new, including Italian art movies and fashion. Unlike our parents, teenagers in post-war Britain were relatively well off and were allowed to keep most of the money they made from after-school jobs. Before, kids were expected to contribute to the family finances from their newspaper runs, etc. What else were these youngsters going to do with their money except spend it on clothes, beer and amphetamines?

The first shops catering for these hipsters opened in Carnaby Street and King's Road, which then became synonymous with Swinging London. Some Mods would go without food in order to buy new clothes. Actually, many of them did, just to squeeze into the drainpipe trousers. Many commentators believe that the new post-war male interest in fashion began with the Mods. It didn't. It started with the Teddy boys. Their interest in how they looked made it acceptable for men to be into fashion. Prior to this, male preening was exclusive to us queens.

'The look' was slick and slim. Lapels were narrow, ties were thin, collars were buttoned down and footwear was tapered (Chelsea boots, etc.) Some Mods even went so far as to steal bowling shoes from the skittle alleys and wear them as a two-tone fashion statement. Some of the daring straight Mods rebelled against the macho norm and wore eyeshadow and lipstick. Mods also preferred scooters over motorbikes as their body panels hid the moving parts, which meant that they were less likely to get their clothes stained with oil. They wore parkas for this reason too.

I was determined to be the coolest Mod on the King's Road, and was bursting with excitement when we arrived at Burton's to collect my suit. My head swelled with pride when I put it on. Bernard told me to keep it on, so I bunged my sweater and jeans into a shopping bag, and he took me for my first Chinese meal. It was a far cry from pie and mash, although the latter is still my favourite food. I spent the entire time trying not to get sticky rib sauce down my lapel. Not too long afterwards, I was ironing the suit to visit the West End with my mate David Pearson, and burned a hole in its crotch. I was devastated, and had to spend that evening with my legs crossed, even while I was walking.

'Never wear more than three colours,' Bernard advised me over our Chinese meal. I still never do. And if I'm ever wearing a tie, I always do a perfect Windsor knot. He taught me how to do that too. He even told me how to wear my hair. This was not controlling, by the way; it was just his way of teaching me how to groom myself.

'Groom' is a loaded word. Today, Bernard would be accused of grooming me for sexual reasons. He didn't. I was his protégé. Although he flirted with me, he never tried anything on. I knew that Bernard loved me, but the spark just wasn't there, which is actually surprising, looking back now. He ticked all the proverbial boxes: he was handsome, witty, interesting … and he wore his sexuality on his velvet sleeve. He pushed being 'out' as far as he could back then without getting arrested. On one occasion we were at the cinema, and the usherette selling ice creams asked if she could offer him anything.

'Madame, you have *nothing* that I would be interested in,' he said with a camp flourish. She laughed, as did the punters around us. It was the closest thing to saying 'I'm queer' that you could get away with back then.

Whereas the usherette was tickled by Bernard's overt homosexuality, his mum was not so impressed. We used to take the steam train out to the suburbs to have tea with her on Saturdays. She was a countess—and looked it. You could see she had been a beauty in her day, and she carried herself with a barely disguised mixture of sadness and disdain for her new surroundings. The house was comfortable but modest, with little clues to the family's former wealth placed about it: antiques, expensive china, etc. Bernard had given me loads of books about antiques, and I recognised some pieces as being worth a few bob. He also lent me his family seal at one stage. It was silver in a red satin box. He used it whenever he wrote to me, which of course made the postman laugh as he delivered it to our small abode in Peckham. 'Well, he had an estate in Italy, and we live on an estate in south London,' Mum used to joke.

Bernard's mum was not a great joker. She was always very hospitable, but clearly thought that it was disgraceful for her son to be consorting with the likes of me. We would sit eating banana sambos and making small talk. His elder brother would sit at the end of the table, looking very count-like. He was next in line to the title and the estate that no longer existed.

I always behaved myself, nibbling genteelly at the sandwiches and cocking my little finger the way that toffs do when sipping their tea. I wasn't from the Salvis' class or privileged background, but I never felt *too* uncomfortable. They were always very courteous, and Bernard always looked out for me. His huge personality bulldozed its way through the walls of convention. And not just at those afternoon 'salons' with his mum; he stood out wherever he went. His dress sense was marvellous, always bohemian and dandified. As I said, he was very funny, but quite intense too. Looking back,

I believe his humour masked the melancholy that defined his later life and actions.

I learned more from Bernard in the six years of our friendship than in all my years at school. We met twice a week for lunch or trips out, and I soaked up everything he told me about the arts and history. When I was older, I would finish up work at the wigmaker's, and he would be waiting for me outside. I don't think we ever fought. There were occasional disagreements, obviously, but no bust-ups.

I had my first drag 'date' with him. I suggested that we go out as a 'couple' one night for a giggle. We borrowed Uncle Joe's wig, and I put on my tightest jeans and loosest top. We spent the rest of the evening walking around the streets, attracting admiring glances. We were the handsomest couple in town. We laughed non-stop, thinking it was hilarious and anarchic. In later years I used to go to the pictures in drag with my merchant seamen friends. That way we could hold hands and snog in the back row. Nowadays, the guys do it anyway: it's no big deal. Back then, you'd have been in serious trouble if you walked around holding another man's hand.

I guessed that Bernard probably had a few more protégés on the side, and I was okay with that. I also knew that he had his demons. There seemed to be something worrying him all the time. His rebellious behaviour would sometimes give way to bouts of sadness, with a touch of madness. I think that something had happened to him in his childhood and he had been diagnosed with schizophrenia. He was always in and out of mental institutions, and would tell me about the characters he used to meet. One person thought he was made of glass and would shatter if anyone even touched his hand. Another had newspapers stuffed up his sleeves and trouser legs to stop butterflies invading his body. We would laugh about this, but then at other times Bernard would ramble incoherently, talking nonsense. I used to let him blather on.

One night, I was doing a drag show with my partner, Bow, in Fulham, and someone came up to me afterwards for a chat.

'It's very sad about Bernard, isn't it?' he said.

'Oh, you know, he is how he is,' I replied, thinking he was referring to Bernard's bouts of madness. I hadn't seen him in a while as I had been busy building up my career as a performer. 'Is he back "inside"?' I asked.

My friend's face dropped.

'You haven't heard?'

He took my hand and led me over to a booth.

'He hanged himself two weeks ago.'

It was like someone had punched me in the gut. I couldn't breathe. I couldn't believe it. There must be some mistake.

'I'm so sorry, Alan. There's no mistake. He did it in an institution. I don't think the poor fellow could take being locked up any more.'

The man who had taught me so much, without looking for anything in return, was dead. The artist, cartoonist, writer ... the light that shone so brightly had been snuffed out. Once the shock had passed, the tears began to flow. They came in torrents, as they had for Dad. The sadness of Bernard's passing has never left me. He was only thirty-two. I still think of him and have his watercolours at home to remind me of his kindness and genius.

I hadn't heard about the funeral, and so never got the chance to say goodbye to him. I never saw his family again and I heard, through mutual friends, that he had asked for his diaries to be destroyed. I hope they weren't and are someday discovered. They would make fantastic reading.

I have had my own dark days. Days you think will never end. Sometimes, in the darkness, I hear Bernard's voice. He is laughing at me.

'Get up, you silly cow,' he says. 'Life is too short. Embrace the world.'

I know then that, no matter how black things seem, I'm lucky to be alive. Unlike Count Bernard Victor Salvo Salvi, who is forever young in the hearts of the few people who remember him.

And, if you were here now, Bernard, *I* would teach *you* everything I have learned about life.

I love you, my old friend.

Chapter Four

Cat on the Tiles in Soho

'Oi, Superman, your mascara's running.'

The drunk pressed his cracked lips up against the glass, screwed his eyes shut and French-kissed the phone box. To my horror, he began to grind his crotch against the door. The veins on his Buckfast-haggard face looked like a map of the Underground.

'Fuck off,' I shouted, without taking my eyes off my reflection in the mirror above the coin slot. I wasn't going to let an old tramp upset my make-up routine. Not while I was on a night out in the West End.

I was in my teens, and no stranger to London's nightlife. I had started going to the West End on a regular basis before I left school and got a job at Jones & Higgins in Peckham. 'J & H' was one of Europe's oldest department stores, and certainly the most salubrious shop in Peckham. It was a big deal to get a job there, in the same way that getting a gig in Arnotts or Brown Thomas would be today. My initial excitement at working there quickly died off when I realised that my post would entail being at the narrow end of a sweeping brush.

I thought to myself: *I didn't leave school to do this crap.* My best mate at the store, David Pearson, who was a window dresser, shared my pain, and we started to go on outings, seeking notoriety and glamour. A lot of the time I would go on my own, taking the night bus and changing in a telephone box. I'd then go to Berwick Street Market and leave my workaday trousers behind a stall and change into my riding boots and skintight jeans. I was 'all zhooshed up with everywhere to go', as we used to say back then. After a night's bopping, I'd head back to the stall, clean my face and get the night bus home. Mum never knew I was out on the tiles.

I loved the West End with its bright lights and bars. I was a very good-looking 'chicken', and used to draw a lot of attention. It was inevitable that I would lose my virginity either on or after one of these trips. The thief of my maidenhead was a man called David Steele—not the politician, I hasten to add. He came up to me in a club and said, 'Hello, pussycat.' I was impressed, and asked him why he'd called me that. 'Because you have cat's eyes.' He was very handsome and charming. We got on like a fire in a petrol station, and arranged to meet at The Oval tube station at 2 p.m. the following Saturday. He had a key to the home of a well-known senior army officer, and we spent the afternoon divesting me of my virginity. I fell in love with him, and we had a relationship for four years. He was my first real boyfriend, and introduced me to the Chelsea set. I don't want to talk too much about my time with him. He was a beautiful man, but I was young, and eventually the sheen wore off and I met someone else.

That 'someone else' was an Aussie called Warwick Sims, who was an actor in *General Hospital* and a bit of a heart-throb. In the late 1970s he also starred in *Against the Wind*, which was an Australian TV mini-series about British rule in Ireland and the development of Oz. It was a big hit, and the first major Australian TV production to be broadcast in the US. He also appeared in a stinker called *He's My Girl*, which was about a female impersonator (surprise, surprise). The *Washington Post* said it was 'A farce so stale the only thing to do is make croutons.' He went on to act with Steve Martin in *The*

Man With Two Brains, and made a few other movies that didn't set Hollywood alight.

Back in the 1960s, though, he was a big star in the UK, and used to hang out with the Streatham crowd of actors. There were parties every night, and I would get up and do my 'turn' in drag, miming to the latest top 10 hit. Warwick and I didn't last. I was young and wanted to party—and there were plenty of parties, especially around Soho, for an aspiring drag queen.

But I'm getting ahead of myself. Before I became a fully paid-up member of the West End set, I had to take my first baby steps into the showbiz world. So I became an apprentice wig stylist at a well-known theatrical syrup factory, Recreations (syrup of figs = wigs). It was an exciting place to work, and you never knew who would walk through the doors looking to get fitted for a rug or a beard.

The main reception area was plush and posh, all chandeliers and respectful assistants. The fitting rooms were downstairs, where the measurements were done. One day, on my way to fetch an order, I passed by one of the fitting rooms and spotted a voluptuous woman in a plastic mac, waiting to be seen to. The coat couldn't conceal her gorgeous figure. She had more curves than Brands Hatch. It was Shirley Bassey.

'You wouldn't get us a cup of tea, love? I'm parched,' she purred in her Welsh accent.

Naturally, as she was one of the biggest names in the business, I wasn't going to let her get dehydrated on the premises, so I asked someone else to get her a cuppa. I wasn't raised to be a charlady, even for Shirley bleedin' Bassey.

Where was I? Oh yes. Then there were the knotting and dying departments, where wigs were hand-knotted, one hair at a time, and coloured with Dylon (the same stuff you use to refresh your faded black jeans). If you're ever getting a syrup, ask for European hair: it's considered the best. You may also wonder how wigs are cleaned. You don't just stand in the shower with them. We used to throw them into a bucket of carbon tetrachloride (CTC). They used to sell it in bottles branded as 'Dabitoff' (which sounds like a good name for a Russian porn star).

Carbon tetrachloride was the stuff that killed Kenneth Williams's father, Charlie. He drank it by accident in 1962, and suffered a horrible death. Apparently, it had been stored in the bathroom cabinet in a cough bottle. CTC stinks like hell—and so did the circumstances surrounding the accident. Kenneth hated his homophobic dad. He once said he had called him a 'namby pamby sod' when he ordered a sweet sherry in the pub. Charlie was a barber, and the family lived over his shop. Guys would come in and innocently ask for a blow wave. He'd say, 'What are you, an iron?' (Iron hoof = poof.) 'Get out, I ain't having no fairies in my shop.' Kenneth refused to visit him in hospital. The next day, Charlie died. An hour after being given the news, Kenneth went on stage in the West End. He put on the best performance of his life.

The coroner's court recorded a verdict of accidental death due to corrosive poisoning by carbon tetrachloride. The police weren't so sure if it was accidental. Kenneth was a suspect, and there is still a lot of speculation about how the poison got into the cough bottle.

I knew Kenneth. I wasn't very close to him, but then nobody was. The first time I met him was when I was descending the stairs in the Spartan Club. I could hear his voice above the din, and the roars of laughter from the group he was entertaining.

'Oh what bona riah and eek!' he whispered theatrically as I rolled into his eyeline.

'Why thank you, dear. I do it myself,' I replied, plumping my hair. He was taken aback.

'Oh, you know the old Polari then, do you? You'd better come over and join us. No point in me wasting my magnificent oratorial talents on these heathens when there's a bona Polari speaker in the house.'

Polari, for those of you who are unfamiliar with it, is a form of British slang, based on Italian and used by gay men during the late 1950s and 1960s. It started out as far back as the sixteenth century, and was associated with Punch and Judy shows. It's still used by camp actors, circus hands, merchant sailors, and Morrissey from The Smiths. And the late David Bowie too. Both included it in songs.

When I was young, it was mainly used by gay men as a common, secret language. Here are a few words to start you off, if you want to learn it.

> *bejax* (nearby)
> *bona* (good)
> *cod* (tacky)
> *eek* (face)
> *lattie* (flat)
> *naff* (unfashionable)
> *nanti* (not, no)
> *omi* (man)
> *palone* (woman)
> *riah* (hair)
> *strides* (trousers)
> *TBH* ('to be had', in terms of sex)
> *zhoosh* (get dolled up)

I'm not going to tell you what 'bona cartz' means. You could hear Polari being used in London fish markets, the theatre, fairgrounds and circuses, where it borrowed a few phrases from Romani. It was also used widely in the Merchant Navy, where many sea queens joined liners and cruise ships as entertainers and stewards. It came in handy when you wanted to discuss a taboo topic openly without the fuzz getting involved.

The popularity of the *Round the Horne* radio show duo, Julian and Sandy—played by Kenneth and Hugh Paddick—led to the straight population being let in on the secret. Peter Wyngarde, who was the star of TV show *Jason King*, even recorded a song in 1970 about Billy the 'queer sexy hippie … trolling the Dilly' (cruising for sex in Piccadilly).

The older queens were a bit unhappy about Polari becoming mainstream, and the younger activists saw it as divisive as it was used to criticise gays and straights who didn't understand the lingo. Personally I loved it, and still throw it into conversations whenever I can.

Kenneth had us in stitches that night, Polari-ing and telling long, hilarious anecdotes. When he was 'on', he was magnificent. When he was 'off', he was terrible. I remember on a couple of occasions witnessing him verbally destroy less quick-witted members of our group. He could flit between being bright and charming and being dark and depressed. He was very unpredictable.

Kenneth used to go to Morocco with the outrageously gay playwright Joe Orton and his set. Everyone knew that he was gay, and he had dalliances he claimed were never consummated, insisting that he was celibate. While Joe would get up to all kinds of nonsense with the local young men, Kenneth would sit by the pool sunbathing. Or sort of sunbathing. A dancer friend of mine, who was one of the Morocco set, told me he always wore a bri-nylon shirt with the sleeves rolled up, even if the temperature was in the nineties. He once asked him why he never fully disrobed. The reply was typical Kenneth. 'Dear, when one is an international star, one never exposes the royal tit.'

Kenneth was very private, but he eventually spoke openly about his loneliness and disappointments in two half-hour documentaries, called *Carry On Kenneth*, on BBC radio. In April 1988 he overdosed on barbiturates, and the last words in his diary were: 'Oh, what's the bloody point?'

Just like his father's death, it's still unclear whether Kenneth's death was accidental or deliberate. What is beyond dispute is that he was an absolute genius and a one-off. He's still funny to watch today. His act never dated.

In my time as a wig stylist, I grew to learn that actors and entertainers—like Kenneth Williams—are 'real' folk like you and me. We put them on a pedestal—and some are arseholes—but in the main they're just earning their crust from making the public laugh or cry. Alec Guinness was particularly nice and polite. I was star-struck when he walked through the doors. Dirk Bogarde was another pleasant man. He came to get a beard done for the film *The Fixer*, and all the staff flew down to the main area and pretended to be working while surreptitiously taking a peek at him. He was gorgeous; even better looking than on the big screen.

Arthur Askey was a jolly, bouncy little fellow and a joy to deal with. So was Clive Dunn. He played Lance Corporal Jones in *Dad's Army*, and had a character called Charlie Quick in *Grandad*. Even as a young man, he could be a really convincing octogenarian when he had his grey wig on. Thora Hird came in too. She used to wear a wig topped off with a hat.

Dick Emery was very smart, well-dressed and polite. I thought that he was very camp and gay, but it turned out he was a real ladies' man. Another TV star of the time, Patrick Cargill, came in and took a shine to me. He asked me to dinner, and then brought me home in a 1950s Bentley. I liked him a lot, and we went out quite often. Nothing happened between us. I think he just liked the company of young men—and being seen with them.

Make-up departments didn't make their own wigs then, so after a fitting and the final 'sign-off' they would be delivered to the theatre where the star was performing. One afternoon I went to drop off an order at the Prince of Wales Theatre. *Sweet Charity* was playing, starring Juliette Prowse. This was the first time I got to see a rehearsal up close. There was a scene where Juliette was carried through a door. Her foot touched the frame, and she said, very firmly: 'Get it made bigger.' It was. I remember thinking: *what a pro*. My theatrical bug was about to become a full-blown fever. I desperately wanted to be up on stage performing.

As I said earlier, Uncle Joe's shenanigans and my mum's shoes played a major part in me getting a taste for drag. By the way, you do know it's an act, don't you? I don't wander around as Mr Pussy all the time. I'm still quite the hip-dude dresser with my leather jacket and tailored men's suits. (Admittedly, I do wear the occasional pair of women's Chelsea boots with my bloke's gear, though.)

My adventures in drag began in earnest at the Vauxhall Tavern. It was an old Victorian pub run by a couple called Jim and Floss who put on drag shows. When they moved to the Union Tavern, another couple, Peggy and Jock Ritchie, took over, and inherited the resident queens. Jock used to play darts in the bar, while Peggy watched the till and oversaw the acts from behind a long counter, which was high enough to act as a stage. The acts were old-school drag: men dressed in long frocks and wigs miming to records. It was all a bit chaotic. The turns would do their number, run down the bar, up the stairs, and be on again before the record changed.

There were some great artistes on that bar/stage. And some crap ones too. One of my favourites was Mrs Shufflewick, aka Rex Jameson. He was hilarious, playing the role of a genteel cockney charlady. He had amazing timing, and was filthy, by the standards of those days. 'Do you like this fur, girls? It cost £200. I didn't pay for it meself; I met 200 fellas with a pound each …'

Rex had been a foundling, dumped on a hospital steps and raised by a well-off couple. It's an old cliché that insecure people tend to head for the stage. Thank God they do. He was phenomenal. Like a lot of performers, he liked his booze, and even changed his name from Coster to Jameson after the whiskey.

He became a radio star and used to drag up for the microphone. Can you believe that? Talk about being serious about your art form. In Ireland they used to have dancing on the radio (anyone remember Din Joe's show?), but in London we had unseen drag. Pure class.

Rex worked with Peter Sellers, Tony Hancock and Harry Secombe, and one of his most memorable lines was: 'I was standing at the bar and this sailor walked in. I think he must have been in the navy because he kissed me on both cheeks. I was doing me shoelaces up at the time.'

Out of drag, you'd never guess what Rex did for a living. He used to read the *Mirror* and the *Sporting Life*, was a gambler, smoked Woodbines, and wore a flat cap and second-hand clothes. When he was on stage, however, he was the finest drag queen in the country. A while back, I read a review by Simon Callow of *The Amazing Mrs Shufflewick: The Life of Rex Jameson*, written by his mate Patrick Newley. According to the book, Rex died from the booze in 1983. His last words, if true, are a comic masterpiece. Apparently, his doctor told him he couldn't find out what was wrong with him.

'I think it must be the drink,' concluded the medic.

'Never mind, doctor,' says Rex. 'I'll come back when you're sober.'

If you bought Rex a drink, he'd be your best friend all night. He was brilliant, but as I said, some of the other acts at the Vauxhall were dire. One evening I was sitting at the bar while an ugly old brute in a wig croaked 'We'll Meet Again'. I was in agony. It was terrible.

'I could do better than that,' I groaned to Peggy, who was polishing her glasses. 'Go on then. If you think you can do better, give it a try.'

There was another punter sitting at the opposite end of the bar. I knew him to see, but being young and pretty like me, we were silent rivals for the older crew's attentions, and had never spoken to each other. We respected each other's space. His name was Jeff Claridge, and he worked in a butcher's shop during the day. He was very good-looking. I took my gin and tonic and sidled down the bar to him.

'Wotcha,' I said. 'My name's Pussy. What do you think of the show so far?'

'Bleedin' muck,' he replied. 'I'd rather listen to our old dog farting than that geezer singing. If you can call it singing.'

We started to chat, and eventually I popped the question.

'Do you want to do a double act? Peggy has given me the nod.'

He loved the idea.

'What will we call ourselves?'

'How about Pussy and Bow?'

He liked the sound of that. I didn't tell him that Bow (or Bobo) was the name of our dog at home. It was his own fault for mentioning canine farts. We spent the rest of the evening going over what we would do—and getting pissed. The conversation spilled over to other tables in the pub, and a builder, Bob Davies, volunteered to be our 'manager'.

The following Sunday we took to the bar/stage. Instead of wearing the traditional long frocks, we had bought Mod gear from C & A: miniskirts and stockings and tight tops. I already had the wigs. We looked great, but that was about it. We were shockingly bad. My brain has blanked out that first performance, we were so awful. We weren't booed, but could see the punters looking embarrassed for us, which is ten times worse.

When we finished, Peggy took me aside to console me.

'You'll do better next time, love,' she said. 'And remember, when you're wearing stockings the line goes straight down the back of the leg, not in a spiral.' I always remember that kindly advice. These days I wear two pairs of tights to give my legs a nice, toned shape. That's a trade secret. Try it, it works.

We worked on the act, and were better the following week, and the week after that. We mimed modern songs to a crackly record player, but after a few weeks we scraped the money together to buy a Grundig tape deck, which we microphoned up to a Vox amplifier. This meant that we could compile our own songs in a set list, and pause it where necessary without having to fumble around with a needle and a turntable. We started to do Sunday mornings and evenings, singing and preening like two young things. We were the first to break with the old guard, and the audience—who were a mixture of showbiz people and ordinary folk—loved us.

Bow and I alternated, taking each song in turn. Peggy loved to cheer us on, and I always imagined she cheered louder for me than for Bow. Whenever she bought a new dress (which seemed to be every weekend), she'd pass on one of her older ones to me. When her daughter's engagement broke up, I was given the wedding dress. I stuffed a pillow up its front and mimed to Sandy Shaw's 'Always Something There to Remind Me'. It brought the house down, and I got my first taste of a real adrenalin rush from performing.

Sandy is a shrink now, by the way. I met her years later at Portmarnock Country Club. 'Ooh, I like your accent,' she said. 'And I like yours,' I replied. My manager, Ian Davey, then chipped in wearily: 'And I'm tired of hearing both your accents.' He had been listening to my Sandy impression for thirty years. She didn't get the gag.

I started to add a few other 'props' to the Vauxhall act: waders and swimsuit for 'These Boots Are Made for Walkin'', and a striptease to 'I Who Have Nothing'. We built up quite a following on the Sunday mornings. Then the papers picked up on us, saying 'Don't miss this act before they get too famous', and queues started to form outside the pub. Stars like the TV broadcaster Daniel Farson and the Bond villain Charles Gray were regulars. Charles played Blofeld, and was very camp. Peggy loved him, and always invited him to stay for lunch. He'd sit at the bar afterwards talking about Sean Connery. He was very down to earth.

Judy Garland was there one night too. She was in disguise, with a headscarf and dark glasses, but everyone knew who she was. She was with her husband, Mickey Deans, and the singer Johnny Ray, who was the best man at their wedding. We got chatting, and ended up back at her Chelsea mews. 'Mrs Deans' was very hospitable, and the drink flowed. I was dying to go to the loo, but too polite to ask where it was. She could see that I was cross-legged, and cross-eyed, trying to hold it in.

'The can is back there, honey,' she said, motioning towards the hall. 'And by the way, you've the best damn legs I've ever seen.' I was delighted with the compliment, and the fact that I could boast I'd had a pee in Judy Garland's bog. The poor woman died not long afterwards in the same house. I hope it was nothing to do with me using the lavvy.

Johnny Ray and I became good friends, and I used to drink with him in clubs like the Merry-Go-Round. He was huge in the 1950s after he scored a hit with 'Cry', but his career was on the wane when I was first introduced to him. I met him loads of times over the years. Once, in the late 1980s, when he was doing a gig in Dublin, I took him out on the town. He was on at the Fiesta Club on Talbot Street (or Toilet Street, as we now call it). The Fiesta was like the Talk of the Town in London. It had hostesses in bathing costumes and brought over big stars from the UK to play cabaret. I sent a note backstage and had drinks with him after the show. He was a very heavy drinker, the poor chap. His piano player used to travel with boxes of Black Tower wine for him.

The following day, knowing he would be hung over, I arranged to have tea with him at the Gresham and avoid the pub. The singer Ruby Murray was over at the same time, so I asked her to join us. Ruby was very softly spoken, while Johnny was half deaf and wore a hearing aid. He couldn't hear a word she was saying. It was like a comedy sketch, with her asking, 'More tea, Johnny?' and him going, 'What? What did she say?'

Johnny's sexuality was well known in the business, but as performers' preferences weren't revealed by the press back then, the public had no idea that he liked men. In fact, as far back as 1951, before he was signed to a record label, Johnny was arrested in Michigan for soliciting an undercover cop in the bog of a burlesque theatre. He pleaded guilty, but the press never picked up on it.

In spite of this—or maybe because she just wanted a challenge— Marilyn Morrison married him at the peak of his fame. She told a friend that she would 'straighten him out'. She didn't.

I remember we were in a club once, and he asked a friend of mine to dance. The friend's boyfriend said, 'If he can dance as well as he can sing, then I've nothing to fucking worry about.'

Johnny died forgotten, and a recluse. I have a picture he gave me, signed 'To Alan, Too Much!' I treasure it, and his memory. It's funny to look back now at my time at the Vauxhall and see Johnny's face. I will always associate him with my rise up the drag ladder.

And I *was* rising. I was even given a key to the Vauxhall, where I had my own bed. That gave me my first taste of real independence. I was still officially living with my mum, but I had the freedom now to crash out across town after a long night out. I used to share a room with one of the barmaids, Marion. I'd stumble in at very late o'clock, and she'd sit up and mock-chide me: 'What bleedin' time do you call this?' Then we'd stay up and she'd interrogate me about my night, interrupting my flow with the occasional, 'Corr, you met so-and-so? What's he/she like?' I loved Marion to bits.

My relationship with Bow was not so great. We had started to do gigs around the city, and our professional partnership was strong, but cracks were beginning to form in our personal one. It wasn't that surprising as we both had big egos, and some of the bookings were a bit of an ordeal.

There was one we did in the East End that was especially horrific. It was a stag night above a pub. Bow arrived late, and I wasn't impressed. We went on stage with a cloud hanging over us. I've never experienced anything like that night in all the years I've been performing. There were blokes with their trousers around their ankles, pissing on the floor and flinging pints around. The strippers had been on before us, and the lads' blood was up. They weren't happy that two poofs were interrupting their evening. I tried to get someone up from the audience to have a lark with, but he wasn't having it, and ended up having to be restrained. 'I'm going to get you, you cunt!' he roared. We fled, and had to hide in the storeroom. We could hear chairs being smashed against the door and the animals outside baying for us. It was terrifying. Somehow, the manager spirited us away. I think I heard him shouting, 'Free beer over here, boys!' to distract them. We survived, but the experience didn't make us bond as it might have done with other double acts.

A few weeks later, we were booked to do another show at a more respectable venue. Bow had bought two new dresses, which he was keen to show off to me. I don't know how the row kicked off—it might have been over lipstick—but we ended up smacking the heads off each other and ripping our frocks to pieces. We knew that our act was at an end. We muddled through the show in taped-up dresses, wearing extra slap to hide the bruises. We made up afterwards and went for a drink.

'I'm getting out of the business, Alan,' he told me. 'My new bloke doesn't like me doing it anymore. I have to respect his wishes.' I told him that I was sorry to lose him, but I understood. He was quitting for love, after all.

Three months later, the little git was doing his own solo show at the Vauxhall. I was miffed for a few seconds when I heard about it, but moved on quickly. I was free now to do my own thing. I told myself that I was going to be a star in my own right. There would be no more changing in phone boxes for me. The cat was finally out of the bag.

Or, to be more precise, with Bow out of the way, the cat was finally rid of the old bag, and heading to the bright lights of the West End....

Chapter Five

West End Kitty

If London was swinging in the late 1960s, then the West End swung both ways. It was the world's showbiz and fashion capital, and offered everything a bright, gay young thing could ever desire.

I was a solo act now that I had parted ways with Bow, and was determined to make a name for myself. In fairness to Bow, he wasn't an old bag. He was all right was Jeff. Sorry, mate, I just couldn't resist the 'cat' and 'bag' pun. If it is a pun. I was never good at grammar.

The bookings were streaming in, and I was playing venues all around town—some great, some dodgy. It didn't matter: I was learning my trade. I was chatting and bantering more with the audience, initially just to fill in the gaps where Bow would have sung his number, then just for the fun of it. Posh people, working-class people ... they all got a mouthful from Pussy. Celebs began coming to my shows, and the numbers swelled. Mick Avery, the drummer with The Kinks, was a regular at the Richmond gigs. Their song, 'Dedicated Follower of Fashion', could have been written about me.

Mick loved my act, and used to hang around and have a drink with me afterwards. Who knows, maybe he had a little unconscious crush on Mr Pussy. I suspect a lot of straight men did: I was, after all, a gorgeous young woman....

Another drummer, Richard Starkie—or was it Starr?—was also a fan from the Vauxhall days. I can't remember the name of his band.

When I wasn't gigging I was out on the tiles. By 1969 I had rooms in the West End, East End and Peckham. I particularly loved hanging out in Soho. Today, it has a bad reputation for being seedy. Back in the 1960s it was Boho Soho, full of celebs and artists drinking their heads off. Count Bernard had fostered my love of art, and I was honoured to wind up in the company of Francis Bacon. I met him first in the Toucan Club, and then would bump into him around town. He was always pissed, and we had plenty of wild evenings together.

He was eccentric, to say the least, and had the beadiest eyes I'd ever seen. He'd bumble about in his black leather jacket, with the collar turned up, calling everybody 'darling', and was never short of a drink as so many people admired him. I don't know how he got any work done.

Most times I met him he was in the company of Daniel Farsons, who was a very famous TV star. Daniel and I became great drinking buddies. Like Bacon, he was always fried. He even owned his own pub on the Isle of Dogs called the Waterman's Arms.

Nobody remembers Daniel now, which is very sad as he was an extraordinary man. He was the son of an American hack, with whom he visited Germany as a child. He had blond hair, and it was said that Hitler patted him on the head and called him a 'good Aryan boy'. He wouldn't have been so friendly if he'd known Daniel was a raving poof.

He was a prolific writer (his grand-uncle was Bram Stoker) and broadcaster, with a sharp, polite, but probing style. In the 1960s, interviewers were supposed to be a bit deferential. Dan was not. One of his best known *Out of Step* episodes tackled nudism, and showed the first naked woman on British television. He also did one on mixed marriages between blacks and whites, which was very controversial.

One of his regular guests was a right-wing nutcase called James Wentworth Day. In the marriage show he referred to mixed-race kids as 'coffee-coloured little imps.' He added that black people were less 'civilised' than whites because 'a couple of generations ago they were eating each other.' I saw a clip of this recently on a compilation show, and it's even more shocking, given the enlightened times we live in. Daniel responded by saying, 'I couldn't disagree with you more, but at least you say what you really feel.'

Wentworth Day got the axe from Daniel's show after he claimed, in a programme on transvestism, that all gays should be hanged. Farson got the show scrapped, which was hardly surprising considering his own preferences. Turkeys voting for Christmas, etc.

In 1962 he made a documentary about pub entertainment in the East End called *Time Gentlemen Please*. He then bought the Waterman's Arms in an attempt to revive old-time music hall. It was a financial disaster, and he lost a tonne of money—enough, said one critic, to buy a row of houses at the time. He continued to write books and did the authorised biography of his chum Bacon, who didn't want it published until after his death.

Daniel was a really bad alcoholic. He used to visit me in Dublin in the 1970s and stay in my place in Mount Street. He loved getting the late boat over as it meant he could drink all night, get off the ship and head to the early house (where you could legally get a drink before general pub opening hours). I loved getting the night boat too (I hated flying). I'd travel over to the UK and drink with the crew down in the mess hall. They all knew me, and would reserve a place in first class in case I needed to snooze. One time I got off the boat and was heading for the train when I was stopped by a copper. I had a Chinese statue for my mum, which he unsuccessfully tried to unscrew from the base, looking for drugs.

'Is your missus pregnant?' I asked innocently. He looked startled. 'Yes actually, she is.'

'You'd have more chance of unscrewing her, mate. That's solid jade.'

He didn't laugh, but muttered 'Fuck off' under his breath and waved me on. I made a mental note never to travel first class again on my own.

It was first class all the way for me in Soho in 1966 though. Daniel and I pissed our way around London picking up strays and getting up to mischief. And there was plenty of mischief. London had several million clubs. Two of the more famous club owners were the Bartell brothers. They were, oddly enough, greengrocers during the day. I still don't know how they got into the nightclub scene. Maybe it was because they were used to looking at vegetables (most of their punters were vegetables by the end of the night). They had the Huntsman in Gerard Street. It was a health and safety nightmare: you'd go downstairs and walk into a wall of smoke, and the ventilation was so bad that the walls were always damp with mould and condensed sweat. The punters were even moister. It was all very bohemian, with people wearing long black gloves and waving cigarette holders about the place. The Huntsman was the first place I ever saw two men dancing with each other. I was shocked and delighted.

I was very friendly with Ray Bartell. He used to do the door, and when police would raid the place for drugs he'd get all indignant about them harassing his customers, claiming that he ran a clean house. It was really amusing to hear him complain as revellers popped Purple Hearts (uppers) there as if they were Smarties. The Hearts cost sixpence each, and were given to pilots during the war to keep them awake. Black Bombers were popular too, although they were too heavy for most clubbers. We popped them so we could dance all night. Kids nowadays think the rave scene is a new thing—we invented it.

At about 7 a.m., the dancing would stop and we'd tumble out of the club into the watery morning light of Soho. The staff would then sweep the floor and keep any lost drugs to resell. I loved those post-club mornings. You'd never see anybody sleeping rough, just a few dealers going to work. Everyone was friendly and the place was electric, still buzzing from the night before. Crowds of us would go to the nearest park and just sit and wait to come down.

The Bartells weren't the only brothers to own clubs in London. There were the Krays too, of course. The first time I saw them was at Esmerelda's Barn. It was a gambling club and trendy hangout, which allowed Reggie to play the part of the celebrity gangster like his Hollywood hero, George Raft. You'd see Francis Bacon and Lucian Freud there quite a bit.

The Krays used it as a front, and you'd be afraid to run up debts there for obvious reasons. There was a story that one of their associates owed £3,000, which was a lot of dosh. Ronnie agreed to write it off in return for the remainder of the lease on his flat and the attentions of his lover, who became a croupier at the club. Ronnie liked to pick the male waiting staff depending on his own personal tastes. He used to get up to all sorts of nonsense with them at his newly acquired flat, or so the story went.

The brothers were terrible social climbers, and decided to bring a broke earl on board for a tenner a week. Mowbray Henry Gordon Howard, Sixth Earl of Effingham, used to drop in a few times a week to mix with guests. He was hanging around the night I first went there. He nodded and said 'Howdy do?' I thought he was a butler or something. I just smiled and nodded back. I was very camp, with my polo neck and long hair. The brothers saw me and didn't bat an eyelid. They had probably batted someone earlier that evening and had no energy left. They liked to use baseball bats on their enemies, apparently.

I thought Ronnie hadn't clocked me, but a few months later I was doing a gig and they walked in. Halfway through my act he let out a cheer and roared up at me: 'Corr, what a bleedin' waste.' Everyone laughed (it would have been dangerous not to). Thankfully, he didn't pursue me.

I was on stage when word came in about the shooting that marked the start of their downfall. Ronnie shot George Cornell in front of witnesses at the Blind Beggar pub. Word spread like wildfire across London that night. Some drunk in the audience started singing Mary Hopkin's song 'Those Were the Days', with some alterations: 'Those were the Krays, my friend, who thought they'd ever bend....' He was quickly ejected from the club.

The Krays were terrifying, but the Richardson brothers were the criminal world's laxative. They scared the shit out of *everyone*. They had a garage in Camberwell Green, not far from where I grew up. One of their favourite pastimes was chaining blokes up and frying their balls with electrodes. For some bizarre reason, members of their gang took me under their wing. They would regularly bring my mates and I to the West End in their Ford Granada. It was very salubrious, and had a portable record player. The first time I heard 'Hey Jude' was in the back of a motor that might have been used as a getaway car.

We'd get out at some club or other, they would walk behind us, and if anybody started they would sort them out. The girls were mad jealous of us. One night during a lock-in at the Vauxhall, one of the boys sat on the steps up to the stage, and I ended up hunkered between his legs with my back to him. There was nothing to it; we were all just relaxing and nattering.

I could see an angry-looking young cow giving me daggers. She took me aside and threatened to scratch my eyes out if I didn't give her a chance with the lads.

'No problem, love, he's all yours. He might pull your todger if you're lucky.'

She nearly spat at me, and retreated to the bar, where she grabbed her mate.

'We're going, Elsie. They're all Iron Hoofs in here.'

I told the boys, and they wet themselves laughing. I have to say, although they were hard men, I enjoyed them. And they enjoyed me. I wasn't a threat to them and was one of their own. They were straight and just liked winding people up.

There were other places we'd fall into on a night out. The Arts and Battledress Club (a favourite among actors and sailors), the Colony Club and the Rockingham Club. You couldn't get into the latter without a tie, and they had a selection at the reception. The place used to be heaving with elegant men swanning around with gins and tonics, listening to a chap tinkling away on the piano. It was all very graaaawwwnd.

There was the Cricketers too, where I met Sir Noël Coward—and was in awe of him. I was with David Steele at the time. David was always a forward bugger, and went up and introduced me to England's National Treasure.

'Delighted to make yourrrr acquaintance,' Coward said. 'Won't you join us for some rrrrefrrrrreshments?' He was rolling his 'r's quite a lot that evening for some reason. As opposed to rolling his arse. Sorry, that was an appalling gag. Let's move on, shall we? Listening to Coward speak was one of the most delightful things I've ever experienced. Can I remember anything he said? No. But that doesn't matter: it was the *way* he said whatever he said that I remember. What I do recall is Noel standing, a little unsteadily, towards the end of the evening, and clearing his throat loudly before launching into 'Come into the Garden, Maud'.

> *Come into the garden, Maud,*
> *For the black bat, night, has flown,*
> *Come into the garden, Maud,* ·
> *I am here at the gate alone…*

Some queen shouted, 'I'm not surprised, Mother!' We all laughed. I'm not sure if Coward did. Shortly after doing his turn, he called for his driver and the party broke up. I remember walking outside and being surprised to see the great man pulling off in a battered Austin Princess. Actually, I should rephrase that—driving off. Tight git, I thought. He hadn't even bought a round of drinks.

I was at the Cricketers another night when a gorgeous man fluttered through the door. I say 'fluttered' because his body movements were as subtle and graceful as a butterfly's. It was the Russian ballet dancer Rudolf Nureyev with dance master Roland Petit in tow. While Rudolf was well known for going cruising after a performance, Roland was married to the beautiful Zizi Jeanmaire, so one presumed the latter was straight, at least most of the time. Neither looked particularly butch on this night: they were swaddled in furs, and Rudolf had some slap on.

I have no idea how we got talking, but somehow we all ended up heading to south London, where, I guaranteed them, we'd get a late drink at the Union pub. The place fell silent as we entered (I love when that happens). The guv'nor immediately recognised Nureyev and came rushing over, ushering us to an occupied corner table (which he cleared in a second with the gentle instruction: 'Sling your hook, we have quality here'). The 'quality' (Nureyev and Petit) attempted to lower themselves into the chair with as much dignity as they could muster. They had had so much to drink, however, that they spilled themselves over the table. The landlord didn't care. He dashed off and came back with a bottle of vodka and an ice bucket.

'What will you have, Alan?' he asked me. It was the first time he'd ever called me 'Alan'.

'A large brandy, if you please, landlord,' I replied. He grinned horribly and went off to get my drink, muttering, 'I'll fucking "large brandy" you.'

We got appallingly sloshed, and stayed until the small hours. It was the first time I'd ever been to a lock-in there before. The

Mum and Dad's wedding day, before the war.

Mum and Dad.

Mum, Dad and me, aged 2 – get the hairstyle! That was Mum's doing.

Me, aged 6.

Santa and me, aged 5.

The munitions factory where my mum worked during the war.
This was a party for the kids. That's me, sitting out at the front on the right
(Mum's behind me in the headscarf).

My first professional photograph
(by Mike Arlen, aka Mike McGrath).

The Count and me.

Me at the Baggot Inn in the late sixties.
Looks more 1860s!

Modelling for Carnaby Street.

Photo for the Baggot Inn, early seventies.

Modelling with Cindy Steeden.
The headline was 'Which one's the guy?'
I'm on the left, by the way.

My first Irish publicity shot (for posters).

Revue with Sil Fox. It was called
The Fox and Pussy Show.

More modelling shots.

Panto with Eileen Reid.
I played the Dame, called Dame Street.

Me, Mum and Jim Sheridan at Café De Luxe on her birthday.

Jim McCann, Luke Kelly and me at the Olympia.

Carrying the coffin at The Diceman's funeral. I'm wearing the hat.

following afternoon I got a call from Roland. He wanted to meet me for a cure. I think he had his eye on me. I agreed, and asked if Nureyev would be there. So, along with my mate Lilah, we made another trip to the Union, and I think Rudolf went there a few times on his own too.

Nureyev was a God. He had high cheekbones, a cute little scar on his upper lip, and a body to go nuts for. He used to go to the Turkish baths in German Street and stand under the shower for half an hour showing himself off. He was such a tease.

In 1992 I was having dinner in the Trocadero in Dublin when I felt someone was staring at me. I looked around and a man at a table nearby caught my eye. I thought: *how do I know that face?* Then the penny dropped. It was Rudolf. He was HIV positive, and his health was failing. He looked very frail. I went over and chatted about London and suggested we meet for a drink. He declined, saying he had to rehearse every day. I didn't take it personally: the man was very ill and had probably given up drink as well. He passed away the following January. He was only fifty-four.

Sometimes, if the Cricketers was quiet, we'd head down to scoff some jellied eels at Tubby Isaac's, then on to a pub called the Coleherne, which was one of the few leather bars in the city, and HQ of the 'Invisible Bikers'. Its 'biker boy' clientele would hang around there in their scuffed jackets and tight jeans, carrying their helmets and looking tough and mean. They never put the helmets down because this was where they kept their ciggies and aftershave. Not one of them owned a motorbike, but they still wore the gear— hence the name 'Invisible Bikers'. They were all 'Hello, dearie. Me on a motorbike? Faaaaaar too dangerous, darling. Would you like a strawberry daiquiri?' They looked bona, though.

London was full of odd bods like the bikeless bikers. There were colourful characters and famous people wherever you turned, and very little snobbery. Everybody was equal because everybody was pissed. Constantly pissed. If you asked what time of day it was, you'd hear, 'Don't be so ridiculous.' Breakfast would be, 'Darling, give your mother a gin and tonic.' If people didn't have money they would scrounge it. You could get a lager and lime for one-and-nine back then. Booze was cheap. Gin was about half a crown, and the bus was only about five pence. Not that I used buses, dear.

It was commonplace to wind up sitting beside someone famous in a bar or café and strike up a conversation. One of the most intriguing stars I ever met was David Bowie. I can't remember the place: it might have been a coffee bar or a clothes shop. It was 1969, and his career was about to take off. We were both featured in a new magazine called *Jeremy*, and chatted about whether it would survive.

My manager, Ian Davey, got us into the control room of a studio where he was recording. He was phenomenal. Weird, melodic and strangely sexy. We had a cup of tea with him afterwards, and he was very friendly.

We were also invited along to the rehearsal for the Save Rave charity concert at the Palladium, and saw him perform 'Space Oddity'. It was as if a light were switched on in my head. I had never heard anything so poetic and melancholic and rebelliously beautiful before. We met him again backstage with my idol, Dusty Springfield.

'Did you like the song?' he asked. I was speechless. He genuinely seemed to want my opinion. In hindsight he was probably being kind, but I did hear that he had a gift for making people feel special and at ease. It was heartbreaking to hear of his death. We thought he'd live forever.

We thought Brian Epstein would live forever too. By 1967, the Beatles manager had the world at his feet. He was rich, in control of the greatest band the world will ever see, and popular around London's gilded streets.

One night I was trying to save money by walking as far as I could when a green Rolls-Royce came towards me. The lights were on inside, and I thought the driver looked familiar. He rolled down the window.

'Would you like a lift?' It was Epstein. I got in, thinking: *oi, oi, he'll be trying it on with me.*

'I'm Brian,' he said.

'I know,' I answered. 'I'm Alan, but my friends call me Pussy.'

'What a charming name,' he replied. 'But you look rather like the opposite of Pussy, if you get my meaning.'

I laughed, and he grinned, and he asked where I was going. He didn't seem in any way put out at the thought of driving me all the way to Peckham.

'I don't sleep, so I drive around at night,' he explained.

I thought nothing of this at the time, but in hindsight it was an obvious indication of the stress he was under. I gave him a hug goodnight, and that was it. There was no nonsense between us. I wouldn't have been Brian's type. He was into 'rough trade', and sought his jollies in the tougher parts of Liverpool and London, often getting the crap knocked out of him. I think he enjoyed the danger, being the pampered son of a posh, well-off Jewish family.

The last time I saw him was in the Cromwellian Club. I enjoyed his company. He was warm and witty, and had a twinkle about him. That twinkle was snuffed out in 1967 when poor Brian accidentally overdosed. This was the same year when homosexuality was legalised in the UK. His timing was pretty awful.

Brian was known to like 'cruising' for sex, like many other men during the 1960s. Probably the most infamous cruising/trolling area was Hampstead Heath. There used to be gay orgies in the bushes, and respectable folk would never dream of going there after dark. The toilets used to be the main meeting point, and as public lavs looked like cottages back then, this is where the term 'cottaging' comes from. Don't say I never teach you anything. Impress your mates with that juicy factoid.

The coppers regularly went down in their civvies to harass the poor chaps. I think they took sadistic pleasure in this. They were a bit less diligent when the Royal Tournament was on in Earl's Court. The shrubbery around there would be heaving with soldiers and civvies bonking and getting up to mischief. No sensible copper would ever dare to interrupt a tough commando while he was at it. It was a risky thing to do.

Naturally, there was a lot of straight sex going on in London too. My mate Blossom and I loved hanging out with the prossies and laughing at their antics. We would often go down in drag to Soho's clip joints, where customers were expected to buy expensive (and shit) champagne for the hostesses. The girls would slip us the champers in exchange for 7UP (as they were working), we'd get pissed, they would get paid, and the John would get fleeced.

We used to frequent one house of ill repute—in drag—where the girls were hilarious. They ran a scam that was pretty inventive, and very naughty. In one of the bedrooms they had a wardrobe with a false back, which was placed in front of a connecting door. The punter would leave his strides on the back of a chair and get down to business with the lady, while unbeknownst to him another lady would sneak through the wardrobe and steal his wallet, disappearing like a Narnian tart the same way she had come in.

When the job was complete, the prossie would ask for her money and the punter would discover that his wallet was missing. All hell would break loose. The prossie would pretend to be sympathetic.

'Oh, you left it at home? Could happen to anyone. I'll just go and see what the boss has to say.' She'd leave the room, and within a minute the scared customer would hear roars and shouts of 'I'll fucking kill the cheating cunt!' coming from below. The prossie would then return and say, 'You'd better scarper. Alf [or whatever his name was] is going to rip your balls off.' The client would then peg it faster than Roger Bannister with a firework up his arse while the girls laughed their heads off in the next room, divvying up all the readies they had stolen from him and writing false cheques as quickly as they could.

It all seems a bit heartless now, but one of them, Frenchy, was putting her son through college, so some of it went to a good cause.

Now you may think, reading all of the above, that England was the most liberal, gay-friendly place on the planet, and men like me were fully accepted by mainstream society. We weren't. I led a charmed life within a subculture. In 1966, loving the wrong person could land you in jail. Smiling at someone in a park could lead to arrest. Even being in someone's address book was dangerous. The coppers liked to arrest gay men because such arrests were seen as easy convictions. The papers sometimes referred to these cases as 'gross indecency'. Modern readers will understandably recoil in horror from those words. Consensual sex between adults is not 'indecent'—filthy sometimes, but never indecent.

Even war heroes couldn't escape the 'wrong arm of the law'. Alan Turing, who had broken the Enigma code and hastened the end of World War Two, was arrested in 1952 and convicted of gross indecency. He was forced to undergo hormone therapy, and later committed suicide by eating a cyanide-covered apple. If a man who had saved millions of lives could be hounded to his death because of his sexuality, what chance was there for the average cottaging-enthusiast?

That's how it was back then. In July 1967, the House of Commons finally passed a bill legalising homosexuality. The old queens saw legalisation as a threat to their old, secret way of life, while conservatives saw it as a threat to the country's moral fabric, whatever that means. Even after legalisation, gay celebrities continued to hide their sexuality.

Frankie Howerd was one of those men. My mate David Pearson knew him well. He was a lecherous old cow, always touching people up and saying, 'Oh, don't tell anyone.'

A cousin of mine had a villa in Malta, and invited Frankie around for dinner (he had his own place called Up Pompeii, after the movie). After the meal they went for a stroll, and he put his hand on my cousin's arse.

'Oh nooooo. Nooooo, missus, don't tell anyone,' he blathered. Howerd was a saddo, and in a lot of self-denial. Everyone knew he was gay, even his fans. The same way everyone knew Kenneth Williams was a queen. Kenneth's *Carry On* colleague Charles Hawtry was another who never officially came out, although he was rip-roaringly obvious. Everyone loved Charles. You could hear him long before you saw him. He was exactly the same as his screen persona.

He used to tell a story about the time his house caught fire while he was in bed with a man. The firemen axed their way through the front door and came barging in. 'Oooooh, fancy that,' he cooed from under the blankets. The butch, and generally unshockable, firefighters were quite perplexed to see their favourite *Carry On* star naked to the waist and wigless beside what appeared to be a drunken sailor. They turfed the tar (sailor) out of bed, snatched up Charles's spindly body and carried it downstairs, while he sang: 'What shall we do with a drunken sailor ... ear*ly* in the *mor*ning? Oh, don't ask. Don't ask!' When he got to the front door he remembered he had left his smokes by the bed. No queen ever likes to be without their fags, so he wriggled free of Fireman Sam and said, 'Hold on, I have to go back. I left my ciggies beside the bed.' He was caught before he could run back upstairs.

Charles later lost both his legs to smoking.

'Fuck it,' he said. 'I'll carry on drinking. I'm not going to live without my legs.' And he drank himself to death, literally dying legless.

Another actor who wasn't enamoured with the new legal status was Richard Watters. You'll remember him from old movies and TV shows where he would play vicars and authority types. He wore tiny, round glasses, and was a bit ferret-faced. He used to sit in the Escort Club and moan all the time.

'Oh, why are we on this planet? When you get to my age, everything is changing…' You'd think he would have preferred to have been banged up inside, the silly old poof.

Then there were the heart-throbs who pretended to like girls to protect their image. Music stars like Long John Baldry. He was a great chum whom I knew from my early Chelsea days. Baldry discovered Rod Stewart and Elton John, who was then known as Reggie Dwight. Reg named himself after John. I've met Elton a few times over the years, the first being at the Garden Club. He was entertaining and friendly. When he got up to go to the loo, he leaned across the table and mock-whispered to me: 'Fabulous jacket … you rotten old cow.' He was joking of course, but somehow I think if he said the same words today he might actually mean them. He comes across as very cranky. I'm digressing. Back to Long John….

One morning he called to say he was doing *Top of the Pops* with 'Let the Heartache Begin', and asked if I wanted to come along. Too bleeding right I did. We sat in the BBC canteen, and I gaped at all the stars there eating buns and drinking tea. Clueless young girls queued up for his autograph, fantasising about him doing all sorts with them. John was more interested in the young chap at the till.

Someone asked if I was famous. John immediately chimed in with, 'This is Alan, girls. He's going to be a huge star,' and insisted that I autograph their books for them. I was mortified, but it was such a kind, generous gesture to an aspiring act. Really typical of the man.

After the show, he said, 'Let' go back to Becky Bart's.' I hadn't a clue who he was talking about. 'Becky' was Lionel Bart, the man behind the musical *Oliver!*, and another closeted gay man.

We arrived at the showbiz legend's house, which was more like a palace, and the first thing I noticed was the enormous weathercock on its roof. It had to be a joke. Sticking a huge 'cock' on top of your house for the entire countryside to see, while not publicly revealing your sexuality, was definitely making a statement.

There was a Bentley Continental in the drive, and a member of staff answered the door. He led us through the long hallway (which had a fountain) into an enormous room with a minstrel's gallery. Lionel was watching telly and jumped up out of a leather armchair to greet us. He then pressed a button in the chair's armrest and the TV disappeared into the wall. We sat there happily chatting with him while his assistant made us cocktails.

After a few drinks I needed to pee, and was directed to the loo. I opened the door to find a toilet that was a faithful replica of Queen Liz's throne. The chain was part of a mace, and when you pulled it it played 'God Save the Queen'.

This is the life for me, I thought as I was driven home to Peckham that night in Baldry's car. I've never managed to get enough money together to buy myself a loo/throne, although I've done well for myself financially over the years. The flitting between the working-class and posh worlds I inhabited could have been head-wrecking, but I straddled both with ease. The 'bi' nature of my social life taught me not to get too enamoured or infatuated with material things. I don't care how much money people have: what counts is that they are decent, kind and entertaining. There were certainly plenty of those salt-of-the-earth types in the East End, even if the world they inhabited might not have been to everyone's taste.

One of those salty, earthy types became my best friend. His/her name was Stella Minge.

Chapter Six

Sequins and Sea Queens

I met Stella Minge indirectly via the telephone exchange and the Merchant Navy. Stella—real name, Derek M—lived down at the East End docks, which were always a great draw for queens. You would see them openly wandering around, as bold as brass, in ski pants and hair rollers, doing their shopping.

There was a popular gay rendezvous pub called the Round House, and once the ships docked the tars would steam up to its bar and get rat-arsed. I went there a lot with my buddies Lilah and Cindy. Cindy had had a sex change and gave me her old sailor's discharge card, which allowed me to get into the seamen's missions and around the docks. One night I had to make a call from the Round House's public telephone and got on to the operator. I heard a voice in the background say 'Bona!' I replied, 'Polari!'

The operator was impressed.

'Oh hello, dear,' he said. 'What can I help you with?' We stayed on and chatted. His name was George, and he lived near me. It turned out that the telephone exchange was heaving with homosexuals. He invited me down, and I got to know the gay mafia there. We had a laugh, and decided to go out on the town. I can't recall where we were when this beautiful Elvis lookalike strode in wearing a leather jacket. All the poofs went 'Oooooh' and then 'Ahhhh' when he pounced on Pussy.

He was an Irishman, Sean Kelly, and he worked as a deckhand aboard a merchant ship. Like many young Irishmen, he had run away to sea to escape persecution for his homosexuality. There were more queers on the high seas than there were waves. We did a line for a while, and I really liked him. He was strong and could handle himself in a fight. There's a stupid phrase: 'handle yourself in a fight'. Whoever 'handles themself' during a scrap?

'Hang on a second, mate. I just want to handle myself.' Better off using your hands to smack your opponent, in my not-so-humble opinion. Anyway, Sean and I were on the way home one night when we were set upon by a group of gougers, who started shouting 'Fucking poofs' at us. He told me to go on ahead, and I ran home. You can call me chicken if you like, but I have always been useless in a brawl.

I was worried to death that he'd be hurt, but we had no phone to call the cops. Half an hour later I heard footsteps on the stairs, and there was a loud knock at the door. *He's brown bread*, I thought.

I opened up and he breezed past me, whistling, without a scratch on him.

'They won't be bothering us again.'

Sean had sorted them out. I threw my arms around his neck and gave him a long, lingering kiss. Three days later I passed the same group of arseholes on the street corner. They actually said hello to me. He must have knocked the stuffing out of them.

Poor Sean died young. He took a fall on board his ship and got tangled in the anchor chain. Such a pointless waste of a life.

There's an old joke that goes: how do they separate the men from the boys in the Merchant Navy? With a crowbar.

The same could be said of the queens and sailors that populated the East End docks. There would be parties every night on the different vessels. Queens like myself would rattle up the gangplank in their wigs and Cuban heels. (I stopped wearing Cubans after I got one stuck between two planks and nearly fell into the harbour.) We'd go down to the cabins and drink and dance, or do a tour of the engine rooms, if you know what I mean.

I fell asleep on a ship and nearly ended up in France once. My mates had gone up on deck to do some early-morning scrubbing or something, and I was snoring on the bunk when someone came in.

'Oi, Pussy. Move yer arse. We're about to cast off for Marseille.' I legged it, slipping and sliding across the deck and down the gangplank. The skipper must have seen me from the bridge—he hooted his horn at me.

Speaking of horns ... I have to point something out here. I was not a promiscuous young man. I was normal in that regard. Our scene was mostly about hanging around with similar people, not bonking them to beat the band. It was a more innocent age in many respects, and seemed to breed memorable characters ... like Stella Minge.

The first time I saw the Minge was down at the Kent. The pub's interior was made up like a ship, with metal nuts and bolts all over the place. There was supposed to be a golden rivet hidden in it somewhere. The owners said that if you found it you could have a drink on the house. I don't know if anybody did, but there was a lot of bending over while punters searched the floor for it. Maybe that's why they said it.

I remember walking through the doors and seeing an apparition—a woman with hair like cotton wool, full make-up, huge rings and bright red lipstick, sitting on a stool that appeared to be different to the others. I started to smile. She/he was the worst drag queen I'd ever seen. The landlady saw me grinning and slipped out from behind the bar.

'Don't cross her, dear, or she'll kill you,' she warned. I laughed, and Stella spun around on her stool.

'What *the fuck* are you laughing at, you West End poof?' she snarled.

'Nothing, dear,' I replied serenely. 'I was just admiring your style. Very camp-meets-butch. Bravo.' Stella's eyes darkened. I noticed a film of sweat across her unshaven upper lip. She could go either way, I thought. The pub was so quiet you could hear a golden rivet drop.

Then she started to laugh, and the buzz of conversation started up again. I bought her a drink and we became (taped-up) bosom buddies.

While Stella accepted me, she absolutely hated what she called 'the West End poofs'. She was a complete 'reverse snob'. Anyone who wasn't from the East End was a West End poof down 'to ruin our night'. One evening she came into the Kent, where a pretty young queen was sitting on her stool. Without any warning, Stella walked up, shouted 'Cunt!' and clocked her. You didn't mess with Minge's stool.

Stella was fifty-three, and served in the navy during the war, where she got a taste for drag, like a lot of other young men at the time. We spoke Polari, and I used to do her hair and make-up. She had two houses next to each other: one was used to rent out rooms to sailors, and the other was her private HQ. There was a secret way into hers via the back garden (it wouldn't have looked good if she had had a steady stream of draggers banging on her front door). We'd climb over her wall and unlatch the kitchen door. If Minge was hung-over, she would hold court in bed, asking, 'Have you brought any bevvy, dear?'

When she wasn't hung-over, she held the best parties in London. She took turns hosting them with her neighbour, another queen called Mental Marilyn. Minge's evenings were more popular than Marilyn's, which peeved the latter a lot. One night I was sitting by the window at Minge's, and a brick came through the window.

There was a note attached: 'Minge, you fucking cunt. How dare you have more parties than me.'

What was particularly unique about this brick/letter/message was that it was covered in sequins. Even when angry, drag queens love their bit of bling.

Minge's parties were legendary, with people stripping off and dancing. Too legendary. I was going back to Minge's one night in drag, and thought I saw a group of men in the back of a van. Minge told me not to be so paranoid. The next night her house was raided by the police. The van had been full of coppers. Thankfully, I wasn't there at the time. They did it under the pretext that she was running an immoral house. There was nothing immoral about it. She didn't hold orgies or anything. It was all drinking and dancing and acting the goat.

For example, one night Minge's friends dug a grave in the back garden and attempted to throw her into it. Another night, someone tried to drive a motorbike up her hole. I was shocked when I heard this.

'Someone tried to drive a motorbike up her hole? That's a bit much, isn't it?'

'No, pet, you misheard me,' said Blossom. 'I said up her *hall.*' Minge couldn't stop laughing when she heard this. They were the kind of 'immoral' shenanigans that went on at Stella's.

I was down at Minge's so much that she suggested I take a room—for free. It meant that I had rooms in Earl's Court, there, and at home in Peckham too. I was an independent woman/man-about-town. I was mad about Minge. We'd sit up late on quiet nights and nibble meat pie, instant mash and beans, talking rubbish and laughing.

There were other nutters like Minge, but none as colourful. Guys like Betty Bagwash (she did our laundry), Cucumber Kate (rumoured to have her own tits) and Gilda Gash. Gilda was a mad cow. She nearly took my head off with a beer can once. She threw it at my head, enraged that I was getting too much attention from someone else's boyfriend. The can left a hole in the wall beside my bonce.

Times were changing, and so was the East End. It was being redeveloped, and the ships stopped coming in. Minge's livelihood depended on sailors looking for digs, so she upped sticks and moved to Southampton, where she ran a successful B&B. She died ten years ago, and must have been about ninety. I loved her/him to bits, and still see her with her horrible wig and pint of gin and tonic clenched between her chipped, varnished fingernails, smoking a woodbine. Minge was the undisputed leader of the East End queens.

It was 1969, and the Swinging Sixties were drawing to a close. My career was taking off, and I had befriended a man who would later become the best-known male nude photographer in the world, Mike McGrath, aka Mike Arlen, aka Millie. He made his living covering the men's fashion scene around Carnaby Street. Somewhere along the line he supplied a German mag with photos of bodybuilders in swimsuits, and was asked if he had more 'revealing' images. His photography career skyrocketed after that. By the by, you may be surprised to learn that back in the bad old days the British censor wouldn't allow the publication of photographs of erections. Mike got around this by tucking the boner under the model's leg. Other times he literally tied down the 'offending' penis.

Mike was an early starter, and was blessed with a supportive mum, who treated him as a grown-up from an early age. Between twelve and eighteen he acted in hundreds of plays, and from the age of fifteen he began his career in journalism, interviewing celebs and getting articles published in *She* and *Woman's Own*.

Speaking of mums, Millie lived with his in an old Victorian flat in Weatherby Mansions. You'd arrive, and the old dear would be having tea in her room while Millie listened to Vera Lynn on the gramophone in the sitting room. Millie would have gatherings most nights, and the place would be full of famous faces: Becky Bart, Peter Wyngarde, Kiki Dee, Epstein … even Veronica Lake, the Hollywood actress, would all go there. Poor Veronica, who was acting in the West End, was pickled the night I saw her. She had a wig on because she'd burned her hair.

It was on one of these evenings that Millie suggested I do a photo shoot. He thought it would be fun to do a 'Which one is the man?' feature article based on Carnaby Street. Being a vain cow, I readily agreed.

The session was arranged for the following weekend at the East End docks. It was a 10 a.m. start, which meant I had to get up extra early to put on my slap, wig, fur coat, etc. I looked every inch the Mod girl. It was a windy day, and when I got to the end of the street my wig blew off, so I legged it back home and grabbed a gypsy scarf to tie it down. I then flagged down a taxi as I was running late.

'Where to, love?' the driver asked. I could see him licking his lips in the rear-view mirror.

'The docks, sweetie. And that's the only rear view you're going to get of me, so keep your bleedin' eyes on the road.' He laughed and held the door open for me when we arrived at the shoot.

'Your boyfriend is a lucky man,' he sighed, nodding at Mike/Millie, who was setting up his gear.

'Hands off, mate,' Millie shouted with mock concern. The cabbie looked past him to our female model, Cindy Stevens.

'You've got the best fucking job in the world!' he roared as he sped back down the docks.

'Well, if we can fool a London cabbie, we can fool anyone, darling,' laughed Millie.

That day is a bit of a blur. Millie took us down by the river when the tide was out and had us posing in a disused printworks. He even made me go topless, which drew a few cheers from the three beer-bellied dockers who were admiring us.

'All right, lads?' I shouted in my roughest Peckham accent. I've never seen three fat bastards move so quickly.

Millie sent out releases to the papers. *Tidbits*, the *Daily Mirror* and the weekend supplements all ran the pictures under the heading 'Which one's the girl?' The snaps ended up on billboards on Carnaby Street, and there were immediate offers of modelling work. I was famous.

I didn't get to reap the benefits of that day, though. When the press came calling for interviews, I was far, far away, in a land that time and the sexual revolution had bypassed. There was a different type of revolution happening there.

I was heading into a warzone called Northern Ireland....

Chapter Seven

Going Down on a Bomb Up North

'Belfast? We're going to Belfast?'

Ian Davy nodded.

'Do you know where Belfast is, Alan?'

'Yes, of course I do you dozy git. It's in Ireland.'

My manager nodded again.

'Will it be safe?'

'Of course it will be safe,' he purred. 'Those riots you see on the telly are all happening in housing estates in Derry, well away from Belfast city centre. We'll be perfectly safe.'

I was horrified.

'What riots? I was talking about the flying. You know I hate to fly. What's all this nonsense about riots?'

Ian sighed indulgently and explained to me that the Catholics of Northern Ireland were getting a raw deal from the majority Unionist powers-that-were. I didn't catch all of it. I've never been into politics.

'Will there be a nice "handbag" in it?' I asked, referring to the fee. Ian smiled and nodded again. He had told me all about the trip a month before but I'd forgotten all about it. The owner of

71

the Intercontinental cabaret club had come over to see one of my London shows, and was so impressed—and excited at the prospect of bringing drag to Belfast—that he had booked me on the spot. I was down to do one week. Ian had deliberately not reminded me because of my fear of flying. The night before we were due to travel, he made sure that I had plenty to drink at a party in my honour at Millie's place. When I boarded the plane I was still three-quarters pissed, and numbed to the idea of my pert little bottom being flown over the Irish Sea.

I recall the plane landing with a loud screech of brakes. Although, in hindsight, that might have been me. I grabbed my fur coat and pegged it to the exit. The Belfast drizzle frizzed my hair and gently smacked me in the face. There was a series of flashes and I thought for a second that I was either being shot at or that a bomb had gone off. It was neither. A large mob of paparazzi had gathered around the foot of the steps and were calling my name.

'To me, Pussy … give us a smile, Pussy … what about ye, Pussy….'

I was being received as a star in a city about which I knew nothing. It was fantastic. I felt like Sophia Loren, and gathered my fur coat around my neck and pouted and posed like mad. The snappers loved it. I was then swept up and hurried through arrivals.

'No customs check?' I asked Ian, surprised.

'No, Alan. That was an internal flight. We're still in the UK.' I was a bit embarrassed, to tell the truth. I thought that Ulster was attached to the Republic. I wasn't alone in this. Millions of Brits hadn't a clue about Ulster and its part in our shared history. That would all change within months when the bombing started in earnest.

I was driven through the grim, grey streets and thought: *what a dump*. Then I saw something that lifted the gloom: my face on a billboard over the busy pavement beside the Intercontinental.

'Drag Comes to Belfast', it read. *Jesus,* I thought, *no pressure.* The sight of the poster made me more determined to make it the most memorable performance in the city's history. I stepped out of the car and into the foyer, like Princess Margaret on steroids. The club's PR had arranged a press conference, which made my head spin. It seemed that Northern Ireland was going crazy at the idea of a drag queen coming to town. I could be a plonker and say it was all about me and how great my act was, but in truth I was a novelty. I didn't care. I was being treated like a star, and that was all that counted.

I did the conference with a legit comic playwright, Sam Cree. That added to the importance of the occasion. I was being seen as a major act. Sam was wonderful. He was massively popular in the North, and beyond. I heard at the time that he had been offered £80,000 for his play *Cupid Wore Skirts*, which he wrote in 1965. The Troubles badly hit theatre audience numbers, but during the height of his success he spent three weeks in Hollywood touring the studios and meeting Jerry Lewis, Frank Sinatra, Liza Minnelli and Dean Martin. He also wrote for the *Carry On* films and Arthur Askey and George Formby. To be on the same PR 'bill' as him was a huge compliment.

After the press conference, I was put back into my posh car and driven to my accommodation. We drove up Serpentine Avenue, a very posh Protestant area, and were met at our B&B by the owners, Jack and Iris Hill. They ran a very upmarket house. They were kind and hospitable, with Jack's loud Ballymena accent trumpeting: 'You'll have a cup of tea, so?'

Iris was very stylish, and was always dressed up with a touch of fur and nice frocks. My bedroom was large, bright and airy, and had something on the bed I'd never seen before: a duvet. They were just coming into vogue then. I remember thinking: *I must get one.* I'd never have to make the bed again. Iris leaned over and whispered to me. 'We have another big star staying with us. His name is Bert Weedon.'

I was impressed. Bert was one of the most influential musicians in the world. He was the first British guitarist to have a hit record in the UK singles chart, in 1959, and he wrote tutorial guides: *Play in a Day* and others. Eric Clapton, Paul McCartney, George Harrison, John Lennon, Brian May, Dave Davies of The Kinks, Keith Richards, Pete Townshend, Tony Iommi, Jimmy Page … they all tugged their long forelocks to him as their mentor. He was awarded an OBE in 2001 for his services to music. Bert was a genius, and a lovely man too.

We hit it off immediately over tea and fruit cake in the dining room. He was playing the Piccadilly Line while I was at the Intercontinental. We became great friends, and even had a near-death experience together. But I'll come back to that.

Later that afternoon I went back to the club to do a soundcheck. I couldn't believe my eyes when I saw a queue of people snaking around the corner to buy tickets for my gig. I was down to do one week only. At this rate, I thought, I'll be here for years—and I was quite happy with that prospect. Everyone I had met was friendly and polite and enthusiastic.

Show time came around, and I knew it would be make-or-break. My knowledge of Ireland was rough, but I had been told that the crowd would be very different and to go easy on them. I was a bit more nervous than usual when I put on my wig and stockings in the dressing room. I just trusted that my mischievous nature would carry me through. I could only do my best.

The music swelled, the curtain went up … and I took to the stage in a long blue chiffon frock. They didn't know what hit them. I started with a song: Bobbie Gentry's 'Never Fall in Love Again', and then launched into the gags.

'What do you think of my dress? I went up to bed last night and told my husband to rip it off. He did. I said, "And don't ever let me catch you wearing it again!"' They roared laughing. I never got any bluer than that. In the second half I wore my mini and floored them.

They were a mixed crowd—from both traditions—and very respectful, which was a shame as I like hecklers. They are always great for getting the audience on side. They just couldn't believe that I was a man. I did my usual routine of stripping an audience member. He was mortified, the poor chap. I think he was with his mum. Or else he had married his missus blindfolded. Another night at the same venue I did the same stunt, and was told quietly and politely to back off. The punter had a gun under his jacket.

The crowd loved the show. They were either out to be shocked, or just to have a laugh. They mobbed me afterwards, and I had my first taste of signing autographs. I could feel my head swelling. Some punters even ripped buttons off my shirt to keep as souvenirs. If you're reading this, I want them back.

A one-week stint turned into a six-week run. The money was great. I got £160 a week, which would be about £2,000 today. That was just when I was starting out, before I became famous all over Ireland. Other gigs rolled in too. Some were a bit 'hairy'. When a promoter gets his teeth into you, you never know what venue you'll be playing next.

One evening I was I picked up by a sturdy-looking car with a very sturdy-looking driver. He took me down a side street and asked me to step out. A Saracen armoured car rolled up, and the back door flew open. Two soldiers jumped out, smiled, and motioned me to step into the back of the vehicle, sharpish. I was in full drag: kinky boots, waistcoat, mini … I did what I was told and squeezed in beside two very handsome squaddies. It was going to be a barracks gig. We didn't say much, and I couldn't take my eyes off the machine gun on the floor. We drove into the camp, and I was led to a dressing room full of nude strippers.

The first show was for the privates, and the second for the officers. I loved sending them up. Some were old-school

Sandringham types. I recall a colonel with a red Lord Kitchener-style moustache and an even redder face standing by the bar. 'Who does he look like?' I asked Ian from the stage. The colonel smiled and twiddled the edge of his moustache. 'Our Doreen! That's right! He looks like our Doreen. Only she has a full beard.' The soldiers howled at that. That was the only time I played for the army. I was really worried that someone might spot me and shoot me, so I always had an excuse when a gig came up. To tell you the truth, I felt sorry for those young chaps. I know it was a war, and all sides were doing terrible things, but some of them were only kids. You knew they probably missed their mums, and being able to socialise like normal young men.

I wasn't thinking about any of that though when I took my bows at the Intercontinental that night. I was just interested in finding a party and being adored. I was a conceited little brat. Ian, my manager, had spoken to a few people about Belfast nightlife, and we headed off to sample the delights of this new city. We were brought to a famous journalists' pub, the Duke of York, which was down an alley in the former newspaper district. I met David Dunseith there—he later interviewed me on BBC TV—and he bought me my first pint of Guinness. I used to go there regularly over the years, and the famous Crown too, where I'd have a laugh and hear the journos talking about what was going on. I got very friendly with 'The Two Gerrys', Messrs Anderson and Kelly, who were big stars up there and, in Kelly's case, the Republic too. I was on RTÉ's *Play the Game* with him twice. There was another Gerry there as well, although nobody knew who he was at the time. Sinn Féin leader Gerry Adams worked behind the bar there during his student days in 1971.

There was another cheerful journo I met there and took a shine to. His name was Jackie Fullerton, and he was the sports anchor on BBC TV. He was always smiling. I was on a show with him once and told him, on air, that he was my type, 'tough and ruthless, not rough and toothless like the men I usually end up with.' The crew laughed, and he went beetroot red.

Northern Ireland's journos were really kind to me. They liked my neck, doing drag in a city run by ultra-conservatives. The TV, radio and print interviews kept coming. The stiff *Belfast Telegraph* even did a cartoon of me, and we used that in our adverts and on billboards across the North: 'Drag comes to Bangor', 'Drag comes to Portadown', etc. It was really exciting to go from London, where I was becoming well known, to Ireland, where I was being treated as a major star. Big fish, small pond, etc. Sam Smyth, today one of the most respected and admired journalists in Ireland, travelled up from Dublin to interview me for *Spotlight* magazine.

Gloria Hunniford, who was to become the first woman to host her own daily show on BBC Radio 2, also did a spot with me. Gloria is a beautiful woman and a lovely singer. She was due to meet me in the Intercontinental. I was wearing a fringed waistcoat, a salmon-pink top, Indian beads, a leather-studded bracelet and Cuban heels. She walked past me three times in the bar. We ended up doing the interview in a stairwell and having a great laugh. She's a bright, smart, bubbly woman who has had her share of pain. Her daughter Caron, also a successful broadcaster, died in 2004 of breast cancer. I felt so sorry for poor Gloria when I heard that.

Despite all this publicity, there was no backlash from the clergy on either side. Drag didn't exist as far as they were concerned. Or they didn't want to be associated with it. I suppose the Catholic side couldn't really have been too critical when you consider that they've been wearing dresses for years.

After the Duke, we did a little pub crawl. Back then, London was bright and more tolerant of gays in many ways, at least in terms of an acceptance that homosexuality existed, although it was still against the law. Belfast had a scene, although it was tiny and a bit morose. It had its gay cruising areas, and some of the favourite pick-up spots were at the Albert Clock, the Customs House toilet, Botanic Gardens and Ormeau Park. There was enough cottaging going on at Victoria Square to start a folk theme park. Actually, they *did* open the Ulster Folk and Transport Museum there. And let's not forget the Giant's Ring. If ever a place was appropriately named....

I recall one old-timer telling me that the cottages/toilets of Belfast were hopping after the infamous German air raid of 1941. I suppose if you've come that close to being blown up, you'll probably go looking for something more relaxing the day after.

When I arrived in the city, the main gay pub was the Royal Avenue in Rosemary Street. It was not openly called a gay pub: this was a city where differences of religious—let alone sexual— persuasion could lead you into serious trouble. The Avenue opened in the 1950s, and was shared at times with deaf customers who often took over the front of the bar. In terms of discretion, you couldn't better this. The managers of the pub were straight, but very tolerant considering the times they lived in. The Avenue eventually closed in the 1970s, and was replaced by the Casanova Club, which was bombed by the IRA in 1976 for allegedly serving RUC men.

As that decade progressed, gay rights activists became more and more vocal. The students at Queen's formed the Gay Liberation Society in 1972, and from 1975 to the early 1980s it ran popular Saturday-night discos in the McMordie Hall, which were attended by hundreds of gay and straight people.

The interesting thing here was that there was no other nightlife in Belfast back then. Gay men were the only people brave enough to venture out into the killing fields/streets. The gays of the North were a hardy bunch, and it was their efforts that ultimately led to the European Court of Human Rights ending life imprisonment for the North's gay men in 1982. It wasn't an easy road to travel. In 1976, the RUC arrested most of the highest-profile activists for sex acts. London intervened and forced the DPP to drop the charges.

The first gay-run pub in the city was the Chariot Rooms in Lower North Street. It had its own disco, and was run by Ernie and Jim through the most savage years of the Troubles. It operated in the central gated area, and punters had to be searched on the way in, which must have been fun. It was popular with a good cross-section of the community, including soldiers bunking off patrol duty.

Then there was the Europa, at one time the most bombed hotel in the world. In the 1970s and 1980s its Whip and Saddle bar was Belfast's only gay venue. Again, it took the North's gays to show enough bottle to drink in a bar that could be blown up at any time. That's not to say that members of the gay community were unscathed by the war. The Dunbar Arms was firebombed by the INLA, and drag queen Aunty Mae was nearly burned to death. She was the last out of the building. In 1997, when it was under new management, the INLA entered it again, and picked out a young man called Darren Bradshaw. He was an off-duty policeman who happened to be gay. They shot the poor man in front of the other terrified customers.

In the 1970s too, another man, Anthony McCleave, was murdered in the cruising area of Oxford Street. He was found, in June 1979, with his head skewered onto a spike on a bollard outside the fire station. The RUC closed the case within twenty-four hours, but was it reopened after a campaign by the Northern Ireland Gay Rights Association (NIGRA) and his family. No one was ever charged with his murder.

That's the overview of Belfast's gay scene. I'm not a historian, so if you want to know more then get off your bum and head to the library. Things were a lot friendlier when I arrived in the city. We wound up that first night in the Royal Avenue bar. My ego was so enormous at this stage that it had to be squeezed through the door. I was determined to be fabulous and make a stir. I did.

The Avenue was quiet when I entered. Then the punters lifted their heads from their drinks, and you could hear the oxygen being sucked out of the room. They had never seen anything like Pussy. I had my hair streaked blonde. This, by the way, was another reason why I was in no hurry to get back to London. If my mother had seen my hair she would have locked me in my room away from the neighbours.

I glided across the room like a diva on casters, and my manager found a table for us. It was clear that the regulars were afraid to talk to this alien vision, so Ian struck up a conversation. Before long we were surrounded by talkative queens, babbling away in their clipped northern accents. This was 1969, and the pub was full of Protestants and Catholics. Nobody cared about religion much on the gay scene back then. Gays had common enemies. I remember being amused by the way some of the men spoke with a whistle, like Jim Molyneaux and Ian Paisley. 'That's tsimply tsplendid, darling. You're tso fabulousth,' etc. etc.

One man stood out from the crowd. His name was Billy Moore, but everybody knew him as Samantha, and he was an ex-beaver-skin-wearing guardsman who had served the Queen at one of her palaces (I can't remember which one). He told me that she used to come down and say, 'Good morning, guard,' knowing full well that he couldn't reply. It was her little joke. I liked him immediately, and we chatted for the rest of the evening.

He became my assistant, looking after all my needs and helping me get ready in the dressing room of the Intercontinental. When I moved to Dublin's Mount Street, Billy came and stayed with me for a year, doing his own drag turn in the Baggot. He used to do his best to shock our neighbours. First thing in the morning he would throw open the window of the flat and address me loudly as 'madame'. As in, 'Would madame care to wake the fuck up?'

When madame had risen, Billy would sit me in front of the window and brush my hair. We loved watching the expressions on people's faces as they hurried by. Billy treated me royally, and would surprise me with a fish and chip supper, served with the best silverware. He was one of the funniest, most caring men I've ever known, and a great mate. When he left to return north we lost touch. I still have fond memories of him.

Closing time came around at the Avenue, and I was getting my second wind, so I asked where we were off to next. My new friends looked at me and grinned. There was no 'next'. That was it. Nightlife stopped at pub closing time. Someone suggested going back to his place with a few bottles and having a party. I can't remember where he lived, but it was one of the dullest parties of my life. At one point, during a lull in the drinking, someone suggested getting some food. 'I'd murder a Chinese,' I said, not realising that, in a murderous city, this might be a loaded thing to say. The boys laughed. My host shook his head. 'No Chinese, I'm afraid. How about some baps from the late-night shop down the road?' And so we spent the rest of the night chewing stale cheese and ham baps and drinking Bacardi. Hardly the West End.

I was forever being asked to parties after that, which I sometimes dreaded. One time I told the host to make sure there was some entertainment other than the radio and baps. He nipped out to his brother's house and came back with a Monopoly set, which he proudly produced when I arrived. Actually, we had a lot of fun playing that, with me making bomb noises every time my piece landed on a street.

The parties weren't all bad though. A man who ran a famous venue had a huge house and threw some fabulous shindigs, with people from all walks of life attending. He used to joke, 'If you're looking for the Teagues (Catholics), they're in the kitchen.' I was out every night, either at parties or hotel bars. I've always had great stamina, and am still the last to leave a bash. I worked hard too. I used to do the Intercontinental for the first half of the night and then over to the Piccadilly Line for the second.

Bert Weedon (remember him?) was driving us both to work one night when the bonnet went up on the car, blocking our view. I very gently and calmly opened the window and directed him. He said afterwards that he couldn't get over how calm I was, but then I've always been a cool cat. It takes a lot to get me wound up. I needed my nerves, as the IRA were starting to bomb the crap out of Belfast, and there were plenty of times when I thought my life was in danger.

The first time I heard a bomb go off, I was standing in the lobby of the Intercontinental. There was a shudder, and the feeling that you'd just got an electric shock. My hair stood on end. Then I heard the bang. There was dust everywhere, which made it hard to breathe. Everyone in the place was terrified, but I didn't run about like a headless chicken, which was my first instinct. The bomb had gone off around the corner at the Clock Tower. The locals knew that sometimes there could be a secondary device primed to go off and catch people fleeing from the first. Imagine planning that? How can people be so cruel to each other?

I calmed down and thought: *at least I can say I heard one now.* Everyone in the hotel just carried on. The same thing happened in another venue. I was in the dressing room, and the bar was full of women and families. Bang. Then two or three seconds elapsed, then silence. It had been very close. Then the buzz of conversation started up again. It was shocking to see how people, even at the early stage, were becoming used to hearing bombs go off. I suppose they were just happy to be able to talk again, unlike the poor unfortunates who had probably just been killed.

You'd regularly hear people sitting in bars and talking very matter-of-factly about the places that were getting hit. 'Such-and-such bar was done last night. They'll be out of action for a while,' etc.

There was another occasion when I was on stage at the Green Briar in Andersonstown, and some masked men just came and robbed the till in front of everyone and left. I carried on singing and the punters didn't bat an eyelid.

The security was increasing, and each time I went back north during the 1970s I'd see some change: from tanks and barricades to flags and red, white and blue painted kerbs. I was always a bit nervous, but I trusted that my drivers knew what they were doing and where they were going. That said, I remember being very scared one night when we were stoned by a group of kids. The promoter's wife was driving and she kept her cool.

I was in a war zone, but I was well sheltered from it. The people had a Blitz mentality I recognised from my folks. Maybe that's why the Northern sense of humour is so black. It seemed like another planet to me. The East End was full of joy. The cockneys had been through every horror imaginable. In Belfast in 1969, they were only starting to go through it.

The Belfast public really clutched me to their bosom. I think they admired my bravery. I was an unusual and daring act for 1960s' Ireland, although, in my mind, there was nothing courageous about doing what I was doing. It was simply my job to make audiences laugh and squirm a bit. I have only ever been about fun and enjoyment. I'm not into politics or activism. I leave that to others. I'm just an entertainer. I think that's why I was never targeted by terrorists during the Troubles. They probably thought: *leave him be. He's not doing anyone any harm. And besides, me ma thinks he's great.*

During the worst years, bands avoided Northern Ireland due to threats from both sides. Only Rory Gallagher was consistent in his loyalty to the North. He was a Ballyshannon man, and continued to cross the border regularly while the bombs were going off. He was never targeted, as far as I know. Other acts were not so fortunate.

I still recall the traffic on the roads late at night in the early days, as we came home to Dublin from gigs in Belfast. We'd be driving along and see the lights of one of the showbands' minibuses in our rear-view mirror. The bus would speed up to pass us by, and the occupants would recognise me. Then they would pull up alongside, stick their arses up against the windows, and moon us. We'd all pull over then for a chat and a cig at the side of the road.

It was all very collegiate, if that's the right word. We were all troupers working hard for our money. It didn't matter that I was a 'speciality' act and they were professional musicians. There was no rock and roll snobbery. If ever there was a showband party going on, I'd be invited.

One of my favourite groups was called The Miami. They were wildly popular in Ireland during the 1960s and 1970s, and had seven number-one singles here. They were originally led by my old friend Dickie Rock (or Sticky Rock as he's sometimes called), and later by Fran O'Toole. They were formed in 1962 by Tom Doherty, and the line-up was Joe Tyrell (piano), Tony Bogan (drums), Clem Quinn (guitar), Martin Phelan (saxophone), Dickie (vocals), Tommy O'Rourke (trumpet), Murty Quinn (trombone), and bassist Denis Murray. Their first gig was at the Palm Beach Ballroom in Portmarnock—hence the name The Miami.

They represented Ireland in the 1966 Eurovision with 'Come Back to Stay', and even made it onto British TV and *Sunday Night at the London Palladium*, which was a major feat for an Irish act.

By the time I knew them, Fran was the lead vocalist. Phil Lynott described him as the best soul singer in Ireland, but also called him a 'bread-head' for being in a showband instead of a struggling rock outfit. Despite being big stars (they were Ireland's Beatles), The

Miami were always down to earth and great fun. Fran, in particular, was a very sweet man. People used to say we looked alike as we had the same hairstyle at the time. I would regularly meet him and the boys for drinks at the TV Club in Dublin on Monday nights. (You couldn't call it the TV Club now or everyone would think it was for transvestites only.)

Monday was the showbands' night off, and everyone would head there, although it was 'wine only'. It was an enormous place on Harcourt Street with a recording studio owned by Eamonn Andrews. There was a reception area with steps going up to the bar, and the main ballroom was overlooked by a balcony where you could see the girls on one side of the room and the men on the other, like the old *Ballroom of Romance*. It used to host nurses' dances on a Tuesday, and the place would be full of guards looking for wives. It wouldn't have been a place that the cooler, rockier young things of Dublin would frequent, but it did host Thin Lizzy and even The Ramones on rare occasions.

I would sit with Fran and the lads and drink brandy punch or pissy Blue Nun wine. If I went in drag, I would always bring a handbag with a bottle of proper booze in it. The doormen never searched a lady's bag. I can't remember any of the banter now, but we would trade stories about life on the road with singers Tony Kenny, Red Hurley (that's an actual name, believe it or not), Mick Roche and the Arrows, Eileen Reid and the Cadets…

Fran was a big hit with the women, and would be constantly under siege. He lived for his family though, and would produce pictures of his little girls, whom he adored. His career ended abruptly in July 1975. The five members of the band were travelling by minibus back to Dublin from a gig in Banbridge when they were stopped outside Newry at a military checkpoint. The gig, as usual, had been a great success, and the lads were in great form. The North was grim, but the kids knew how to boogie. When The Miami rolled into any town, the grey streets would be ablaze with colourful checked cheesecloth shirts, blue eyeshadow, platforms, and loud flapping flares as youngsters swarmed their way to the gig. The Miami left a lot of happiness wherever they went.

The soldiers ordered them to get out and line up by the roadside. You've probably guessed at this stage that they weren't real soldiers; they were members of the Ulster Volunteer Force. They tried to hide a time bomb on the bus, but it went off, killing two of the bombers. Their 'comrades' then opened fire on the band, killing Fran, Brian McCoy and Tony Geraghty, and wounding Des Lee and Stephen Travers. Two serving Ulster Defence Regiment soldiers and one former UDR soldier later received life sentences for the savage, stupid, mindless murders. Fran was twenty-nine. He would have been seventy this year.

I wouldn't normally quote politicians, but the Taoiseach, Bertie Ahern, nailed it when he said at the unveiling of a monument to The Miami in 2007: 'Their murder was an atrocity which had such a profound impact on everyone on this island. Their popularity crossed all boundaries and all traditions. They simply wanted to entertain everyone … At a dark time, they were a shining light for so many.'

They really were. Show-people like us just want to entertain. To make punters happy. That's why we do it. Oh, and the money too. That's nice as well.

Bullets and bombs was the future that awaited Ireland, north and south, back in 1969. I had no idea things would get so bad as I sang and slagged my way across that tragic province. Besides, my mind was beginning to wander elsewhere. I was curious to see what Dublin was like….

Chapter Eight

Drag Comes to Dublin

Grey, dull, overcast, miserable, depressing … the Dublin skyline looked like a giant sodden Brillo pad waiting to be squeezed over the equally grey, dull, miserable suburban rooftops. *Belfast was like Las Vegas compared to this*, I thought as we chugged through Finglas.

All I can see now in my mind's bloodshot eye are TV aerials. Each house had what appeared to be coat-hanger sculptures clamped to their chimney pots. Aerials that scraped the low-hanging clouds, which threatened to burst into tears like a hormonal nun. This was my first view of Dublin—and I wasn't impressed.

Ireland in 1969/1970 was a vastly different country to what it is today. For a start, it was more insular. Those TV aerials were tuned to catch one station: Radio Telefís Éireann. The broadcaster's 1973 Annual Report said that 77 per cent (542,000) of households in the Republic had a TV; 530,000 had a licence, and 27,000 had colour televisions. I just thought I'd throw those statistics in there to show how clever I am.

RTÉ started broadcasting in the mid morning and finished before midnight—probably because the bloke who pushed the buttons had to get the last bus home. There were programmes like *Wanderly Wagon*, *The Late Late Show*, *Dáithí Lacha* (about a duck), and *Quicksilver*. The latter was a quiz show hosted by a man named Bunny Carr. If that's not a drag name screaming out to be used, I don't know what is. Bunny was very softly spoken and used to award prizes of 2p for correct answers. He had a sidekick called Norman, who played awful musical 'clues' on his organ. The contestants were, consistently, thick. On one occasion—and this may be a myth, but it's true in spirit—a man was asked what Hitler's first name was. He scratched his head for a second and replied: 'Heil?'

The Late Late Show was still in black and white, and was a groundbreaking show by any international standards. It was presided over by Gay Byrne, and featured people discussing sex and other things that decent, God-fearing Irish folk would never have dreamed of talking about before.

Throw in a few repeats of *Gunsmoke* and some Polish cartoons (*Bolek and Lolek*), and you more or less have a handle on what TV was like here back then. The only international programming came from HTV Wales. If you wanted to watch Welsh television, you had to angle your rabbit's ears towards the Irish Sea and hope it wasn't raining in Snowdonia. Sometimes, after this, you were rewarded with a TV picture that looked like Scott's last hours in Antarctica.

The radio was equally foreign and bizarre to me. The first time I heard the Angelus, I thought it was a bomb warning. The Angelus, if you're from out of town, is a twice-daily call to prayer, which features the bing-bonging of church bells over the airwaves. Muslims have their own call to prayer, with an imam calling '*Allahu akbar*' (God is great) from a minaret. The Angelus is the Irish equivalent, from a church steeple: 'Ah sure, isn't God only great?' This was an Ireland that was still struggling to free itself from its rosary bead chains: divorce, homosexuality and contraception were all illegal, and the Church influenced most parts of daily life. In 1971, the Irish Women's Liberation Movement highlighted the crazy state of social affairs in the Republic when they boarded a train from Dublin to Belfast to buy contraceptives, which were legally available in Northern Ireland. TV crews from around the world filmed the ladies as they arrived back at Connolly Station waving rubber johnnies and spermicidal jelly over their heads. Some even swallowed their newly purchased pills rather than surrender them to customs. It later emerged that the women had been filmed arriving at a chemist's and being informed that they needed a prescription to buy the pill. Someone hadn't done their homework. So they bought a load of aspirin instead, which they proceeded to swallow for the cameras.

One thing is for sure: contraceptive pill or no contraceptive pill, they couldn't use the old 'Not tonight, love, I have a headache' excuse when they got home.

Rubber johnnies weren't the only thing Northern Ireland was exporting to the Republic. Like the six counties, the Republic didn't know that a war was about to break out on the island and last for twenty-five years. The first sign of that war spilling over into the south occurred at RTÉ's Donnybrook HQ. In August 1969, a bomb badly damaged the front of the main building. Nobody was hurt, and the Ulster Volunteer Force (UVF) claimed responsibility. The bombing took place during the protests by the (Catholic) Northern Ireland Civil Rights Association. It was a foretaste of things to come.

Let's not dwell on that too much. There was another, far gentler, northern explosion in 1970. In March, a seventeen-year-old Derry girl called Rosemary Brown won the Eurovision Song Contest in Amsterdam. Her song, 'All Kinds of Everything', was a sweet antidote to the mayhem that was taking place in her home town. When you look at the camp pantomime that the Eurovision has now become, you may be inclined to ask, 'So what?' This was a big, *big* deal for Ireland at the time. The Republic was just over thirty years old, and it was less than fifty years since the War of Independence. Ireland never won *anything*. This was a huge confidence booster.

Dana's win showed that it could achieve things internationally, in terms of the arts at least. It also gave me great material for my shows. Some of it would be too un-PC to do now, especially the bit where I wore a bra pad as a skullcap to illustrate the early morning dew/ Jew. God, I hate PC. It seems that the PC brigade are just waiting to be offended these days. And they often feel discriminated against if they *haven't* been offended.

Anyway, this was the Ireland I was entering. I had decided that I just wanted to have a look at the place, so my manager, Ian, Samantha/Billy and I headed south for a gander. After the grim, grey northside, we entered O'Connell Street, where I saw my first splash of colour: flowers on the bridge.

Ian had heard of a bohemian bar called Bartley Dunne's, and we decided that this would be our first port of call. We parked on the street. You could park anywhere in Dublin in those days, and traffic was much lighter. Grafton Street, which is now pedestrianised, was 'two-way', with buses snorting up and down outside Switzer's department store and the other swish shops. I always loved the Christmas windows in Switzer's, with crowds of kids goggling at the robotic elves and polystyrene snow.

I realised straight away that I was in a different country, with different traditions and a defined culture. The architecture, though, was the same as at home. I really loved the Georgian buildings. They hadn't been bombed like their counterparts in London or the North. The only places bombed here during the war were the synagogue in Donore and the North Strand. I didn't know it then, but I would later do my own 'bit' for preserving Georgian Dublin.

As I said, it was only fifty years since the War of Independence, and many parts of the city seemed to be stuck in a time warp, with the old colonial areas falling into decay. Georgian Dublin was being bulldozed and allowed to fall into ruin. I think many politicians associated it with the old regime and wanted to modernise the city. That's why so many ugly new buildings were going up, like the appalling Bank of Ireland HQ on Baggot Street. I may have, indirectly, helped to slow down this process by 'influencing' Senator David Norris.

David is one of the most impressive men of his generation. When homophobia was rife in Ireland, he had the guts to stand up, and out, and challenge the status quo. He has more balls than any of his macho critics. In 1977 I was involved in a club in North Great George's Street and David was involved in one on Parnell Square, The Phoenix Club, which ran discos. One night he came down to check out the competition and spotted a Georgian house across the road. It was occupied by tenants, and he fell in love with it, vowing to live there. Being David, he made his dream come true and he went on to devote a lot of his energies to saving old Georgian Dublin. If it wasn't for Mr Pussy muscling in on his disco turf, it might never have happened.

I like David a lot. I can't praise him enough. We've met plenty of times over the years, and I always find him to be entertaining, smart and funny.

Our club days were seven years away, though, as I stepped out of my car onto a Dublin street. I was wearing a fur coat, black velvet suit, Cuban heels, and looked and felt sensational. As I walked through the doors of Bartley Dunne's, I thought: *I'll make an impact here.* I didn't care if I appeared too OTT because, as far as I was concerned, this was just a visit and I would probably never be coming back. How wrong was I?

The pub was dim and atmospheric. The piped music was French, and candlelight flickered and spilled off the beer-glass-ringed tabletops. The bar was stocked with an astonishing array of bottles: it had the biggest selection of spirits in Europe. I sensed a hundred pairs of eyes running me up and down. The entire pub had stopped talking to view this exotic creature who had silently glided across its threshold.

Samantha helped me out of my fur coat and then went out to put it in the boot of the car. You couldn't be too careful: someone might have pinched it. I was standing there with a lager and lime, a twenty-eight-inch waist and a bum so toned that you could open beer bottles on it. Not that anyone ever tried. And nobody tried to pinch it either. The punters, while clearly captivated by my unusual and colourful appearance, were too shy to talk. Ian quickly remedied this, starting up a conversation at the bar. Within minutes we were sitting at a table surrounded by chatty Dubs, all eager to know more about me. It was like Belfast again, only Dubliners, unlike their Northern cousins, are a more open breed of folk. When they ask you about yourself, it's not to pigeonhole you into Loyalist or Nationalist or Catholic or Protestant; it's genuine curiosity. I was *out* and they were *in*. They loved my 'fuck it' attitude to the conventions of the day. And I loved their accents. Some were soft-spoken and posh, but the real Dubs spoke in a tone that I could identify with as a south Londoner. It was bluff, bassy and fast. The Dublin accent seems to come pre-loaded (if that's the right word) with humour. The 'slagging' took a bit of getting used to at first, but after you realise that Dubs love to insult newcomers as a sign of welcoming affection, it's easy to fall in love with the citizens of this quirky and unique city.

'Nice hair, Alan. Did you drive down from Belfast with your head stuck out of the sunroof?'

'No, I had my toe plugged into the cigarette lighter. It's great for giving the roots a bit of a lift.'

The night flew by, and I played the visiting diva for all I was worth. I loved the attention I was getting. They were like flies around caviar. The clock struck eleven, and the barman came around looking for last orders. This was a shock to the system as in the UK the glass would have been wrested from my delicate hand and we would have been turfed out. We stayed for another two drinks, and then someone suggested we continue the evening elsewhere.

'Oh great,' I purred. 'I'd love a bop. We going to a club?' My new friends exchanged glances and smiled.

'Dublin's not really a nightclub city,' explained one, who was dressed in a brown suit and looked like an Open University professor. I was about to ask him to explain this when someone else made a suggestion that caught my attention.

'Let's go to Manhattan.'

Man-bleedin'-hattan? These were flash gits, I thought.

'I don't have my passport.'

'You won't need it. It's in Rathmines. We can refuel there and have a party back at my place.'

'I only *give* parties,' I said grandly, and immediately regretted it as I sounded like a twat.

The Manhattan turned out to be a late-night café with a jukebox in the corner and loads of dodgy types hanging around. It specialised in 'soakage' food: fried breakfasts designed to keep taxi men on the road and jarred revellers awake and off the road. I was starving, and glad I had agreed to go with my new buddies. A rasher sarnie wasn't going to hurt my lovely figure.

We squeezed through the door, and I was expecting the same reaction I got in Bartley Dunne's, but nobody so much as turned their head. The customers and staff (it was a family business) were used to seeing odd characters, and also knew better than to stare at anyone: this was a favourite haunt of Dublin's criminal fraternity too.

After eating, we finally got around to thinking about where we were going to stay.

'It's too late to start looking for a B&B now,' said Mark, who was one of the more sober members of our gang. 'You can stay with me tonight.' We thanked him, and ended up staying longer than the one night. Ian was delighted. I think he fancied him. Already, I had the feeling my day trip would turn into something a bit longer.

The following afternoon, we regained consciousness in Mark's. He suggested a walk into town for a cure. So, slightly (only slightly) bedraggled, we meandered through town to Baggot Street, which is the gateway to Dublin's beautiful ambassador belt in Ballsbridge.

'Here we are,' said Mark, nodding at a sign that said 'Baggot Inn'. The pub didn't look much like an inn, but Mark assured us that it was good fun and served a great pint of Guinness. I looked across the road to O'Donoghue's, which was very traditional-looking and homely.

'What about over there? That looks more like an inn.'

'Not really your scene, Alan,' said Mark. 'Mainly chaps with beards playing diddly-eye music. The Dubliners gig there a lot.' I had heard of The Dubliners and later became good friends with them. They had a big hit in the UK with 'Seven Drunken Nights', selling 250,000 copies and appearing on *Top of the Pops*. They were sometimes considered politically controversial because of the material they played, and RTÉ had unofficially banned their music between 1967 to 1971. An English queen might not have been welcomed there with open arms.

'The Baggot it is,' I decided. I had no idea then, as I crossed its threshold, that I was taking the first steps towards a career in Ireland. Once I entered the Baggot, there was no returning to England.

As it was early, there were only a few people in the bar: one or two workers having a late lunch, a Dáil reporter or two, and some punters just taking a break with a quiet pint and the paper.

I was introduced to a very nice man named Frank Kenny. After a few bevvies he spotted the owner, Jim McGettigan, and called him over. Jim was a Donegal man and went on to found the Regency Hotel Group. He had emigrated to Southampton in his late teens, and worked as a first-class waiter aboard RMS *Queen Elizabeth* (the QE1). He returned to Dublin eight years later and entered the pub trade. When he bought the Baggot in 1969, he became one of the city's best-known businessmen.

Over the next twenty-six years, the Baggot became one of the most popular music venues in the country. Very few pubs can boast such a colourful history: a young Bono was almost turned away once for looking underage; Tracey Chapman (of 'Fast Car' fame) launched her career there; and Bob Geldof whined and begged for a month before the Boomtown Rats were finally given a gig. Christy Moore, Phil Lynott and Thin Lizzy, The Waterboys, Mary Coughlan, Danny from The Script, Brendan Grace ... all learned their craft at the Baggot before becoming famous. And Mr Pussy did too of course—although I'm getting ahead of myself.

Jim and I had a great old natter about the Merchant Navy, and he fell around laughing when I regaled him with yarns about Stella Minge and her shenanigans with sailors on shore leave. He was very open-minded and warm, and had been to his fair share of drag shows in the UK.

'Put him on, Jim,' said Frank. 'The customers will love him. It's about time Ireland was introduced to drag.'

Jim considered the matter for a second or two.

'Why not? The upstairs lounge is empty and could do with an injection of life. Let's give you a go and see how you get on.'

Jim's missus, Patricia, was equally keen on the idea, and would go on to fix me a cocktail religiously before each show.

Frank and Ian got to work on drumming up publicity. The former went out that day and ordered a stack of gilt-edged wedding invitations with the words: 'Mr Pussy, Drag Artist, Opening Night at the Baggot Inn'. The pair lashed up a release and sent it to all the newspapers and magazines. Our press reception was stuffed to the rafters with hacks and hackettes and fellow performers. Shay Healy was there. A decade later he would write Ireland's winning Eurovision entry, 'What's Another Year?' We've been friends for years. He's one of the most inventive all-round entertainers on the planet. Mary Kenny was there too. She was woman's editor in the

Irish Press, and a flamboyant character in her own right. She is still one of the most respected and sometimes controversial journalists in the business. She interviewed me, and we got along famously.

I did the conference in mufti, saving the drag for the show itself. We had papered the walls with newspaper cuttings from London and the North, including the pics from my photo shoot as a girl down the docks. Just like in Belfast, I was being treated as a fully formed star. The idea of a famous drag act playing in Catholic Ireland was hard to resist for the mischievous Dublin press. They played it up to the hilt.

There was another Englishman at the reception. His name was Terry Willers, and he was an established cartoonist and performer. His work was a high point in RTÉ's satirical TV show *Hall's Pictorial Weekly*. Frank Hall's take on modern Irish life and politics was hilarious and surreal, and the sketches were wonderfully acted by Eamon Morrissey and a future household name, Frank Kelly (aka Father Jack Hackett). Terry's cartoon round-up of the week was my favourite part of the show, as I've always been interested in drawing and cartooning. We later agreed that he would come on at my interval with a large sketch pad and draw and crack jokes. He was truly gifted, and his presence on Mr Pussy's stage gave my act a little extra 'cred' with Ireland's satirists. He christened the place 'Mr Pussy's Parlour'.

The first night was stuffed. Between the interviews and the ads we had taken out in *The Irish Times*, there was a great cross-section of Irish society in attendance. I sipped my cocktail, touched up my lippy, checked my miniskirt was the correct length, and breezed out to a loud cheer.

'Helllllllllloooooooo, Dublin!' I cooed, with a saucy wink. The crowd went mental. They were determined to love me. The gig, which was based on my London show, flew by. I could do no wrong. Ireland was crying out for something new and anarchic. I could have drop-kicked a kitten off that stage and the punters would still have cheered for an encore.

I was an overnight success in a foreign country. Ian cancelled my London gigs, and we decided to stay and give Dublin a try. More dates were added, and Mr Pussy's Parlour became a hip new meeting place. The Dáil was around the corner, and politicians started to drop in for the show—and a few drinks between debates. The Establishment accepted me. My fellow proles had accepted me.

Alan Amsby had arrived.

And Mr Pussy was hot on his tail.

Chapter Nine

Pussy is Born

Pussy's Parlour went from strength to proverbial strength. The press was generally very fair, and there were no protests from the clergy damning my vulgar, innuendo-fuelled shows. I stayed with Mark until I found a place in Rathmines. From there I moved to Mount Street, which is in the heart of Georgian Dublin.

I loved living there. It was in the centre of town, and had a genteel, elegant atmosphere. I always felt safe going home to my flat, even after Samantha left and went back up north. Well, nearly always. One morning, after a very late post-Baggot bender, I woke to hear voices in my sitting room and the sound of furniture being moved around. *That can't be the bailiffs already*, I thought. *I definitely paid the rent.* The voices were coming closer to my bedroom door. I leaped out of the scratcher, hid my rings under the chest of drawers, and grabbed the short, frilly blouse I had been wearing the night before. I then jumped back into bed and watched, from behind the duvet, the door handle slowly turning. I let out the butchest scream I could muster, despite my thumping hangover. The handle stopped moving and there was a short, muffled discussion behind the door, which terminated with a distinct 'Fuck it'.

The door burst open, and two young burglars gaped in horror as a semi-naked drag queen levitated off the bed and flew at them head first, screaming and flailing her/his arms. They were so shocked that they actually stepped back from the doorway and let me through. Not that they would have had any choice. I was going through that door, and nothing was going to stop me. I was bursting with adrenalin … and pee. I was dying to do my early-morning wee. The adrenalin kept me pumped up, which was what they call a 'curate's egg' in Ireland. It was both good and bad in equal measure. Good because it unnerved the burglars; bad because it made me run around like a headless chicken. I was so fired up that I couldn't remember where the front door was, and so ran around the living room in circles. This gave the crims enough time to regroup, and they quickly joined in, running around in circles after me as I bounced off the settee and the coffee table.

'Bleedin' fairy!' one of them roared. 'Get him!'

Now to be honest, I have no idea what they intended to do once they got me. They were skinny and undernourished-looking. I could probably have kicked their arses if I had been thinking straight. In fairness to them, I doubt that they knew what they were going to do with me either. The best thing for all concerned was for me to get out of the flat before this ridiculous chase became really embarrassing. One of the desperate duo was clearly thinking along the same lines. He broke off pursuing me and held open the front door. I remember thinking briefly: *how thoughtful of him*—and flew through it like a bird on Purple Hearts.

I ran down the street, still shrieking, and hid in a gateway, trembling, cursing … and *naked from the waist down*. The shrieking began again after a few seconds, although this time it wasn't me doing it. I looked up and saw a group of schoolgirls across the road … outside a convent school. A figure in black was herding them through its front door. She dashed—if it's possible for a nun to 'dash'—over to me and asked if everything was all right, which it clearly wasn't.

'I've been burgled,' I gasped. She arched an eyebrow and looked me up and down.

'They stole your clothes?'

'I hope not,' I replied, thinking of the thieves ransacking my wardrobe of beautiful frocks. I must have been in shock. Then the penny dropped: I was semi-naked. I made a vain and rather pathetic attempt to cover myself.

The sister sighed deeply, as if she was used to encountering semi-naked female-impersonators.

'I'll walk you home,' she said. And so a dishevelled and half-dressed Mr Pussy was escorted back to his flat by a nun. God knows what the neighbours thought of that.

The thieves had fled, empty-handed. I was never burgled again at that address. Word must have gone out in the burgling community that there was a mad queen living there. I thanked the sister, and she headed back to the school as if nothing had happened. Irish nuns are great like that. They're completely imperturbable.

As were the people who came to my shows. Ian had managed to get us gigs in other venues, and the punters were flocking in. The cheekier and more risqué I was, the more they loved it. I was really enjoying myself, and my act was improving all the time, as I honed it for an Irish audience. It was still largely my London act though: Mod girl singing and being mischievous. I had no idea how it would go down in the more traditional and tougher parts of town. Would they be more anti-English than homophobic? Well obviously they wouldn't be homophobic if they were coming to my show, but Brits weren't very popular back then in Ireland, as a result of what was going on in the North. Two years later, a mob would burn down the British Embassy not far from my Mount

Street home. I remember it well, not so much for the violence, but because I couldn't do my Baggot show as the upstairs lounge was full of police in riot gear.

I had 'earned my dues' in the tough East End of London. I would have to do it in Ireland too. My first date with real Dublin came sooner than I had expected or hoped for. Ian, who had decided to return to England, had booked me in at the Drake Inn in Finglas through Aidan Maguire. Aidan was a great help to me when I was establishing my act.

Finglas was one of the toughest parts of Dublin. It's a few kilometres north of the city, and was very deprived in the 1970s. It was developed in the 1950s with sprawling estates to rehome people during a 'clear-out' of the inner city. Many of these estates were named after famous republicans: Plunkett, Casement, Barry, Mellows, McKee ... and here was a London poof planning to storm those nationalist barricades.

I was nervous when the gig day dawned. Not because I believed I was going to be tarred and feathered (I already had the boa feathers, dear), but because I'm always nervous before gigging at a new venue. First night nerves, etc. I had decided that, as this was the real heartland of Dublin, I was going to do something different, but I wasn't quite sure what that was going to be. I intended to liberate my alter ego completely and see where she took me. I was going to go with the flow of the audience and ad-lib as much as possible. That was the plan, at any rate.

I arrived early to look the place over and do a soundcheck. The Drake reminded me of the clubs in Belfast: it was vast, with a community-based audience. Big stars used to come over from the UK and play there, so they were well used to English acts. That was a bit of a relief. What was an even bigger relief was the sight of the queue at the door. It had started at 5 p.m., and punters were happily lining up to shell out two and six to see my set.

I was sharing the bill that night with legendary crooner Sonny Knowles. Sonny was the housewives' favourite—an Irish version of Tony Bennett. He was famous for his 'window-washer' dance, where he circled his palms in the manner of a chap polishing windows. Or, indeed, a pervert fondling a pair of tits, depending on your point of view.

Sonny, I hasten to add, was not a pervert. Or a window washer. He was a consummate professional and a real gentleman. I was doing my make-up with a long blonde wig on, and topless to the waist, when he came into the dressing room. I had my back to the door. He was mortified, the poor dear.

'I'm terribly sorry, love. I didn't know anyone was in here,' he gushed, red-faced.

I turned around and beamed at him. He nearly fell back out of the door in shock when he saw I was a man.

'Awright, mate?' I said. He started to laugh. Sonny was the first to see the birth of the new Mr Pussy. Something had clicked in my head when I entered that dressing room after exploring the Drake. It was as if a fully formed character was biting and scratching to get out. I knew that this would make me or break me in Ireland.

Billy Hughes was the compère of the show, and while he was doing his patter I sneaked a peek at the audience from the wings. It was a good, working-class crowd. I knew what I had to do: hit them with a killer song at the start, followed by my strongest gag. It may seem obvious, but if you win them over at the start, they will root for you throughout your set. They *will* you to be funny. You've probably watched stand-up shows on TV and wondered why the performer only has to raise an eyebrow to corpse the audience. This is because he or she has hit them hard in the first minute.

It's down to crowd psychology—that and basic economics. An audience, like the one at the Drake, had paid hard-earned money to be entertained. Very few people were there to have a bad time. They were with their friends and family, and had a few bevvies on board. Once the dominant member of a group starts to laugh, the others follow suit. If you give them a reason to like you, or in a worst-case scenario, feel sorry for you, they will stay onside. If you come out and dither or show weakness, you will irritate your audience. If you're not confident, they will subconsciously think: well, if he thinks his material is crap, it must be.

My material is not crap. And I never give an audience a reason to feel sorry for me. That night, Mr Pussy stormed the stage in full metal (gold lame) jacket, long dress and big hair. I hit them once, twice, three times … not allowing them any space to analyse what they were witnessing. I wasn't just a man in a frock. I was a woman—a woman with balls. I scanned the room and picked the fattest, baldest man in the place.

'Ooooh, look at the big baldy fellow. Stand up straight, dear. Pussy is going to play with her baldy fellow for a while….' The women in the audience shrieked as I led him up on stage and began to strip him. I looked at the mark's female companion and winked. 'Is this your husband love? He is? I can see now why you're looking so bored.'

'I did a gig in Coolock once,' I said. 'Is there anybody here from Coolock? I have relations in Coolock … twice a week, if I'm lucky.'

For the second half, I changed into my mini, let my hair down, and taped up my boobs. This is an old drag trick: using Sellotape to enhance your cleavage. Try it sometime … just be sure to wax your chest first.

I played tricks on the crowd, sang, humiliated the tougher members … and completely won them over. I could see Sonny and Billy peeing themselves in the wings. Now, I *am* blowing my own trumpet here. They loved Mr Pussy—they had never seen anything like him/her before. There was a standing ovation, and I was mobbed by well-wishers afterwards. Young girls tried to steal the sequins off my gown to keep as souvenirs. Blokes, even real hard men, were shaking my hand and saying, 'I can't believe you're a fellah. There's no way you're a fellah!' There was such warmth and sweetness and humour being fed back to me that I knew then that I couldn't live anywhere else. I had a little cry for myself back in the dressing room. I loved London, from Peckham to Trafalgar Square, but I felt I was finally home.

Mr Pussy was born, and like all beautiful felines, needed grooming. I needed a steady supply of new dresses and accessories, so I began to shop like a mad thing. I became a well-known fixture at the city's theatrical outfitters, especially Burke's on Dame Street. Burke's had connections with the Gaiety, and there were family ties with the DJ Gerry Ryan and TV legend Eamonn Andrews.

The first time I popped in, the staff all came out to say hello. They had heard of me, which wasn't surprising as I was a novelty and festooned all over the newspapers. Old Mr Burke was a great character with a great intellect. He had grey hair, and always seemed to have his glasses perched on top of his head. He wrote and collected theatrical books. The downstairs of his shop was part library, part costumier. Upstairs, there were suits, dresses, hats, helmets and his (sweet) sisters. One of them was very light on her feet, and seemingly unflappable. The only time I saw her move at speed was when I brought Danny La Rue in to meet them. She literally ran downstairs she was so excited. Mr Burke was far more stoic; he'd seen it all before. Everyone in the profession was all right by him, no matter what they did. He gave me preferential treatment as he admired my chutzpah. He once loaned me a fox fur stole worth hundreds of pounds, and a beautiful, expensive gypsy dress, which I wore in the Drake. All the women wanted to know where I bought it. I lied and said I had it made specially. Being a flash git, I also shopped in Brown Thomas—the most expensive store in Ireland. The staff were lovely there, and were tickled that I had chosen them as one of my suppliers. I ended up modelling for them on the strength of my Carnaby Street photo shoot.

Even though I was becoming firmly ensconced in Ireland, I still travelled over and back to London to see my mum. Sometime in the mid 1970s I took a trip over to go to Jean Fredericks's drag ball. Jean was a famous drag performer who had come to England from North America. He was an ex-schoolteacher, weighed roughly twenty stone, and played the trombone. After a straight role in a West End musical, he concentrated on his drag act, singing mock-opera. In 1964 he released an LP, *Recitals are a Drag*, and the following year he was featured in the first issue of *London Life* magazine. He was quite a trailblazer.

In 1969, he and Ron Storme began organising five, or sometimes more, drag balls a year in London at Porchester Hall. It was a big deal to get on the guest list. I was asked to judge the contestants, and even the contestants couldn't believe I was a man. Afterwards, when we got back to Jean's place, I said I had a headache and needed to lie down. So I went into his bedroom and fell asleep. Not long afterwards, Jean blustered in.

'Get up, Pussy,' he said, gently prising the pillow out from under my head. I had been sleeping on the night's takings from the ball— thousands of pounds. If Jean hadn't been a drag queen, she could have been the tooth fairy.

Unable to go back to sleep, I joined the rest of the party and was introduced to a handsome young man called Noel McNeil. He was a singer, and had taken over from Butch Moore in the Capitol Showband during the late 1960s, but left after the travelling became too much for him. We got on brilliantly, and he came to see us off at the airport the following day. I liked him so much that I decided to kidnap him. Before he knew what hit him, I had bought him a ticket and he was bundled onto the plane for Dublin.

Noel had no clothes. While this suited me fine (he was a fine figure of a man), we couldn't let him wander around Dublin in rags. So we dressed him and got him a few gigs. He was a brilliant singer—a cross between Matt Monro and Perry Como—and very, very funny. We fell in love, and he moved in with me.

Noel and I used to have mad parties every night and invite people over to dinner. Then, after everyone had left, we'd have equally mad rows, wanting to smash each other's heads in. I'd say, 'Not the face; I have to do a show tonight,' and we'd start to laugh. It was that kind of a relationship.

We had a housemate called Tanya. I met her in the Baggot. She was a model and a dancer and did shows with me. The blokes went mad for her, although she was very skinny and had no boobs. She was very loveable and great fun too. That said, I could have killed her on one occasion. I had a beautiful blue sequin dress I bought in London. One evening I went to Tanya's show and saw her wearing it on stage. Or what remained of it. She had cut it up into a blue bikini. I nearly throttled her.

'I thought you wouldn't mind, dear,' she said serenely. She was such a sweet thing, I let it go. The three of us had such a laugh living together. I think some people believed he was living 'in sin' with Tanya with me as a housemate. Noel was very well known in Dublin, and had to keep his sexuality a secret as the showband world was very macho and all about attracting girls. There were a few active gay men on the showband scene, but it's not my business to 'out' them. We all looked out for each other, and still do.

After a year, the bright lights of London called Noel away. The end of any relationship is hard, but we had run our course. He died very young. I still think of him with the fondest of memories.

I was quickly building up a devoted following through my Baggot gigs. The next obvious step was to introduce Pussy to the rest of

Ireland. Before that happened I had a chance to go 'legit' and tread the hallowed, scuffed boards of a real theatre. An offer came in that I really couldn't turn down. Was it to star as Lady Macbeth, you ask? Or Eliza Doolittle? Perhaps a young Miss Marple? Nope. It was a leading role in Ireland's first untraditional panto, *Little Red Riding Would!*, at the Eblana Theatre, directed by Chris O'Neill and starring Maury Taylor (as the Wolf), Virginia Cole, Brenda Doyle, Des Nealon and me. I co-wrote the show, and it was a real thrill to see my name in the credits at the top of the bill.

The Eblana Theatre was underneath the Busáras terminus just off the north quays. Someone unfairly referred to it as 'the only public toilet with its own theatre'. It was very small and cosy and had no wings, but it was a great place to work.

Despite its location and size, the Eblana had a reputation for breaking new material in the days before the Project or Andrew's Lane. It was the first theatre company to produce John B. Keane's *Big Maggie* and *The Field*. Ray McAnally played 'The Bull' when it opened. He went on to become a massive international film star.

Our little panto, which was produced by Alan Gibson of Amalgamated Artistes, was set in a disused tube station and was double-entendre-laden from start to finish. We had great fun staging it and ad-libbing. At one point in the panto, Red Riding (me) was tied to a totem pole. I was desperate for a fag, so I called for a last cigarette and a drink of water. My request was unscripted, but our runner, Maggie, didn't let us down. She slipped out to the bar and returned with a smoke and canteen full of liquid. I took a slug and nearly choked—with delight. She had filled it with scotch and Coke. The show got even ruder after that unexpected refreshment.

We smashed new ground with *Little Red*. It was considered very risqué for its time: the *Sunday Independent* called it 'off-beat, way out by traditional panto standards'. The critics and the punters loved it. I even received a congratulatory telegram from the two greatest theatricals in Ireland: Hilton Edwards and Micheál Mac Liammóir. I'll tell you a little bit more about them later.

I had half-expected to get read from the altar for staging such an 'immoral' show, but the clergy kept quiet. Ireland was ruled by the Church back then, in particular by one man called Archbishop John Charles McQuaid. He was God's stormtrooper and the moral guardian of the nation. Oddly, he never tackled my evangelical mission to bring drag to Catholic Ireland.

I met him once at a gala night. I can't remember the venue, but he came backstage to greet the performers after the show, much like the Queen does at Royal Variety gigs. I was back in civvies, and he didn't recognise me. He stuck out his hand to greet me.

'Hello, young man. I'm sorry but I don't recall your act. What do you do?' he politely inquired.

'I do bird impressions, your grace,' I replied, and could hear stifled giggles all around me.

'How nice,' he said. 'Can you do a chaffinch?'

I nearly fell over.

'I could try, but I'm not sure the chaffinch would like it.'

He was swiftly ushered on with a rather confused look on his face.

I'm not religious, but if I had a tendency towards any church it would be the Catholic one. I suppose I like the costumes. I see a lot of humour in all that pomposity and how the clergy were treated by the public back then. One of my all-time favourite shows is *Father Ted*. I'm proud to say that I gave its star, Dermot Morgan, his first real break.

In the late 1970s, I put on a show at the Oscar Theatre in Ballsbridge called *Mr Pussy's Midnite Folies*. It was very popular, and ran for six weeks after the main play at the venue. We did sketches, and I had strippers sent down from the North to perform for the randy punters.

As part of my routine, I'd go on stage in my finery and strip down to a bikini. I'd then go behind the curtain and a stripper would emerge in the same colour bikini and wig as me. She'd continue to strip, thoroughly melting the audience's heads.

One week they sent a new girl down from the North without telling me. I stepped behind the curtain and 'emerged' as usual as a gorgeous, busty woman with a body to die for. The only problem was that the girl that emerged was black. Not only had I undergone a sex change on stage, but a race change too. That really confused the audience, but they loved it. The poor girl wasn't familiar with the act and didn't know why they were laughing so hard. And no, dear, it wasn't a racist thing. The audience bellowed because it was such a mad mistake. They nearly had a collective heart attack when they caught sight of me peering around the curtain with tears of laughter streaming down my face.

One night, one of our cast didn't turn up and we had to look around for a replacement. I knew Dermot Morgan from around the circuit, where he did a guitar/comedy routine. He was a schoolteacher at the time. We decided to call him and give him a chance. He went out on stage and was really well received. So well received, in fact, that he wouldn't come off. I stood in the wings, wearing a wedding gown, waving my arms like a crazed swan. Eventually, I let out a roar.

'Turn the bleedin' lights off when you leave, Dermot!' He started to laugh, took his bow and went off to huge applause.

I really liked Dermot. I went around to his house a few times and even slept on his floor. One night his German wife, Susanne, cooked us a special meal. She produced long forks, a plate of meat and a bowl of hot oil. I was too polite to say that I liked my meat cooked, so I nibbled at the raw steak thinking it was some German delicacy. Dermot looked at me and smiled. I took another bite.

His smile grew even broader. I thought: *he's delighted. He thinks I'm enjoying this.* Eventually, after a nudge from his wife, he started to laugh.

'You've never eaten fondue before, have you, Alan?' he asked, pronging a piece of meat and dipping it into the oil to fry. He was a little git like that, and a natural, classic comedian, unlike a lot of the other 'alternative' acts that emerged in the UK during the 1980s. I hate alternative comedy. These guys just come in off the streets and think they can do it all, pint in hand, looking scruffy. When I was starting out, acts weren't even allowed to sit down in their costumes. Billie Barry was very strict about that. I went to see Frankie Vaughan in the Drake once. He was sitting in the dressing room with his flies open. 'Mr Vaughan,' I said, 'I know you're Jewish; you don't have to prove it.' He was unbuttoned because that stopped the pants getting creased.

Unlike the 'alternatives', Dermot could do stand-up, sketches and act. One of his sketches, by the way, was 'Ireland's first full-frontal nude'. He would walk out in a suit and tie and stare at the audience. Then he'd turn around to reveal the back of the suit, which was completely naked. That's a lot funnier than Alexei Sayle shouting about his mate John getting a new motor.

Mini-rant over. Another sketch involved Dermot doing a brilliant turn as a pirate radio DJ. He and the cast would be rolling fake joints on stage, and I would walk through the auditorium dressed as a guard. I played it straight and the well-jarred audience would believe I was a rogue copper coming in to clamp down on drugs and immoral behaviour in the theatre. I'd walk up and, ignoring the dope, ask if they had a valid radio licence. That always got a laugh. Then I would sit on the stage and fling off my cap and reveal myself. Dermot never fluffed a line, and his timing was always perfect.

I'm very proud to say that I gave him his first theatrical dog collar for a skit we were doing that involved a parish priest. I was heartbroken and shocked when I heard that he had died of a heart attack after the final episode of *Father Ted*. I can't watch that show without thinking of what he might have gone on to achieve—*Ted* really is one of TV's all-time greatest sitcoms.

But back to me. The *Folies* were a great success and, briefly, became a cult place to go after the pub for many celebs and business types. The play we used to follow every night was a Victorian melodrama called *East Lynne*. We had to share dressing rooms with legit actors. One evening I arrived to find a note pinned to the door. It was from one of the *East Lynne* cast. 'Please don't touch what belongs to me'. I was a bit miffed by her rudeness, so I hung two of my tennis balls, which I used as boobies, behind the door with a note that read: 'Please don't touch my balls'. She never left a note again.

Our little group of *Folies* folk were very close, and we were always playing tricks on each other. We had a piano player who looked like a school ma'am while playing the keys and reading the sheet music over her glasses. She was the very picture of respectability. One night, I got a picture of a gentleman with a ridiculously large chopper and put it in with her music. She didn't so much as flinch when she turned the page to find 'Mr Big' wagging his manhood at her. At the end of the show, she folded the picture up with her sheet music and put it in her handbag. And completely forgot about it.

Then, in the best comedy tradition, something unexpected happened. While she was stopped at traffic lights on her way home, someone smashed in her side window and stole her bag. You couldn't make it up. By some crazy stroke of luck, the bag was found the following morning, and she had to go to the cop shop to collect it.

'Here's your bag,' said the old guard, handing it to her with a knowing look. 'They took everything but your sheet music.' He paused for effect, and there was a guffaw from the back office.

The poor woman was mortified. I told her later that she should have said it was a holiday snap of her husband.

It has been said that the *Little Red Riding Would!* panto, and my shows in general, paved the way for similar acts to perform here. Of course, I was the original of the species. And the best. It was inevitable that, shortly after my arrival, the greatest show on Irish TV (there was only one channel), would come knocking. *The Late Late Show*, hosted by Gay Byrne, had been running since the early 1960s, and was considered to be the real weathervane of Ireland. It challenged the moral majority and discussed things publicly that families wouldn't even speak about in their own kitchens.

Ireland was a homophobic country, with cruel and outdated laws, and an attitude to gays that was dismissive, derisive and fearful. 'Queers' were seen as predators, always ready to pounce on some unsuspecting, innocent young man—or woman. In 1974, Jonie Crone, a young gay activist, became Ireland's first lesbian to out her sexuality on national TV on *The Late Late*. Predictably, there was uproar in Catholic Ireland over this shockingly unnatural behaviour. You could almost hear the thunderous hammering of nails on wood as conservative Ireland built a new closet to throw her back into.

I was brought on before Jonie broke that taboo. I wasn't there to talk about being gay. I am the way I am, and either you accept that or you don't. I don't care. Anyway, the thought of talking about homosexuality with a man whose name sounded like a friction injury wasn't on the cards.

It was (still) 1971, and I met Gay on the afternoon of the show. He suggested I sing a song as Mr Pussy and come on as myself afterwards. He wouldn't introduce me as a drag act, and the audience would be unaware that I was a man until the 'reveal'.

'Try to look butch,' I was told by a researcher. 'Wear a suit and stick your hair down the back of your collar before you come back to talk to Gay.'

The audience loved the song—'I'll Never Fall in Love Again'— and were blown away by the revelation that I was a chap. You have to remember, nobody had ever seen this kind of an act on Irish TV before. Gay asked me about my modelling in London and a few other things, but nothing invasive. I must have acquitted myself well as I have appeared on *The Late Late Show* countless times over the centuries. That night, I remember the studio was full of taxi men—I think there was a taxi strike on. Cabbies are always a great barometer of a city. They all came up afterwards and shook my hand.

The next day I couldn't go anywhere without being mobbed. (Now I can't go anywhere without being mugged.) It took me almost an hour to get down O'Connell Street. People kept stopping me to chat or sign an autograph. Nobody was nasty or homophobic. Real Dubliners are the funniest people in the world (with the possible exception of Cork). They love a character: Bang-Bang, Fortycoats, Mad Mary ... and now Mr Pussy. I think the more outrageous you are, the more they like you. Dubs like people with an 'eff you' attitude.

It was time to see what the other inhabitants of this island made of me. Mr Pussy needed to go on tour. I had been taken on by the Ray O'Sullivan agency after the success of the Drake Inn. They looked after the big cabaret acts (Sonny Knowles, Fr Cleary...) and I was now top of the pile. We put together our own band called Pentagon, a compère (Dale King) and an opening act: Eithne Dunne, the blonde bombshell. We took to the roads, Ted Ray and me in the Jag, the others in the bus. We must have played every venue in Ireland, and held local records for crowd attendances. There was always a friendly competition going on between us and the showbands we'd bump into on our travels. I made a lot of friends on that tour. Tony Kenny, Red Hurley, Mick Roche and the Arrows, the tragic Miami, The Indians, Joe Dolan (what a showman), Dickie Rock.... Dickie was—and still is—well hard. He's a master at karate. I'd love to have seen him and Elvis fight it out. Unfortunately, Elvis was never good enough to play any of the venues we played, so that never materialised. Then he died, God rest him.

Some of the venues were huge, like the Cork Opera House. Others were miniscule. I recall doing one and asking where the dressing room was. I was shown to a small cupboard.

'Where's the chain and the toilet paper?' I asked. 'This isn't a dressing room, it's a lav.'

'Well, Big Tom used it last week,' came the reply.

'He should change his name to Tiny bleedin' Tom. And he didn't have to change into a frigging dress. Or did he?'

I've always liked Big Tom, by the way. Great sense of humour, but a different audience to mine.

We drove and drove and played and played. One Saturday we drove from Caherciveen to Malin Head for a gig. I can still hear the Saturday afternoon radio on in the car, with Mícheál Ó hEithir's odd squealing voice commentating on the races. The tour was becoming so well known that Mike Murphy from RTÉ joined me on the road with a crew when we were doing the Curragh Camp. The crowds were enormous. I'm not exaggerating. Look up that piece on RTÉ's archive if you don't believe me.

Our first gig in Longford was memorable for its crowds too. On the morning of the gig I was condemned from the pulpit by a bishop. He warned his flock not to go to that night's show. Word spread and, Ireland being Ireland, I ended up with a sell-out crowd—more than he'd preached to in a year. I forget his name. I really should send him a card to thank him for helping me on my way.

The constant driving took its toll. My 'chauffeur' was a very careful and capable man called Frank. He was great for a chat while on the road, but knew when to shut up when I was tired. One night I put the car seat back and fell asleep. Frank, somehow, hit a kerb and the car spun and spun and spun before crashing into a tree. All the gear flew out of the back. Miraculously, we were completely unscathed. If I had been sitting upright I'd have been dead. A branch had come through the windscreen and missed my head by inches.

The roadshow was hard work, but a lot of fun and a great introduction to the real Ireland that exists outside of the Dublin bubble. The hospitality was incredible. We generally stayed in the venue where we were playing or at a nice B&B. After the show, everyone would retire to the kitchen, where there would be a vat of tea and a hill of sandwiches waiting for us. Then the singing would begin and the whiskey would be produced.

You were always conscious of the fact that you were in somebody's home when you stayed in a B&B. The family would come to the show and expect you to come back for tea afterwards. Hotel post-show parties were wilder affairs. We stayed in Youghal one night and returned to the hotel, pissed, in the small hours. We couldn't get into our room—I think the key was broken. So, rather than spend the night in the van, the lads from the band scoured the place looking for a vacant room. Somehow they managed to find one, unhinge the door, carry it up a flight of stairs and replace my locked door with it. It was even more miraculous considering that they couldn't breathe they were laughing so much.

It only struck us the following day that they didn't need to go to all that bother. I could have just stayed in the vacant room.

They were crap carpenters. The new door stuck fast in the jamb and couldn't be opened, so I just unloaded all my gear through the window as it was a ground-floor room. I climbed out after it and was collared by the porter, who thought we were doing a runner without paying. I think he thought we were The Who, only instead of TVs being thrown out of the hotel window, the Pussy Posse was defenestrating drag queens.

I looked that word up, by the way. It means 'to throw someone out of a window'. English lesson over, kids.

Of all the places I toured, Cork is my favourite. In my prime I used to head down there every six weeks for shows in Midleton, Mallow, Clonakilty … My first Leeside venue was Moore's Hotel in the city. Noel Magner had come to see me play in Molloy's, Tallaght, and booked me for a week. The accommodation was lovely, and when I looked out of the window I could see a crowd queuing around the hotel. I asked a waiter what they were lining up for.

'You,' he replied.

I broke box office records in Ireland's real capital that week. It was a very special introduction to Cork for a number of reasons. We drove down the night before the first gig as the roads were so bad back then that travelling took forever. Nowadays it's a two and a half hour drive. It was a Friday evening and there were no rooms available in our hotel, so I kicked off, and they brought a bed down to the residents' bar. We got locked in there for the night—and well locked too. The night porter was pissed, and kept us well supplied with drinks. He even made us a 'salad' from some hard cheese he found behind the bar and some leftover crisps, 'to give it a bit of flavour'.

Actually, I'm not sure if he *was* the night porter; he might well have been a customer. It doesn't matter: that first night set the boozy theme for the rest of the run. We would do a gig, go on the batter, end up in the early houses and then home to sleep for an hour before the next show. I had immense stamina. I still do, and am always the last to leave a party.

The management at Moore's were quite apprehensive about my material before the first show. 'Keep it clean,' they said. I did. I also did a striptease down to a swimming costume and a pair of wading boots—and the crowd went nuts. I followed this by firing tennis balls out of my bra. They always love that. It's crowd participation, I suppose, as they have to throw them back for me to catch in my bra. I always make them return them, by the way. Tennis balls aren't cheap.

The last crowd-pleaser was the Cinderella routine, where I pick five ugly brutes from the audience and dress them up as fairies, ugly sisters and Buttons. The crowd, and the papers, loved it. 'Drag comes to Cork' ran the following day's headlines. I was 'in'. So 'in' that I was invited to a civic reception held by the Lord Mayor. I don't remember much about that as it was 10 in the morning and I was well pissed on brandy. I do recall that there were a lot of nuns there. That's about it.

Later that day, once the brandy had worn off, I went on a pilgrimage to the birthplace of my hero, Danny La Rue. That was a real high for me as we were the greatest of friends, and I really enjoyed sharing my Cork experiences with him whenever we used to meet up. He was always a huge fan of the opera house, as am I. I have such happy memories of my times there. I said a short while back that playing at Moore's was special for a number of reasons. One of those reasons is that I fell in love with someone after one of my gigs there. Platonically 'in love': we were never an item. His name was David Gordon.

David was Ireland's leading ballet master, and began his career as a boy soprano in his local church in the docks area of Belfast. When he was just fifteen he was chosen to represent Northern Ireland at the Queen's coronation as a soloist. During the show he was spotted by Dame Ninette de Valois, the founder of the Royal Ballet, who was in the audience. She asked to meet him afterwards, and he told her about his dream of becoming a dancer. The Dame was impressed, and offered him a scholarship to study at the Royal Ballet.

His backstory reads like *Billy Elliot*: coming from the tough, macho Shankill Road to become one of the Royal Ballet's principal dancers, and later a respected teacher. David toured the world and danced with

Margot Fonteyn and my old mate Rudolf Nureyev. When Joan Denise Moriarty founded the Irish National Ballet, she asked Dame Ninette to recommend a ballet master. David was her only suggestion. He packed up his tights and codpiece and headed to Cork, thinking, like me, that he would only be staying for a few months.

He stayed there for the rest of his life, and became a widely loved, respected and flamboyant part of Cork life, with his balletic posture, jewellery and long shawls. Everybody adored David, and he became known as 'Mother Gordon' around the city. He wasn't just an endearing figure; he was a pioneer of Cork's gay scene, uncompromisingly camp and 'out'. He gave a lot of youngsters the courage to be themselves.

He was irrepressibly funny and outrageous. I remember at a party, David woke with a raging hangover and declared: 'I've arrived! I've arrived! I've always wanted to sleep in a four-poster bed, and now I've done it!'

He had passed out under the kitchen table.

David was well known around the city's pubs. He threw a party one evening, and the next morning/afternoon we were looking for a cure. He picked up the phone and called his local, ordering fifteen Bloody Marys to be delivered to the house. Five minutes later he had forgotten the phone call. So he rang another pub ordering another fifteen Bloody Marys. Five minutes later he repeated the order to another bemused publican. Three lounge boys arrived in three separate cars with trays of drinks and handed them through the window of his flat as if it were the most normal thing in the world.

Another time, we went to the boozer and he spotted a big, muscle-bound guy ordering a snowball.

'Ooooh, a snowball…?' he mused, looking at the chap sitting down by himself with the gayest of gay drinks. 'Barman, every time that gentleman orders a drink, put two up on the bar for me.'

Within an hour, there were ten snowballs on the counter. David smiled across at the man and motioned to the drinks. The He-Man laughed and joined us. David had pulled. The snowballs were decanted into a bottle, and they left to have their own private party....

Another time, he got us invited to a bash in a stately pile. We were cross-eyed with drink, and I remember two very rough stable-hands vying for my attention. Things got so heated that they went into the great hall and pulled two swords off the wall to fight a duel for 'my hand'. (I'm sure it wasn't my hand they wanted, but let's not get into that.) I stood on the balcony and watched them stumble about the place with the heavy choppers.

'Sweetie, you look just like Juliette,' laughed David. 'Throw down your handkerchief to the winner. I'll have the runner-up.' And he did.

Ireland lost one of its most colourful characters when David passed away in 2007 at the age of sixty-nine. And I lost a great friend. He was one of those people who spanned the yawning divide between gay and straight in a time of rampant homophobia. That's the peculiar thing about Ireland. While it was legally an anti-gay country, in practice most people really didn't care about your sexuality. If you didn't ram it down their throats, so to speak, and just behaved honestly and remained true to yourself, you would be accepted—and in David's case, taken in to their hearts.

The Irish are the kindest people you could ever meet ... for the most part. That said, the 1980s were approaching and the relationship between gay and straight Ireland was about to be severely tested. The decade kicked off with one of the most brutal murders Dublin had ever witnessed.

And the backlash from the gardaí still makes my blood boil.

Chapter Ten

The Grey, Gay 1980s

'I wish to talk to you this evening about the state of the nation's affairs, and the picture I have to paint is not, unfortunately, a very cheerful one. The figures which are just now becoming available to us show one thing very clearly. As a community, we are living way beyond our means.'

That was Charles J. Haughey speaking. It was 9 January 1980, and the country was so shagged that the taoiseach felt it necessary to record a state-of-the-nation address. The hard-pressed people of Ireland were being asked to 'tighten their belts' by a man who looked like he was about to unbuckle his own and ravish your sister.

More than a million workdays had been lost in 1979 through strikes, and unemployment was rising. Ireland also had a trade deficit of IR£760 million. That kind of dosh could have bought a lot of belts, or Charvet shirts. While Charlie was telling us to live more frugally, he was living it up royally, flying to Paris to buy tailored shirts and running a stately pile in north Dublin.

I was introduced to Charlie once in the Dáil bar. The reprobates from Leinster House were always sneaking off to my show in the Baggot, and someone had decided to reciprocate by bringing Pussy to the seat of power. I went with my new assistant, George Woodhouse, and we joined some Fianna Fáilers in the bar. As soon as Charlie walked in with his entourage, the Soldiers of Destiny were up like a shot, offering him a drink and pointing him towards our table. Charlie was famous for his poker face—you never knew what was going on behind those hooded eyelids. I swear, though, that his eyes twinkled when he saw me. He had been to a few of the shows and was well known for his gritty sense of humour.

'Ah, Mr Amsby,' he said, stretching a manicured hand in my direction. 'You're well used to hanging out with comedians and prima donnas. I don't expect you'll ever get to rub shoulders with as many clowns as you'll find here tonight.' His face was impassive. There was silence as his terrified lackeys were unsure whether to laugh or not.

He was gone before I had a chance to say something witty or clever. That was the only time I ever met him. He was painted as a pantomime villain for the rest of his life. I could see why. There was an air of unearned wealth about him. Not so much a whiff of sulphur as a nose-caressing scent of expensive cologne.

He lived like a prince while the Great Unscented population lived from hand to mouth—something that constantly annoyed his critics, but was largely ignored by his supporters. Haughey epitomised a lot of what was wrong with Ireland in the 1980s. While he was seen as a colourful character, he presided over a country that had become grey overnight. Young people were starting to leave again, and the Troubles were sapping the island's morale. Anti-Paddy racism was on the rise in the UK as a result of immigration and Republican violence. Ireland was, to put it kindly, buggered.

He had a mistress, the gossip columnist Terry Keane, and together they flouted the 'moral conventions' of Catholic Ireland. Terry was a controversial character. Her *Sunday Independent* column could be exceptionally bitchy, and she often made veiled references to 'sweetie', who everyone took to be CJ. She wasn't the most popular person in Dublin as she came across as arrogant. That said, I liked her—not just because she was kind to me in her columns, but because she was her own woman. She was always very entertaining and had a strong personality, and if you didn't like her, well, that was your loss.

While our Prime Minister was living a life of 'moral' double standards, gay sex was still against the law. It annoys me to think back on this. All CJ and his friends had to do was legislate in the Dáil and a considerable number of Irish people would have been free to live as gay couples. The hypocrisy was dreadful, but typical of the new (and beloved) country in which I had to chosen to make my home.

I'm not sure how Haughey personally felt about gays, but the legend goes that he christened RTÉ 'Fairyhouse' because of the high number of gay men working there. One of those gay 'Fairyhouse' men was to make headlines two years into the new decade. His name was Charles Self, and he was a set designer who shared a flat with pioneering DJ, Vincent Hanley. Charlie suffered a horrible death.

He was well known on the pub scene. I drank with him in the South William Bar and knew him from *The Late Late Show*, and liked his company, as did the rest of our peers. He was outgoing and popular and openly gay.

Charlie was brought up in Scotland, and had been living in Dublin since 1978, when Alpho O'Reilly, head of design in RTÉ, had brought him over from the BBC. He was the main set designer on *The Late Late Show* and was highly regarded in the business. Charlie had a good income and a good life, never bothered anyone, and just generally enjoyed himself as best he could (like the rest of us).

On the night he was murdered, Charlie had been cruising around Dublin and left the city centre in a taxi with a young man. Vincent Hanley was working in London, and his room had been taken by another man, who said he was disturbed at 2.30 a.m. by someone coming into his bedroom and saying, 'Sorry, wrong room.' He told the gardaí that it wasn't unusual for Charlie to bring men home, so he wasn't worried.

The following morning, he found Charlie lying dead in a pool of blood, slumped against the front door. He had been stabbed fourteen times; six of the wounds were so vicious that the blade of the carving knife went through his chest and out his back. He also had three slash wounds to his throat, one of them five inches long. Part of the cord from Vincent Hanley's red dressing gown was also wound around his neck.

Whoever killed Charlie was fuelled by anger and hatred. The flat had been ransacked, but there was no sign of a burglary. It was believed that his murderer escaped through a window, leaving bloody footprints across the carpet.

There was widespread shock and sadness at his death among the gay community, and fear that a homophobic serial killer was at large in Dublin. Word of his murder quickly spread across town hours after he was discovered. This was in the days before social media: gay men are miles better than Twitter at getting the latest news and gossip across. There was wild speculation as to who might have killed Charlie. Some said it was a merchant sailor who had slipped back onboard his ship after the crime.

In the wider world there might have been a touch of 'well, he deserved what he got for being gay'. That's not an exaggeration. Dublin was becoming more homophobic, and one group in particular seemed more anti-gay than the rest of the country combined: the gardaí.

The police response to Charlie Self's murder was to round up Dublin's gay community. Around 1,500 people were questioned, fingerprinted and photographed during the investigation. They were asked who they slept with and for their partners' names. It was almost as if the gardaí were more interested in compiling files on gays than solving the crime. It was disgraceful and certainly wouldn't happen now.

I was living in Finglas when it was my turn to be questioned. I had been in hospital for blood tests that morning, and had decided to spend the afternoon on the couch, relaxing. The doorbell rang, and I answered it to a sheepish-looking young guard.

'Mr Alan Amsby? We'd like to ask you a few questions in connection with the murder of Charles Self.'

Nobody wants to hear a guard speak their name followed by the words 'in connection with … murder'. I kept my cool, though. I could see the guard looking at the needle-prick on my arm from the tests. I laughed.

'Just the annual check-up. I'm not a junkie.' He looked relieved. I looked over his shoulder and saw a squad car with another young officer behind the wheel. 'I'm happy to help you, but I'm not going to stand here talking to you with a police car outside my door. God knows what the neighbours will think.' The guard shifted uneasily.

'Let's go for a drink,' I suggested. To my surprise, he thought this was a splendid idea. I grabbed my coat and he led me to the car.

'You'll have to sit in the back,' I said. 'I'll get in the front.' I didn't want it to look like I was being arrested. I am sure the other men who were being similarly harassed felt the same way. Again, to my surprise, the young guard agreed, and we drove to the Drake, where we had a brief chat—and in my case, a double brandy. I had nothing to tell them other than that I knew Charlie from the pub. We finished up with them requesting that I go to Pearse Street Garda Station to have my fingerprints and mugshot taken. I was really angry about this, but could tell the young guards were only doing their job and were embarrassed. I went along to Pearse Street the following day and had my prints and photo taken. The staff there knew me from the papers (and maybe from the Baggot), and were polite and as friendly as they could be. In fairness to Pearse Street, it had a reputation for being relatively sympathetic to gay men. The station is just behind Burgh Quay and its public toilet, which was a notorious pick-up area for rent boys. The guards knew that 99 per cent of these rent boys had tragic backgrounds and were renting because they had no alternative. They were the most vulnerable group in Irish society. Many members of the force unofficially kept an eye on them for their own safety.

Nothing came of the investigation. The police narrowed their search down to two young, gay prostitutes. One had an alibi and the other couldn't be identified by a witness. Nobody has ever been charged with Charlie's murder. It has since been said that the murder scene was staged by the killer to cover his/her tracks. The window was too small for anyone to escape through, and there were other anomalies. The guards still hope that the case may someday be solved. But then, today's gardaí are a more enlightened breed to those around in the 1980s.

The Charlie Self case faded out of the public eye as the months progressed. There were bigger news stories afoot. Charlie Haughey was trying to boot Charlie McCreevy out of Fianna Fáil, the DeLorean car factory in Belfast (remember that?) was closing down, and then there was the Bridie Gargan case. She was a twenty-seven-year-old nurse who was beaten to death with a lump hammer after being abducted from the Phoenix Park. A few days later, a man called Donal Dunne was shot dead with his own gun. Their killer was a man named Malcolm MacArthur. I knew him to see in Bartley Dunne's, where he sometimes drank. He was arrested in the apartment of the then Attorney General, Paddy Connolly, in Pilot View in Dalkey.

Despite Charlie's death being pushed from the main headlines, gay Dublin was still living in fear. Before the year was out, there would be another murder which would, ultimately, change everything.

In the summer of 1982, a series of what seemed like systematic beatings was carried out in Fairview Park. Gay men used the park as a meeting place, and were being targeted by thugs. The public and media called it 'queer-bashing'. Obviously, most of the population thought this was despicable—and some straight men were mistakenly beaten up too—but there was an undercurrent of disgust at the lifestyle these men chose to lead. In some quarters, the bashings were seen as cleaning up the area. It's hard to imagine people having that attitude now, but this was only thirty years ago.

On 10 September the bashers struck again, and chose thirty-one-year-old Aer Rianta worker Declan Flynn as their target. One of them was used as 'queer bait'. When Declan sat next to him on a bench, four gang members rushed out from the trees and attacked him. He ran towards the gate but was caught just inside the park, where the 'vigilantes' kicked him and beat him with sticks. When they had tired of this, they stole his watch and £4. Declan choked on his blood and died hours later.

Two of his attackers were members of the Defence Forces. One of them told gardaí: 'We were part of the team to get rid of queers from Fairview Park. A few of us had been queer-bashing for about six weeks before, and battered about twenty steamers. We used to grab them. If they hit back, we gave it to them.'

When the case came before the courts in March 1983, the judge gave the attackers suspended sentences for manslaughter and they walked free. 'This,' he said, 'could never be regarded as murder.' Now, I'm not a lawyer, and I'm not qualified to have an opinion on the finer points of the law, but natural justice was not done that day. What's more, the gang's leader went on to rape a pregnant woman ten years later.

The ruling caused an outcry in the papers and in the Dáil. David Norris said it seemed to give people a 'licence to kill' gay men. Within days, almost 1,000 people marched from Liberty Hall to Fairview Park for a rally with speakers from the Dublin Lesbian and Gay Men's Collective and the Dublin Rape Crisis Centre. That June, Ireland held its first Gay Pride march, from St Stephen's Green to the GPO. It was 200 people strong. There are now over 10,000 participants, and the Pride festival takes place over ten days.

Many young people are unaware of its origin. Now you know.

Despite the non-violent fightback by the gay community and its supporters, queer-bashing didn't disappear overnight. The 1980s continued to be a scary time. Being gay was like being a child molester in the minds of many stupid people. Homosexuality was seen as a 'condition', and the Legion of Mary ran special meetings for 'people with that problem'.

Then, of course, Rock Hudson died in 1985, and Aids appeared on the public radar. Gay men had yet another stigma to contend with. I remember the idiotic 'joke' that some straight people would crack when introduced to me at the time. It was supposed to show that they were liberal and enlightened enough to know that Aids was not leprosy.

'I better not shake hands with you in case I catch Aids! Hahahahaha.' I once, publicly, threw a drink over someone for saying that. Word must have travelled around as it was the last time I heard that 'gag'.

Rock, by the way, came to Ireland a number of times. He was here in the mid 1950s while filming *Captain Lightfoot*. It was an appropriate title for someone who was as light on his feet as Rock. He was also a regular in Rice's and Bartley Dunne's during the 1968 filming of *Darling Lily* with Julie Andrews. I missed him by just a year. Damn it.

Nineteen eighty-five was also the year when a major tragedy was averted in Dublin due to the quick thinking of one man: David Norris. The senator was one of the people who set up the Hirschfeld Centre on Fownes Street in 1979. The Hirschfeld was what we would now call a 'hub' for gay Dublin, and was named after a German gay rights activist whose institute for sexual research was torched by the Nazis. Fownes Street was chosen because it was so run down. It was out of the public eye and away from queer-bashers.

The Hirschfeld ran all the usual community centre facilities during the day, and at weekends ran a disco called Flikkers, which is Dutch slang for 'faggots'. It wasn't what most straight people would have expected. It was kind of a like a local disco with people dancing slow sets as opposed to running around in G-strings and having orgies. It was a very cool place, with great music and chic decor. There was a recycled RTÉ National Song Contest set, and the floor was painted black. There was no booze to be had, so punters drank tea or soft drinks. There was food on offer too.

The dancing was the main thing, though. It staged all-night discos and really changed the face of Dublin nightlife. When it closed, the DJs who had spun discs there moved on and applied what they had learned in other clubs. You could argue that the Hirschfeld gave birth to the city's dance scene of the 1990s.

There was a feeling among many of the gays who frequented the centre that they were outlaws—which, technically, they were. This added to the attraction of the place. The guards generally left the club to its own devices, although sometimes they would come in to just harass the club's patrons, taking names and addresses. Occasionally, they would be called to deal with a punch-up between two queens, and would enter very cautiously—as if they were going to catch 'The Gay'—and leave to a slow handclap and whistles from the dancers.

In 1985, there was a firebomb attack at the centre. In his autobiography, *A Kick Against the Pricks*, David Norris describes working late in his office at the centre and noticing sparks coming from the roof. He went to investigate and discovered a milk churn filled with explosives and surrounded with firelighters and two barrels of petrol, and the roof's felt was on fire. He very bravely put the fire out. If he hadn't done so, the petrol would have dripped down and incinerated everybody below. He saved dozens of lives that night.

Nobody was ever caught for the crime, and two years later the centre burned down. Despite David's representations, no official money was offered to help to rebuild the place. That was 'Official Ireland' at the time: dangerously homophobic and unsupportive.

That said, I don't want to paint Ireland as a bleak, gay-bashing hell. It wasn't. Although there wasn't a 'scene' in the same way there was in London, the life of gay Dublin continued as before. We still had our places to meet: Rice's … Bartley Dunne's … Tobin's … The Viking Inn on Dame Street. Our pubs were not known as 'gay bars' in the way that places are labelled today. They were 'gay friendly', with a mix of artists and professionals, straight and homosexual.

The Viking, by the way, was the first pub in the city to have a gay manager and be specifically aimed at a gay clientele. I was the first drag act to appear there. Once in a while, a straight rustic type would innocently wander in and the locals would mischievously set out to let him know that it was gay turf.

After Declan Flynn's death, attitudes slowly began to change towards gay people. The Irish, as I've said before, have an incredible sense of decency. No matter how stupid or entrenched their 'beliefs' are, they always leave 'wriggle room' for kindness and common sense to survive, if not thrive. Gay men were being seen less as perverts and more as people with the same human rights as heterosexuals. This slow change was largely down to pioneering work of people like David Norris. The senator—who was the first openly gay person to be elected to public office in Ireland—can take a large share of the credit for liberalising Ireland.

There were others, too, who helped to changed attitudes by being … well … 'fabulous'. I was one of them. Another was the

DJ Vincent Hanley, affectionately known as 'Fab Vinny' due to his upbeat delivery. Vinny was from Tipperary, and became a pioneering radio and TV presenter. He was our first gay media celebrity.

He began his radio career in RTÉ Radio Cork in 1976 and did turns on Radio 1 and RTÉ TV before moving to the new Radio 2 in 1979. Radio 2 was a totally new idea: a national station dedicated to doing what the pirate stations had been doing up until then. Vinny was so popular that he was drafted over to Capital Radio in London, and then moved to New York, where he co-produced the groundbreaking *MT-USA* (Music Television USA). This was a three-hour-long music video show modelled on the new American channel, MTV. Vinny was Europe's first video jockey.

He was a lovely man, and did a lot for mainstream acceptance of gay men, although he was never an activist or vocal about his sexuality. The public knew that he was homosexual and loved him for who he was. He didn't camp it up: he was just likeable, enthusiastic, and very good at his job. In 1987, Vinny passed away at the very young age of thirty-three. He had physically deteriorated over a relatively short time, and there was speculation about whether he had HIV, although he denied this.

His denials reflected how the disease was stigmatised in Ireland and abroad. Vinny had the virus and died from a related illness. He's largely forgotten now, with his name only cropping up in stories about Charlie Self's murder. Hopefully these few paragraphs will be a small testament to a man who opened many eyes to the fact that gay men are capable of achieving great things. More importantly, that they are human and, in an age of desperate homophobia, not just camp figures of fun.

There were two other men who did their bit to open Irish eyes to the bigger picture. While my lovely Paddyland was officially homophobic, two of its best-loved 'theatricals', Hilton Edwards and Micheál Mac Liammóir, lived an openly gay life in the city centre.

'The Boys', as they were universally known, made their home on Harcourt Terrace, where Michael Collins had a safe house and the playwright and mystic George Russell used to host soirées for Dublin's artistic set. Michael and Hilton didn't believe in being low-key, and their house was a landmark for many Dubs. People would pass it hoping for a glimpse of Micheál doing something flamboyant. On one occasion, when their cat died, the mourning 'Boys' blacked out their windows as a mark of respect to their fallen feline comrade. The city's population would have expected no less from them.

One evening in the mid 1970s, my mate Tony McCann suggested dropping in to see them for a drink before a night out on the tiles. I remember being impressed by the house's posh, red-brick Regency facade … and even more impressed when the door was opened by a striking-looking man in full make-up.

'Dear boys, won't you please come in?' he intoned with a flourish. I noticed that he was wearing an enormous chunky gold bracelet. Perhaps the flourish was to show it off. Theatre types like 'The Boys' never had much money. I wondered if it was real gold. The interior of the house was very nineteenth-century, with antiques and prints of Sarah Purser paintings and playbills. We drank, and Michael (to his friends he was Michael, professionally he was Micheál) held court as Hilton sat and listened with a twinkle in his eye.

The pair were 'divils', to use the Irish saying. Mac Liammóir once claimed to have had an affair with General Eoin O'Duffy, who was the head of the fascist Blueshirts. Nobody has ever been able to prove or disprove this. Maybe Michael was being mischievous—he was certainly capable of telling a few porkies!

He sold himself as an Irish language expert and Hibernophile from West Cork. He wrote three books in Irish and translated them into English. In fact, he was born Alfred Willmore in London, and had no Irish roots whatsoever. He had been one of the leading child actors on the English stage in the company of Noël Coward, and studied painting at the Slade School of Art. He was delighted when I told him I 'knew' Coward from London.

'Oh, my dear boy, we appeared together in *The Goldfish*. I played King Goldfish in amber tights, a tiny crown on my head, and a sort of orange bathing suit bristling with gold sequins and a short and saucy cape to match. Noël played Prince Mussel in a scheme of slate-grey and blue-green velvet.'

I was impressed with his attention to all the costume details. He would have made a great drag queen. Whatever about that, he was a delightful man, sweet, thoughtful, clever, funny and supportive.

The evening Tony and I spent at the Boys' place was full of anecdotes about the Gate's early days and the films both men had acted in. I was surprised to hear that James Mason had got his break at the Gate. He is one of my all-time favourite actors. What was even more surprising was the revelation/claim that Michael and Hilton had discovered Orson Welles. I didn't really believe them at first, but the story is 100 per cent true.

Welles had come to Ireland in 1931 as a sixteen-year-old and spent some time travelling around the countryside on a donkey and cart. After twatting around the Aran Islands, he found himself in Dublin and, being an aspiring actor, visited the Gate. He immediately fell in love with it. 'Everyone works for the joy of working,' he said. Which was just as well, as there was piss-all money in the place.

Teenage Orson presented Hilton with an exceptionally cheeky note, which read: 'Orson Welles, star of the New York Theatre Guild, would consider appearing in one of your productions and hopes you will see him for an appointment.' He got the role of Duke Karl Alexander in a play called *Jew Suss*. Hilton recalled that his first performance was all over the place, but he got a standing ovation. I came across this description from Michael: 'Welles put on an astonishing performance, wrong from beginning to end but with all the qualities of fine acting tearing their way through a chaos of inexperience.'

As Welles found out early on, the Gate had sod-all money. I heard a story that illustrates this. Sometime in the early 1970s, the Boys hadn't paid their rates or rent, and the bailiffs came calling. A number of burly men rolled up the pathway to the house and banged on the door. A few moments went by, and they knocked again. A disembodied voice called to them from an upstairs window: 'I'll be down presently.' Another few minutes went by, and the heavies were just about to break down the front door when it swung open. The gasps and the sound of jaws hitting concrete could be heard across the road.

'Won't you please come in?' Michael was standing, in full make-up, wearing a short silk kimono, which revealed two elderly but shapely legs. The terrified bailiff's men backed out of the gate and legged it, citing some other pressing matter across town. They never returned, and the couple continued to live on Harcourt Terrace.

While they were known to have an open sexual relationship, the Boys were devoted to each other. They met in 1927 at the Athenaeum Theatre in Enniscorthy, and it was love at first sight, apparently. Now I don't mean to be harsh here, but I doubt that it was love based on overwhelming physical attraction. Hilton was a wonderful man, but he wasn't blessed with matinee idol looks like Michael. He wasn't a 'looker'.

That never matters of course. What's important is love and companionship. The Boys were both brilliantly gifted actors, designers and theatrical producers. Their love was one of those deep-rooted, soulmate affairs, which are rare to find anywhere, for gays or straights. While David Norris was an early icon for gay rights activists, Michael and Hilton were equally important as an example of how love will insist on prospering despite prevailing attitudes and phobias.

Their greatest achievement as a couple, aside from finding true love, was their establishment of the Gate Theatre in 1928. It was experimental and new, while the Abbey was floundering at the time following the poor reception of O'Casey's *The Silver Tassie*. I'm not going to start into a history of Irish Theatre here. There are loads of great books on the subject, if you're interested.

Michael passed away in 1978, and a little wash of limelight disappeared forever from the Irish stage. Hilton never recovered from his death. For the next six years he pined for his great love, and barely left the house, where he would sit in front of the TV, flicking through the channels—Ireland now had a second station.

Few of us who attended Michael's funeral will ever forget the great display of Irish political hypocrisy in evidence that day. The president, Patrick Hillery, and the entire cabinet lined up to shake hands with Hilton. This was a public acknowledgment that he was a 'widow'. Many of those politicians were actively against lifting the laws that had criminalised the Boys' 'marriage' in the first place.

It would be another eighteen years before that first, most important, step down the road to equality was taken. In the meantime there would be more beatings and a handful of deaths on the island of Ireland.

Change, as Yeats said about peace, comes dropping slow. But it would come.

Up North.

Celebrating two years at the Baggot Inn.

Olympia Theatre, Dublin.

On the way to Cork.

I didn't make it …

Ireland's first midnight revue.

Ireland's first adult panto,
written and directed by me.

LITTLE RED RIDING ~~~WOULD!

Ireland's first untraditional panto.

'Drag' comes to Dublin

By Tony Wilson

"DRAG" has come to Dublin, in the form of "Mr. Pussy", alias Londoner Alan Amsby.

For the uninitiated "drag" is female impersonation, or more bluntly, a man dressing up as a woman.

It's an area of entertainment that has blossomed in recent years into a fashionable showbusiness category. At its best, it can be very funny and clever, or its worst a vulgar...

The tremendous rise in popularity of Danny la Rue, the Cork-born "drag" star, has given female impersonation a respectability that has lifted it from East End pubs and dubious clubs to the television screen and the West End stage. Danny la Rue has made it a kind of art form, with his "send-up" of famous female singing stars and light-hearted swipes at the feminine sex.

'I'm in it for the money'

Of course, female impersonation is nothing new. In Shakespeare's time, the female roles in his plays were taken by boys, before it was considered decent for women to act in plays, and the pantomime has a tradition of Dames. The late Jimmy O'Dea was famous for his characterisations, while Noel Purcell at one time also played "Dame" parts and today Cecil Sheridan carries on the tradition.

These, however, were and are, much broader and obvious comedy presentations of women. "Drag", if it's good, is a deal more subtle and sophisticated.

Alan Amsby came to Dublin some weeks ago from Belfast, where he went for a week's booking and eventually stayed for a month. Now he has established his own nightspot in Dublin's "Pussy's Parlour" at the Baggot Inn, Baggot Street.

Says Alan, 23: "I came to Dublin for a weekend when I was in Belfast and it bit me so being something new and exciting."

Alan started in the "drag" game by chance four years ago. "I used to drink in a pub in South London where they had a 'drag'," he recalls. "I said that I could do better, and so I borrowed a frock and it just went on from there."

Alan was working as a wigmaker—a trade which has obviously stood him in good stead subsequently — and he decided to go into full-time female impersonation following his successful debut.

He worked clubs in London first of all, gaining experience and polishing his act and then graduated to clubs and cabaret all over England, which, in turn, led him to Belfast and Dublin.

As "Mr. Pussy", Alan tries to project an extremely glamourous image of a slightly dimsy dumb bird. He's certainly one of the best "drag" acts I've ever seen and refreshingly different from some of the tired, middle-aged female impersonators who only end up by making the thing a tasteless mockery.

Off-stage, he's quiet, intelligent, witty and well dressed and enjoys a pint. And there's little hint of the attractive young lady we'd seen miming to pop records and joking a few minutes before on stage.

He takes his job seriously, from a business aspect. "It's just not dressing up," he says. "I'm in it for the money and I've done very well so far. To me the dressing up is just the end product."

Alan reckons it costs him in the region of about £30 to dress his act. "I'm very particular about the wigs, naturally, and I try and go for a mod type of image.

'It would be nice if someone would say the act was terrible'

"I don't believe in shaving my legs—I wear three pairs of tights. I buy most of my clothes off the peg but I do sometimes have special costumes made. I've paid up to £120 for a costume."

Alan has found that his act has a strong appeal for women. "I think they like to see themselves sent up. They seem fascinated by it but they try and find fault as well."

At takes Alan 20 minutes to get ready, especially with the eyebrows. "I've got that to a fine art now". And funnily enough ask him about his makeup, practically to the point of advice.

He says reaction to the "Mr. Pussy" act has been very good. "I can go on stage and sum up an audience almost automatically now. If they are going one way and I'm going the other, then I have to go their way, if I don't use a script. I just judge what's best for a particular audience."

So far Alan has had no complaints. "Nobody's come up and complained yet. I'd appreciate it if they would. It would be very nice if someone was to say the act was terrible."

As well as the stage act, Alan also models girls' clothes and has been photographed in this side of his career in a number of newspapers and magazines.

He has an ambitious, though, to go into straight comedy acting one day. "What I do now, I taught myself, and I started

Mr. Pussy in action

off with all miming. I never dreamt I'd be talking as well. Actually, I've been offered a couple of film parts in London but I turned them down because — well, they weren't suitable."

Alan intends to stay in Dublin for as long as he can and feels that the setting up of "Pussy's Parlour" is something of an achievement. "To do that in London would take years," he says. "I'll still go back to London for bookings and work in other parts of Britain and in Belfast but I want to use Dublin as a base. I lived at home before I came over and I'm hoping that I can bring my mother over to live here as well."

I've arrived!

The first of many visits.

A revue …

Couldn't agree more!

Can you tell the. difference ?

Have a good look at the picture, on the left and decide who is who, or, perhaps, which is which. One of them is a man's man — when he is out of costume.

When he isn't Mr. Pussy, Alan Aimsby is a 21-year-old Londoner, the youngest Drag Queen on the English scene. At one time Alan was involved in the wig business. Now he concentrates on raising a few eyebrows.

Drag hasn't really come to Ireland yet. We have had our share of pantomime dames and gross music hall madams, but nothing l'ke the slinky Mr. Pussy, who is being tipped strongly as the heir apparent to Danny La Rue.

MINI-SKIRT

Tomorrow night at The Drake Inn, Finglas, Alan, or Mr. Pussy if you prefer, will be showing his first Irish audience, what drag is all about.

It is not really his first Irish audience, though. He was booked for a week in Belfast an stayed four. That is the sort of girl he is. His make-up and general appearance are so good that he scorns the concealing folds of long dresses and purrs his way through his act in tight mini-skirt. He has even modelled trendy clothes in London and nobody has known the difference.

Out of costume, Alan is a perfectly normal healthy male. He only took up drag because of a silly bet, but there is nothing silly now about the upward trend in his career. Alan plans to stay in Ireland for about a month and that should give a lot of people time to see Mr. Pussy

Footnote: Mr. Pussy is on the left.

SHAY HEALY.

One from my modelling days, written by my mate Shay Healy.

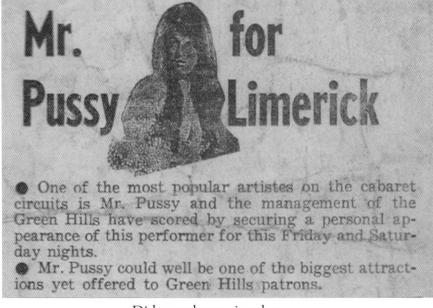

Mr. Pussy for Limerick

● One of the most popular artistes on the cabaret circuits is Mr. Pussy and the management of the Green Hills have scored by securing a personal appearance of this performer for this Friday and Saturday nights.

● Mr. Pussy could well be one of the biggest attractions yet offered to Green Hills patrons.

Did a week at a time here …

Children's panto – great fun!

Cover girl at last!

Nice feature by Eddie Rowley.

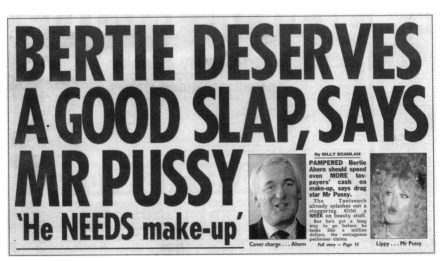

Front page again!

Chapter Eleven

Dublin in the Not-so-Rare Old Times

That last chapter was a bit grim, wasn't it? Gay-bashing, Aids, emigration … we're in danger of turning this book into a misery memoir. This isn't Angela's bleeding Ashes. Things start to get brighter again from here on, although we still have to get through the Greyties (grey eighties).

This might be an appropriate point to talk about my love life. You're probably wondering why I haven't done a roll call of former lovers and conquests. The reason for this is quite simple: I don't like to talk about that part of my life. Also, more importantly, there isn't much to tell. The first and last long-term relationship I had was with David Steele in the 1960s. A few other people have passed through my life since then, but in the main I'm a solitary man. I'm happy living on my own, and couldn't see myself sharing my home with someone else. My sexual preferences are my own business—the same way as if I were a straight man. As a teenager, my sexual awakening was more about discovering that I wasn't straight rather than realising that I was gay.

I have plenty of people in my life: good friends, and of course my 'nieces' from the drag scene. The current crop of wonderful drag stars call me 'Auntie Pussy'. My life is still spent in the public eye, although less now as I'm not in the first flush of youth. I'm always surrounded by people, and when I go home I switch off and read a book. In short, I'm not looking for love or sex on tap. I'm a bachelor, and that's the way I like it.

Even though I'm not a bed-hopper, I had to be careful, like everyone else, from the '80s on. The virus took a number of my friends. Poor George Woodhouse, who I mentioned earlier, succumbed to it. He was a wonderful man, and a great help to me. He used to come on trips with me, carry the cases and generally look after all the stuff I couldn't be bothered managing.

He had been a chef in the Mater Hospital, and was well known and loved around Dublin. Crowds of gay and straight mourners, including Bertie Ahern, turned out for his funeral, and rock and roller Brush Shiels sang for him. By making that small gesture, Brush did his bit to help de-stigmatise the disease. Brush is one of those people who will forever be known as a Dublin Character. Not because he's mental or wanders the streets shouting at people, but because he epitomises the spirit of the city. He's funny and warm and manly and creative, and completely devoid of crap. He is cut from the same cloth as his old pal Phil Lynott. Phil died too young: he had a rocker's booze-fuelled death. He was one of the nicest and coolest men you could meet. I'm great friends with his mum, Philomena. I love her dignity and her sense of fun. She is still stunning-looking, despite having her bus pass.

There were other Dublin Characters who made the city a more colourful place during the drab 1980s. One I remember in particular was Thom McGinty. Thom was known as 'The Diceman'. Mention him to anyone over forty and they will generally go into a reverie about Dublin in the Rare Ould Times and how Thom was a landmark (person-mark?) in their youth.

Like me, Thom had come from the UK looking for work, and ended up staying. He was born in Glasgow and arrived here in 1976 to work as a nude model in the National College of Art and Design. Sitting still must have come easily as this was how he would spend most of his time on Grafton Street during the late 1980s and early 1990s—the first 'human statue'. The monicker 'Diceman' came from a shop he did promotion work for that sold role-playing games, and when it closed he was snapped up to advertise various other businesses, including Bewley's Café.

Through his art, Thom also highlighted political causes such as the Birmingham Six and gay rights. Most of his costumes were mad and outrageously funny. He performed as the framed Mona Lisa, or as a teapot, lightbulb, clown, Dracula.... In 1991 he crossed over the line in the eyes of our moral guardians when he wore a tiny loincloth that didn't cover his bum. He was charged with causing a breach of the peace and with wearing a costume that could offend public decency. How times have changed. Head out into town on any Saturday night now and you'll see a lot less being worn by the city's young ones.

Where London had the bear-skinned guards outside Buckingham Palace to annoy, Dublin had the Diceman, and it was commonplace to witness youngsters trying to break his concentration by throwing things at him or pulling faces (theirs, not his). Sometimes he would chase them off in a playful manner, other times he just suffered on for his art. Then there were the occasional idiots who would throw lit ciggies at his feet, but Thom always stayed in character, earning his celebrity status the hard way. He lived in Galway for a spell during the 1980s and founded the Dandelion Theatre Company. He appeared in the Gate's production of Oscar Wilde's *Salomé*, directed by hammy old Steven Berkoff. Thom also did his act across Europe and in the US and Russia, and was one of very few people to perform on both sides of the Berlin Wall and in Red Square.

I knew him from around town, and we appeared on TV numerous times together, on *Play The Game* and *Saturday Live* in the mid 1980s, and became great mates. He was a lovely, sweet, gentle man, and a regular at my café on Suffolk Street in the mid 1990s. He was always the last to leave a party, and I remember in 1991 he left my place like a corkscrew to perform at the St Patrick's Day parade. I think he did it in fishnets and suspenders. I can't remember if they were mine.

Thom has gone down in the Irish record books as having performed the slowest ever getaway from the gardaí. During one of their periodic clampdowns on busking, members of the Fun Police attempted to make life difficult for the Diceman, claiming that he was causing an obstruction (which he was, due to his popularity). The constant 'move along there' from the underworked gardaí would have become a major source of irritation for a lesser man, but Thom used it to enhance his act.

He would walk at a painfully slow pace, moving his feet almost in slo-mo, sometimes taking over an hour to walk down the street. For a bit of variety he would occasionally leg it at great speed across the road and would then stop, standing stock still for minutes on end before winking or blowing a kiss or running after a group of shrieking schoolgirls.

In 1990 he was diagnosed with HIV. He dealt with the disease very bravely, but towards the end there were signs that it was taking its toll. He would come into my café with a bag of sweets and lay them all out on the counter. He would then spend ages 'sorting' them. I think the medication was affecting him. In 1994 (I can't recall why it took so long), his friends held a Hallowe'en benefit gig for him at the Olympia Theatre. I sang a duet with Gavin Friday, and Thom was crowned High King of Ireland, and the money raised went to pay for his medicines and his funeral. He was only forty-two when he passed away in his sleep, not long after that gig.

His funeral was one of the saddest, and yet oddest, I've ever attended. I helped to carry his coffin the length of Grafton Street, at almost the same pace he walked it. We stopped for a minute's silence outside the café I ran with Bono and Gavin (I'll tell you all about that later). It's still strange to think that he's gone. There really should be a statue erected to him somewhere near the Green. In 1997, the Lord Mayor of Dublin, Brendan Lynch, renamed a corner of Meeting House Square 'The Diceman's Corner'. Spare a thought for him the next time you pass it.

I've leaped ahead of myself into the 1990s there. Let's get back to the 1980s. It was a bleak time, but there were signs that Ireland was still alive. The music scene was bright and vibrant. You had bands like The Boomtown Rats, The Pogues, Sinéad O'Connor, Aslan, The Saw Doctors, and of course U2, putting Ireland on the musical map. You also had The Blades, Cactus World News, That Petrol Emotion ... and loads of great acts that didn't make the international big time, but added colour and a soundtrack to the lives of those young people who chose to stay here.

The cabaret scene was not so healthy. Venues were closing down all over the place and being replaced with snooker halls. People just didn't have the money to spend on a good night out, with a meal, drinks and a couple of live acts. Work was getting harder to come by.

The nightclub scene was still trundling on though. There was Sloopy's, Barbarella's, Good Time Charlie's (where Fab Vinny Hanley was a DJ), the Revolution Club, Lord John's.... The Revolution Club was a bit of a rough kip, and was well known for fights. It served the usual nightclub food (chicken in/out of a basket) under low lights. The punters could barely see what they were eating, which was probably just as well.

Perhaps the best known club in Dublin was Zhivago's off Baggot Street. It was started in 1970 by Freddie Bailey and Pat Gibbons, and its cinema ads ran with the (now legendary) slogan: 'Love stories begin at Zhivago's'.

It portrayed itself as a sophisticated club where you could pull, game, dance and have a nice meal, all washed down with a bottle of wine that would melt Shane McGowan's liver. It was very well run and policed by another Dublin 'character', Jim 'Lugs' Brannigan. Lugs was a former garda who was famous for keeping Dublin's streets safe. If you messed about and he was in the locality, you could expect a good ticking off and an order to go home. If he caught you a second time, you might get a boot up the arse from him. He was both feared and respected.

You would roll up to Zhivago's, and Lugs would examine you through a peephole to see if you were respectable enough to gain admission. If you passed muster, you paid your 90p at the cash desk and had two floors on which to amuse yourself. There was a good restaurant called Lara's where you could get a steak for about £1 in the mid 1970s, a curry for 60p and a bottle of horrible Spanish 'Sauterne' for £1.35. You'd often see big stars there enjoying a natter and a nosebag. I brought Long John Baldry there, and as usual he was mobbed by fans.

On the second floor, there were pool tables, and from about 1980 on, *Space Invaders* and electronic skittle machines. Thousands of punters would dance the weekend away there. Whatever about love stories beginning there, I'm sure a few pregnancies started there too.

I was having a quiet drink there on 13 November 1984, when someone rushed up to me, I can't remember who it was, and said that the club was closing early. The messenger was pale and looked like he was in shock.

'Why?' I asked, irritated that my evening was being interrupted.

'There's been a plane crash,' he replied. 'Pat is dead.' The words were like a kick in the stomach. Pat was a legend on the nightclub scene, and a really lovely man. He had gone on a trip to France to bring back the first Beaujolais nouveau wine of the year with a group of journalists. Their light plane crashed during a rainstorm, hitting a hill near Eastbourne on the English coast. Eight passengers and the pilot, Jack Walsh, died.

Among the deceased were *Evening Herald* editor Niall Hanley, *Herald* columnist John Feeney, former *Sunday World* editor Kevin Marron, and Tony Heneghan, columnist with the *Irish Independent*. Businessmen Cormac Cassidy, Pat (who also owned the Sands Hotel), Francois Schelbaum (manager of the Sands), and restaurateur Arrigo Chichi were also killed.

The showbiz and media worlds were in shock. I knew Kevin Marron quite well. I'd been the first entertainer to advertise in the *Sunday World* when it was launched in 1973. He always stopped for a chat whenever we bumped into each other. It's still hard to believe that such an awful waste of life could happen during a pointless junket.

Naturally, the atmosphere in Zhivago's was never the same after the tragedy.

Another favourite club of mine was Elisabeth's on Leeson Street. I arrived there one night in the 1970s, straight after a show, and spotted Peter Sellers having a meal with some friends. I was a huge fan, but had never met him. I hemmed and hawed over approaching him to tell him how much I admired him.

'Tell you what,' suggested the manager with a wicked glint in her eye, 'why don't you serve him this bottle of wine?' Sellers had ordered a second bottle of the club's plonk—something no regular would do, given that it was fermented camel piss. I was still in full drag, so I adjusted my wig, took the bottle and sashayed over to the table.

'Your wine, sir?'

'Oh yes, thank you,' said Sellers, gripping the arm of his spectacles and examining the label. I could see his eyes move from the bottle to my waist and up over my cleavage. I cleared my throat and said, in my deepest, blokiest voice: 'And how was your meal?'

He nearly jumped out of his seat in shock. I had heard that Sellers was absolutely crackers, so the joke could have gone either way. Thankfully, he began to roar with laughter and stood up to shake my hand. We shared a few words about London, and I left him alone.

In terms of nightclubs and the gay set, probably the most innovative venture was Sides DC on Dame Lane. It opened in 1986, and was the first proper gay dance club in the country. That was not the only reason why it was innovative. It was straight on certain nights of the week and gay on others. Those boundaries eventually blurred, and you had gay and straight young people dancing shoulder to shoulder (and hip to hip) on its dancefloor. Sides is credited as being one of the birthplaces of the 'rave' dance scene of the late 1980s and 1990s.

While this new fledgeling club culture was finding its wings, the traditional world of Irish entertainment was getting older and less relevant to younger people. As I said, the cabaret venues were closing, although Jury's Cabaret was still in full swing for the Yanks. I was brought there not long after arriving in Ireland. I enjoyed it for all the wrong reasons: I thought all those waggling legs and diddly-eye music was hilarious. I've always wanted to do a strip to Irish music. I might still do it.

Despite the sad state of the cabaret circuit, the old troopers were still giving their all to their craft. I especially looked up to and admired Maureen Potter and Danny Cummins. They were two of the best entertainers these two islands ever produced.

Maureen, or Mo to her friends, had a seventy-year career in variety, pantomime, TV, films and legit theatre. She began her stage life at the age of seven when she became the junior Irish dancing champion. Three years later she was discovered by the legendary comedian Jimmy O'Dea, who put her in one of his pantomimes. She never looked back. As a child she was billed as the Pocket Mimic, and toured Britain in the 1930s as a Shirley Temple impersonator with Jack Hylton's band. She even trod the hallowed boards of the London Palladium.

She told me that she performed in front of Hitler in Berlin in 1938. The Führer was so impressed that he sent her a medal. Maureen, being a child, was delighted, and proudly showed the medal to her mum when she arrived home to Fairview. Her mum wasn't so impressed, and threw it onto the fire. I wonder how much that would be worth on eBay today…

Her variety shows were huge in the 1970s, particularly *Gaels of Laughter*, which ran for fifteen summer seasons. They featured Mo, with her trademark glasses, clowning about with Danny Cummins, dancing, singing and doing her various characters, such as the Dublin 'ma' who was constantly exasperated with her son.

Gaels featured speciality acts: jugglers, magicians, the Billie Barry kids, and one of my favourite performers, Monica Bonny. She was a xylophone player who entertained the troops in the Congo in 1961. Her dad, Joe, taught U2's Larry Mullen to play the drums. If you're a fan of *Britain's Got Talent*, you would have loved *Gaels of Laughter*.

Comedian Hal Roach was a top draw. He was one of the funniest gag men anywhere, and had a sixty-year career in the business. (He influenced many of our top comics, including my great friend Brendan 'Bottler' Grace.) Hal aimed his act at the Irish-American market, and holds the record for the longest-running comic show for his twenty-six-year stint at Jury's Cabaret. There was a lot of blarney in his act, but he was hilarious.

His catchphrase was 'Write it down'. A typical gag would be: 'He told me I had a cult following. At least that's what I thought he said.'

Here's another. 'The teacher said, "Seán, what is a cannibal?" He said, "I don't know." The teacher said, "Well, if you were to eat your mother and father, what would you be?" He said, "An orphan."'

One night there was a fire in the Baggot, and I had the evening off, so I went to see a *Gaels* show. Hal spotted me and said, 'There's been a fire in the Baggot. Gardaí are blaming Mr Pussy's hot pants.'

I shouted back, 'Yes, but I put it out with my panti-hose.' He corpsed.

I was reminded not so long ago by the singer Joe Cuddy about a day I spent with Hal in the Phoenix Park doing a showbiz donkey derby for charity. I did it in drag, along with Joe, Maureen Potter and others. There was a lot of drinking going on, and my mate David Carter, who was well sloshed, decided to liven things up a bit. We were up in the VIP commentary box with Eamonn Andrews, who was a huge star. David grabbed the microphone and started doing his own commentary: 'And here comes Danny Cummins riding Maureen Potter....'

The place went into uproar, and we fell about in stitches. He was asked very politely to leave. I remember seeing Eamonn pissing himself. He looked at me and said, 'What the hell has this country come to?'

David's reply was: 'It's your own fault. You shouldn't have left the fucking mic on!' I don't know if Maureen found it funny. I didn't hang around that long.

When variety was in decline, Maureen reinvented herself as a critically acclaimed straight actress, appearing in Seán O'Casey's *Juno and the Paycock*, and later *The Shadow of a Gunman*. She also wrote children's books. There was no end to her talent.

Maureen was a titch. She was just under five feet tall, but made up for her tininess with a huge personality and voice. Ireland loved her and her 'Real Dub' persona, with its disdain for authority and funny, snappy putdowns. Despite offers of work from abroad, Mo chose to spend most of her career here. She was desperately lonely when touring as a child, and appreciated her native city.

I first went to see Mo at a Gaiety show in the early 1980s. After the gig I retired to the green room, where she was having a jar with her stage partner, Danny Cummins. They were a fantastic duo, on and off stage. Mo was drinking scotch and milk.

'Hello, Alan,' she said. 'This is your first time in the green room, so let me buy you a drink.' It was the kind of sweet, supportive gesture which was typical of the old pros at the time. On another occasion she spotted me in the audience during her panto and name-checked me.

'There's Mr Pussy. Isn't he gorgeous?' The audience gave me a round of applause. I was delighted and honoured, but knew that Mo treated everyone she met with respect and generosity. I remember reading somewhere that even the grumpy poet Patrick Kavanagh walked up to her on the street and said, 'Do you know what? You're not a bad little woman at all.'

She was tough, though, and could be a strict disciplinarian. If you didn't get it right on stage, she'd let you know. She'd have a go at you, but then it would be forgotten.

That first visit to the Gaiety green room was magical for me. Maureen is recorded as saying that the Gaiety was/is 'the most aptly named place I know'. It's as if its walls are stained with laughter (among other things). It may surprise many readers to know that it started out as a grocer's shop and a bakery. It has played host to innumerable international stars, including Sarah Bernhardt and Anna Pavlova— who must have felt at home there given that it was once a bakery.

When I entered the green room it was as if the clock had stopped sometime in the 1950s. There was a piano in the corner and ancient theatre bills on the walls. I needed a pee, and was escorted to the loo by legendary stage manager George McFall. He worked in the Gaiety for forty-eight years, and was married to the equally legendary Mai McFall.

George once referred to the Gaiety as the only place that could take you into the future or the past and keep you in the present. That one statement sums up the theatre for me. Whatever about taking me into the past/future/present, George led me down the stairs to the gents. The basement was enormous: vast and deep. George told me we were at the same level as the Liffey, so there was water just beneath our feet. He showed me the wind machines and the trapdoor, and led me to an area to the right of the loos. The smell of pee and damp fur was outrageous. This was where they kept the animals for the panto: camels, horses, llamas....

They were in cages, but there was one Gaiety animal which was free to roam wherever it wanted. The theatre had its own cat, named Bobby. Bobby got star treatment and, no matter how big the act, he always came first. He would walk out on stage during performances and the actors, generally, never flinched. I say 'generally' because I can recall him strolling along the boards past Spike Milligan once. That gorgeous madman stared at him, aghast, and said: 'It's Mister Pussy!'

I love animals. I've owned two dogs since moving into my current Drumcondra mansion: Lily and Danny. I also had a very special cat, named Bobby after the Gaiety feline. They say that cats have nine lives. Well, Bobby gave me one of his.

I was out and came home a little worse for wear, and accidentally threw my clothes on an electric fire that I thought was off. Sometime during the night, I felt something warm and furry scratching my neck and waking me up. It was Bobby. He had an expression on his face that said: *wake the fuck up, Joan of Arc—the bedroom is on fire.*

I shot up, and grabbed as many bowls of water as I could. If I hadn't been pissed I probably would have legged it out of the house, the fire brigade would have been called, and the place would have burned down.

Once the fire was out, I went back to bed.

The next morning I woke up, realised what had happened, went to the bathroom, and when I looked in the mirror I saw Al Jolson staring back at me doing three choruses of 'Swanee'. I was covered in soot. Bobby was curled up at the end of the bed, purring his head off.

The amazing thing was that the bedroom door had been open all night, and Bobby could have just buggered off out the back window, which I kept open for him, but instead he chose to wake me and save my life. And they say dogs are loyal…

I loved the Olympia as much as the Gaiety, and one of the things I enjoyed most was the arrival of old-time music-hall acts from the UK. The bar would be full of variety pros, air-kissing and chatting about the old days. The noise could be unbearable at times as these 'oldies' had learned how to project their voices in the days before microphones were introduced on stage. I had learned to project too. Brenda Doyle taught me the technique in the Eblana. 'Do it from the diaphragm, through the top of the head,' she would say.

I liked listening to the old stagers and learning about the trade as they quaffed gin in their pancake make-up. One trick I learned was to draw a red dot on the corner of your eyelid. This makes your peepers look brighter on stage.

Their tales of mischief and naughtiness used to make me cry laughing—although some of the yarns involved nastiness on an almost psychotic level. Billy Carroll was a drag queen who had performed in a show called *Splinters*, which entertained the troops during World War One. He told me that the bitchiness among the queens was terrifying. If they didn't like a fellow performer, they would leave booby traps for her in the dressing room. One 'wheeze' was to put ground glass in the face powder. Another was to stick a razor blade in a lipstick. One leading lady was so hated that her co-stars nailed the tail of her dress to the stage.

Little did I know, as I was listening to Billy and his peers, that one day I would be the old pro telling anecdotes and dispensing wisdom to young stars and starlets. History repeats itself, etc.

I miss the atmosphere of those old, fun days. I miss the little tubs of ice cream with wooden spoons, the usherettes smiling and cursing under their breath about the kids ('The fucking little brats…'). I even miss people smoking. If you sat in the middle of the stalls you'd barely see the show for the cig smoke. It all felt more 'real', somehow. Simpler.

I did the *Summer Revels* show in the Olympia, and enjoyed every minute of it. Like its King Street rival, the Olympia has a long history. It's been running shows on Dame Street since 1879, and was credited with screening the first movie in Ireland, on 20 April 1896. It was by the Lumière brothers, and had a deep effect on young James Joyce, who subsequently opened Ireland's first cinema, the Volta Electric Theatre, with his sister.

Noël Coward, Charlie Chaplin, Marcel Marceau, Laurel and Hardy, and many other huge stars played there in the mid twentieth century. In 1974, however, disaster struck. Parts of the roof and stage collapsed during rehearsals for *West Side Story*, and the theatre's future was in doubt as a venue. The show must go on though, and the Olympia's staff fixed the place up and saved it from immediate demolition. The public got involved too, and lined up outside the box office to donate money to save the theatre. Then Dublin City Council placed a preservation order on the building and gave money towards the cost of refurbishment, which ran to £250,000.

My old pal Maureen Grant has worked there since 1949. I recently celebrated her ninety-first birthday with her. She is a fantastic woman, and still runs Maureen's Bar there. I was the first to give her a photograph of myself to hang in the bar. Now there are dozens on the wall.

The spirits behind the bar aren't the only ones Maureen has encountered. The theatre is haunted by the ghost of a child the staff have christened 'Charlie Parker'. Maureen first encountered Charlie when she was just starting out on Dame Street. She was freshening up before her shift when the door opened. She was in her underwear and asked, 'Who's that?' There was no reply, so she closed it thinking that it was just the breeze. Then, suddenly, the door went *bang* and her coat came off its hook and her tips went flying in all directions. She rushed out into the café, but there was nobody nearby who could have slammed the door.

On other occasions, unwired lights would turn on and off, and a baby could be heard crying. Eventually they brought in a medium, who discovered a boy's spirit lurking in the toilet. The spirit then moved to the bar, and nowadays frequently messes with the tills and smashes glasses. There's also a ghastly pall-bearer who walks up and down the aisles. You may not believe any of this of course, but I've felt presences there. It's an odd feeling, like someone is standing beside you. WoooooooooOOOOOOOOOOO!

Speaking of spirits, there was one actor who was very fond of his gargle and 'gave up the ghost' during a famous non-performance at the Gaiety. His name was Alan Devlin, and he became mildly famous for his appearance in the 'Sally O'Brien' Harp ads. (Look them up.) He was a great actor, admired by Anthony Hopkins, but a chronic alco who drank everything he earned and fell out with people all over the place.

In 1987 he was appearing in *HMS Pinafore* at the theatre, when drink, and nerves, got the better of him. Dressed in full admiral's regalia, Alan turned to the audience and said, 'Fuck this for a game of soldiers,' and walked off the stage … and into Neary's pub next door.

He was still wearing his mic and the audience could hear him cursing and battling with the stage door, grumbling across the alley to the pub and then sitting down for a chat with the barman. Legend has it that the audience also heard him taking a piss in the loo, complete with sighs and an 'Ahhh, that's better.'

Unsurprisingly, he was fired. Then, when the play transferred to the West End, Cameron Macintosh (of *Miss Saigon* fame), ordered his agents to get Alan back on board, as he was worth his weight in gold when it came to publicity. Sadly, his West End break didn't save him. He continued to drink and to squander his money.

Poor Alan died in Dalkey in 2011. He really had wasted his talent as an actor, but added to the anarchic atmosphere of the city. He'll always be associated with the Gaiety—for all the wrong reasons. Or the right reasons, depending on your point of view. Dublin loves a rebel. And Alan was a rebel.

Around the same time that Alan was throwing away his stage career, I was starting to wonder if I was wasting my talent too. Dublin was lovely, the people were lovely, but some of the sparkle was wearing off. I had been here for seventeen years. I was feeling disillusioned and restless. I missed the bright lights of London.

I wanted to go home.

Chapter Twelve

Sour Puss Camps it Up

'Let's do a panto. It might cheer you up.'

'Oh, no it won't!'

'Oh, yes it will!'

It was 1985, and Eileen Reid was concerned that my bouts of doubt and grey moods were becoming more regular. Eileen, who is one of our most enduring performers, is an old, old mate. I've lost track of the times we've been on stage together. We even had a residency at Butlin's Holiday Camp in Mosney. That was during the early 1980s, and was a very strange time for me, contributing to my growing disillusionment.

I was booked to do two seasons. I knew Butlin's from my childhood. It opened in 1949, and my mum decided we should take our summer holiday abroad, so my dad booked us on the boat to Dublin. I don't know what age I was (and if I did, I wouldn't say), and my memories are scattershot. We did the full two weeks there. I remember that the steward brought us tea to the cabin in the morning. Dad and I went up Nelson's Pillar, and I can still see Mum standing outside the GPO and waving. I won first prize at the kids' fancy dress competition. Mum dressed me as a railway porter with a strike sign.

One thing I remember clearly was that signs used to go up on the side of the stage during the shows: 'Baby crying in chalet number ten'. Nowadays, the idea of leaving your baby in a chalet while you go on the piss would be enough to get social services in a lather. It was a different, less paranoid world, then.

Mum and Dad were great dancers, and used to fly around like Fred and Ginger. The ballroom had one of the best parquet floors in the world. The whole camp was world-class. It was vast when I was a kid, and had expanded further by the time I arrived there in the early 1980s with Eileen Reid. There was a funfair, amusements, 'the Gaiety Theatre', a cabaret lounge, and a swimming pool with a window below the waterline that faced out onto the bar. You could have a pint and look at people flailing their legs about in the water. Maybe they were drowning. Who knows? Who cares? Sometimes, as the pool was full of kids, a yellow 'cloud' would blossom and spread across the window. I often wondered if there was more piss in that pool than water. I certainly never tried swimming in it.

We were booked to do the camp's Gaiety venue. Our little group included Eileen Reid, Mai McFall and Val Fitzpatrick. The dressing rooms were like cupboards, but we didn't mind. Mai, who I mentioned earlier was married to George McFall of the real Gaiety, would bring our personal 'star bar' in a bag. There would be vodka, gin, sandwiches, cheeses, ham, pickles … the best picnic you could imagine. After shows we would sometimes go to the staff bar and drink with the Redcoats. It was all great fun.

Eileen and I did 'The Grass is Always Greener', which is a lovely little two-hander featuring me as a posh laydee and Eileen as my common housewife neighbour. We did six shows every three nights, playing to thousands of people. It was a great success.

The show's popularity didn't prevent me from getting the sack. When Butlin's changed ownership and just became 'Mosney', I was asked to do a rehearsal … which was really an audition. I wasn't very happy about that, and that night I went on and cracked a couple of blue gags.

'My husband came home and said he had bought me a present. I asked what it was. He said, "It's a gravestone with the words: Here lies my wife, cold as usual." I came home the following day and told him I'd bought him one in return. "What's it say?" he asked. "Here lies my husband, stiff at last."'

The audience roared with laughter, but the management was not amused. I got a note saying that they had decided to replace me.

I was delighted. I used to be driven home every night, and the travelling was driving me mad. I was also sick of the screaming kids. One evening I was carrying my wig on a block from the car to my dressing room when one little charmer shouted, 'Look at the fucking head on that!' I thought to myself: *if the kids are cursing and I'm getting told off for being blue, then it's time to go.* As luck would have it the show transferred to the Olympia, so I could give Mosney the two fingers. I nearly got the sack there too. After the first night, the Olympia's head honcho, Brendan Smith, called us all on stage and started to deliver a lecture, telling everyone how to do their job. I walked off.

'Where do you think you're going?' he asked.

'I'm going to get changed,' I snapped. 'When you know how to put a frock and make-up on, then you can tell me how to perform.' I could see my fellow stars smirking behind his back. He was a miserable old sod. Afterwards, I was worried that he might give me the boot. I didn't hear any more about it.

Eileen reminded me of that narrow escape when she asked me to do the pantomime in 1985. (Remember the pantomime I started this chapter with? You don't? Please start paying attention.) We had already done one together in 1974, although it wasn't your typical panto. *Cinderfella* at Gulliver's Inn on New Street was Ireland's first ever adult panto. I wrote and directed it, and it was very saucy. The public loved it. I got a standing ovation when I downed a pint of lager in five seconds as part of the routine. I was half-cut for the rest of the show. It was that kind of a gig.

My mum, who used to come to Dublin with Auntie Rose on a regular basis, was there for *Cinderfella*'s first night. Customers and staff kept coming up to her and saying, 'I see where he gets his looks from.' She was chuffed. I had to do a strip as part of my act, and was mortified that she was in the audience. We went for an Italian meal afterwards, and she leaned across the table and whispered, 'I'm proud of you, son.' It was the first time she had ever told me that. I was really moved.

'And what did you think of the strip, Mum?'

She looked at me and started to grin.

'Too much lipstick, Alan. You need to tone that down or you'll look like a tart.'

Eileen Reid and I followed *Cinderfella*'s success with another Amsby-penned revue called *Hello Duckies* at the same venue. I wore less lipstick. Nobody noticed. Anyway, this time Eileen wanted to do a 'proper' panto.

'We'll do *Jack and the Beanstalk*,' she announced. I jumped at it as it was something different and a chance to tour the country again. The show starred Eileen, Sonny Knowles, Helen Jordan and me. It was a tonic for me, and was hilarious on stage and off. I can't remember who played the giant, but his casting was one of the strangest stage decisions ever made. He was tiny, and had to wear specially constructed platform boots.

One night one of the boot heels snapped, and our giant had to spend the entire performance looking up at the cast. We spent the show trying not to laugh and improvised our way through it. Eileen and I still giggle about it whenever we meet up to chat about the 'old days'. The former Cadets singer has had an extraordinary life in the biz since she first started out in showbands. She was one of the most popular warblers in Ireland in her twenties, then she became 'legit' on Dublin's theatre circuit in the 1970s and 1980s, and joined the Carmelite religious order in the 1990s. She wrote a wonderful memoir with her husband, Jimmy Day, called *Eileen*. Read it after this. It's a brilliant story. End of free book advert for Eileen.

The panto tour with Eileen took my mind off my homesickness for a few months. The respite didn't last, though. I was still missing London.

Life is funny. Maybe it was God, or the universe, or just plain good luck, but an opportunity to revisit my old home city presented itself out of the blue. I was asked to judge a drag ball across the pond. I'll have some of that, I thought. My mind was made up: I was going to use this as my 'bridgehead' back into the UK. I settled up my affairs in Dublin, packed up my frocks and slap, and headed for the boat—I still hated flying.

The drag ball was an eye-opener. Jean Fredericks's lavish balls used to be held in the Porchester Hall and were world-famous. This wasn't anything like one of Jean's bashes. It was staged in a town hall, and whereas Jean's had been elegant, glamorous and 'old school', this event was fetishistic, leather-clad and, to be blunt, tacky. There were trannies and bondage types and a few dirty old men leering at the contestants. There was no glamour, mystique or straightforward fun.

I was seated beside Cynthia Payne—possibly the most famous 'madam' England has ever produced. Madam 'Cyn' made headlines in the 1970s and 1980s when she was acquitted of running a brothel at her house in south London. Police first raided her knocking shop in 1978, and interrupted a sex party where punters paid with luncheon vouchers (remember those?) to dress up in knickers and be spanked. The coppers found fifty-three chaps in varying levels of undress, including a peer, an MP, a few solicitors and company directors, and several vicars. One of the papers ran a cartoon featuring a vicar in bed with a prossie, demanding to see his solicitor … who was in the next room.

Cynthia was obsessed with willies. I suppose it was her specialist subject. Throughout the drag show she kept referring to 'cock'.

'Oh, I bet he has a lovely big cock under that dress.' It was funny the first few times, but after a while it started to grate on me.

I visited my old haunts, and dropped into the Vauxhall to see if the place had changed. The new owners, Pat and Breda, knew me from Ireland. They worked with Paul O'Grady's partner, Brendan Murphy, and he booked me to do a gig. He also did the sound, and looked after me really well.

The place had changed a lot. There was a new stage area—I didn't have to perform standing on the bar—and a dressing room. The gig went well, and Breda really enjoyed it. I picked on her from the stage:

'How many kids have you got, love?'

'I've six, Mr Pussy.'

'It's no wonder they called you "Breda".'

Despite the warm reception and the ovation, something didn't feel quite right. Something was missing. I couldn't put my finger on what it was. Afterwards, two old friends, George and Stan, took me out to the Garden Club in Kensington. Elton John was there. The place was packed with celebrities, many of whom I didn't know personally as I'd been so long out of London. Again, something just didn't feel right. Eventually, the penny dropped. The element that was missing was the Irish people. Londoners weren't my audience anymore. I missed the Paddies (and I say that with affection). I knew their rhythm and their humour, their kindness and their warmth. I had an English accent, but I was Irish now. Later, in the 1990s, I would come back to do gigs in Kilburn and be booked as 'Ireland's Mr Pussy'. I was an Irish act.

I spent three weeks in the city of my birth, meeting old friends and feeling out of place with all the changes Margaret Thatcher had ushered in. I was booked to do a gig in Belfast, but it was cancelled. Eventually I decided: sod this, I'm going home.

I returned to Dublin and booked into the Waldorf Hotel in the city centre. I threw my bag onto the bed and looked down from my window over the rain-slicked streets below. People were scurrying along, heads bowed to the rain, under a mercury sky. I heard the buses belching as they settled down at their stops on the quays. I smelled the eggy Liffey, and saw one of Dublin's resident mad women, Holy Mary, reading the bible aloud at the O'Connell monument. She used to carry a crucifix around, and I sometimes had afternoon tea with her. She was the poshest Dublin character you could meet.

I traced the drops of rain meandering down the window pane until my eyes grew cloudy. I realised, then, that I was crying. With tears of happiness and relief. I was home, and I was never leaving here again.

'How do you fancy a trip to America?'

My decision never to leave Ireland again didn't last long. After I arrived home from London, I was presented with two choices: mope around and complain about the economy, or get up off my pretty arse and find work. I remember counting the change in my pocket one evening and weighing up the options: go and get fish and chips or put on my best suit and head out on the town.

I always believe in putting your best face on. It's the showbiz way, so I chose to re-engage with Dublin. I found myself enjoying the city's nightlife more than I had in years: hanging out in Suesey Street and meeting my good mate Jean, who ran the club and is now the queen of Lillie's Bordello, which is my home from home.

One night in the Tudor Rooms, where I was doing the odd gig, I started chatting to George Hilliard. George had a great contacts list and used to book acts. He started to get me shows around the country and in the UK. I'm eternally grateful to him for helping me get back on my feet.

George got me a gig in Queens (appropriately enough) in New York. I was looking really good at the time. I had lost four stone in weight (the Yanks are so weight-conscious) and was a slip of a thing. I got around my fear of flying by manning up—and dropping a Valium. I hated the flight, but knew I couldn't let my phobia cost me the chance to play in America. I arrived in JFK, full of excitement, and was met by a driver in a Jaguar. I was arriving in style. We were brought to our hotel and I flopped on the bed, listening to the sounds of the Big Apple below me. The traffic, the horns, the occasional gunshot … it was like white noise, and I quickly got used to it. That city has the most extraordinary energy: it perks you up and beats the crap out of your jetlag. It refuses to let you sleep or feel tired.

My show was very well received. Queens was full of young Irish people, so it felt a little like playing in Kilburn or Archway in London. They 'got' the act. While the younger Americans enjoyed the show, they couldn't get their head around why a man would want to dress as a woman.

'For the handbag, dear,' I explained. Of course, they didn't have a clue what I meant. 'Handbag' is a slang word my mate Rory Cowan and I invented for 'money'. Politicians have brown envelopes, drag queens have handbags. The Yanks didn't have a clue what I was talking about, and probably thought I was getting a sponsorship deal from Mulberry or Burberry. God bless them.

George didn't drink and wasn't gay, so I headed off after the show with a friend from Dublin, Eugene, to explore Greenwich Village. The bars were nothing like I'd ever experienced before. Gay pubs are pretty much all the same nowadays, but back then each one had its own personality. There was the Monster, which featured a fabulous pianist who had a top hat full of money on his piano. Whenever anyone put a dollar in it, he would produce a toilet plunger and stuff the cash down. It was all screamingly camp. Then there was the Whip and Saddle, which was one of the sleaziest kips I've ever been in. It was full of leather boys with caps and nothing on underneath. There was even a chap being led around on a leash.

'Get me out of here, dear,' I said to Eugene. 'I can't be doing with any of this.'

The place had dark rooms where strangers could get up to all kinds of nonsense, and two-way mirrors in the loos. The only head you were likely to receive in the respectable old Bartley Dunne's was the beige one on top of your pint.

We went on to Mineshaft, which was more of the same. Actually, it was a lot worse. Monster's seemed tame compared to it. We pegged it back there as quickly as we could. And that was only my first night out in New York.

I was booked for more gigs in the Bronx and then Boston, so I had to pace myself. The bar I was playing at in the Bronx was underneath an overground railway line. It was just like in the movies. You could hear the glasses rattling behind the bar when a train passed over us. There were a few yuppies there, but it was mainly old-timers: proper Bronx people. It was a good crowd, and the act went over well.

I travelled on to Boston. All I can remember is that Boston closed at 11.30. It bored the arse off me. The show was really enjoyable, though. I had to get ready in the bar cellar and climb up a ladder onto the stage. There were lots of Irish kids on visas there. Obviously I didn't know it at the time—and neither did they—but this was the generation that would come home and power Ireland into the Celtic Tiger. They were powering into the sauce when I assaulted them with my saucy humour. Although boring, Boston is a beautiful city. I did a tour and loved the architecture, which was the same as Georgian Dublin. In a sentence: Boston is Dublin with a poker up its hole.

The first time I ever saw a stretch limousine was in Boston. They're hideous. I wouldn't want to be seen in one. I was getting a great profile in the local papers, and someone offered me a ride to one of my gigs in a horrible white stretch limo. I turned it down. The following year I was asked back to New York for two weeks of gigs. One of my closest friends, Tony McCann, came with me. We were picked up at JFK by a guy driving a hatchback. It was a bit of a comedown. I remember making a mental note: next time, keep your mouth shut about hating limos.

I stayed with Eugene in Queens, and paid a visit to Washington, where a hairdresser mate, Paul Hayden, put me up. We did the sights, including 'Bouffant Square', where the campest of queens sped about on rollerblades whilst wearing the tiniest tiny shorts.

When we weren't having mad parties at Paul's place, we would go out on the batter. I remember one evening we went to a bar, and the waiter who served us was wearing a T-shirt and no pants. I looked down at his manhood and said, 'It's all right, love, my drink doesn't need stirring.' He didn't get it. The dozy cow.

I left Tony in Washington as I had to go back to NY to do some shows. I don't know how I managed to get the train there as I get lost on O'Connell Street. I did, though, and was very proud of myself. I felt very safe all the time I was there. The only occasion I was nervous was when we were coming out of a club and a guy came over and put his arm around me. Eugene knew he was trying to pick my pocket and told him to fuck off. Thankfully, he did.

I've been back to America a few times since then, and met some great people. In 2002 I went on holiday to Chicago, which included a gig in Rochester. The trip started off well as I was recognised at the check-in desk and upgraded to first class. Thank you, Aer Lingus. The show had been organised by a wonderful friend of mine, David Byrne.

David was a former showband booker who had followed his vocation into the priesthood. He is a very funny man and has a great soul: he's totally open-minded and Christian in the real sense of the word. I suppose he'd have to be open-minded as he's the chaplain in the Mayo Clinic. He did my mum's funeral for me. That's how close we are.

The gig was at Love Uglies, which was a lot like those biker joints you see in the films, with women dancing on the bar, etc. The show was 'in the round', and David had brought a group of wealthy Rochester matrons along. They adored it. The following day, he said, 'I have a surprise for you.' We flew to New York, and were met by one of the oddest and most loveable geezers on the planet. He was a monk, and his name was Brother Patrick.

I couldn't believe my eyes when Brother Pat hovered into view. He was chain-smoking and wearing a brown monk's habit and a Muslim hat, and carrying a big stick—I still don't know what the stick was for. He cursed like fuck, and looked like the grim reaper's mischievous cousin. I didn't know what to make of him.

'This is my driver,' he said, nodding to a man who had more earrings than Corrie's Beth Lynch. 'You keep your mouth shut and I'll give you $100.' The driver nodded back at him. I couldn't resist a one-liner.

'Give me $200 and I'll keep mine open.'

Brother Patrick threw his head back and laughed, and the car sped off on a mystery tour around New York. I had no idea where we were going. I don't know if the driver did either. Eventually, we pulled up outside the Waldorf Astoria. David had got us a deal as it was the year after the Twin Towers attack and nobody was going to New York. My room was dreadful. It was roasting hot in the city, and I had to sleep beside a radiator I couldn't turn off. I complained, and we were given a suite. Which was nice.

Brother Pat had arranged for us to go to a piano recital. Afterwards, we went back to his apartment above the shelter he ran, looking after Aids patients and the homeless. He was suffering from cancer, and should have been dead years earlier. David had met him while working at a rehab clinic. It was probably the booze that had kept him alive so long.

It was sweltering, and Brother Pat had the windows closed to get the benefit of the air conditioning. I suspect it was turned on especially for us. It was rubbish. A penguin's burp would have kept us cooler. I felt ill, and couldn't take my jacket off as I'd managed to tear my shirt.

'Dinner's on the way,' Pat announced.

'I hope it's ice cream,' I panted.

It wasn't. The door opened, and two young men arrived in with platters of … prawns. I don't know about you, but the last thing you should be eating in 80 per cent humidity is prawns. I nearly threw up. Nearly. I didn't want to insult my host, or the two blokes who were serving it. They were all over each other, cooing and pawing and generally letting it be known they were madly in love.

'We're madly in love,' one of them said.

The operative word there was 'mad'. Six months later, one of them killed the other. Probably served him prawns once too often for his tea.

After that disgusting supper, Pat brought us around the shelter and showed us the work he was doing: stuff like needle exchange, counselling Aids victims and feeding and washing the homeless. He was an extraordinary man. David's 'surprise' hadn't been about seeing New York again; it was about introducing me to a man who was a walking saint. He was rough-edged, but there's no doubt he's bossing Jesus about in heaven as I write this. And making Our Lord fall about the place laughing.

Pat brought us back to our hotel in a people-carrier. He was still dressed in his monk's gear and played rap music, at full volume, all the way there. Every few yards he would jerk the brakes in time to the beat, like the gangstas do in LA. People were shouting 'Asshole!' at him from the sidewalk, and he replied by giving them the finger and roaring, 'Up yours, cunt!' Everyone was a cunt to Brother Pat. He dropped us off with a wave and a 'So long, cunts!' and nearly caused a five-car pile-up.

Before we left, we paid a visit to Ground Zero. It was really eerie. New York is the capital of the West. It's a city that thrives on people's energy and their drive to forge their own place in the world. It's dreamland, and those sick, fundamentalist bastards turned it into a nightmare. But only briefly. It has risen again, and I love it.

Anyway, I've leaped into the future again. That visit to meet Brother Pat was in 2002, fifteen years after my first trip. We're back to 1987 now. I returned home to rain and greyness, but it didn't matter. I was re-energised, and loved being back in my dear old Dublin. Less than a year later, Ireland would be energised in a way that it could never have foreseen.

An Englishman named Jack Charlton would lead a band of half-Englishmen in Irish jerseys to victory over England at the European Championships. Euro '88 was the turning point in modern Irish history. Economist David McWilliams goes on about the Pope's Children being responsible for sowing the seeds of Ireland's economic success. Bollocks. It was Jack Charlton's children. For the first time, people on the streets were chanting, 'You'll never beat the Irish.' Our soccer fans were charming everyone, everywhere. 'Everybody loves the Irish' was the catchphrase of the day. It was true. My adopted country was throwing off its national inferiority complex. The Celtic Tiger was but a sperm, but it was coming.

The Greyties were over, the 1990s were here, and the Celtic Pussy was about to have a revival of his own.

Chapter Thirteen

A Snog with Danny La Rue

'This is, for me, a happy day, for my fellow legislators have chosen, as the lawmakers of a free and independent republic, to liberate the gay community from an oppressive, corrupt and deeply damaging law, whose origins are shrouded in the mists of ancient religious prejudice. Young people will no longer have to grow up in the shadow of the taint of criminality, which has blighted the vulnerable youth of so many of our citizens with terror and shame.'

A round of applause for David Norris, please. That was the senator speaking in 1993 after the government finally decriminalised homosexuality. It was a momentous day for civil rights in Ireland. The campaigners, rightly, rejoiced, and David, who spearheaded the campaign, would have been canonised if the Catholic Church went in for making gay saints.

The people who celebrated the most were the TDs who passed the bill. It was sickening. That stupid law had been in force since 1861, and they had done nothing to amend it until David started to wage his crusade. For the rest of us, life went on as normal. We partied, worked, had sex, ate, slept, drank ... nothing really changed. It was a great symbolic gesture, but what was really more important was getting society to change its attitude towards alternative lifestyles.

Ordinary people needed to get used to the idea of homosexuality being as natural as heterosexuality. That is still an ongoing battle, but huge strides have been made. People are fundamentally good and kind.

Anyway, enough pontificating. The early 1990s were also an important year for me on a personal level. It was the year that I cemented my friendship with my all-time idol, Danny La Rue. Danny created 'modern drag', and his artistry and resilience always inspired me. He was one of the most beloved friends I've ever had. I'm not exaggerating when I say that an evening I spent with him in 1991 was a landmark for me.

Before I get to that, let's have a few biographical paragraphs about Danny. His real name was Daniel Patrick Carroll, and he was born in Cork in 1927, to a cabinet-maker dad and a seamstress mum. Dan never knew his father, who went to New York in the late 1920s, intending to bring the family over once he'd found work. Sadly, he died before he could achieve this. Danny was just eighteen months old at the time.

His mother, who he adored, moved the family to Soho in London and managed to raise five kids on a widow's pension and her wages as a seamstress. She was determined to see Danny do well at school. He remembered her crying one day because she didn't have the money for his uniform. She was an amazing woman. During the Blitz they moved to Devon (oo-arr), and Danny got a post-school job in a bakery. He always liked his buns did Danny. After that he got a job window dressing before entering the drag world.

He used to say that he got the bug after watching Jimmy O'Dea perform as a panto dame, but the seed must have been sown, or sewn, at his mother's knee. He was used to seeing piles of dresses and costumes lying around.

Danny made his first stage appearance while in the navy, playing a native girl in a send-up of the play *White Cargo*. The marvellous Sir

John Gielgud saw it and told him to take his ability to make people laugh more seriously. Danny listened to the advice and auditioned for a show called *Forces Showboat*, which featured a young Harry Secombe. The Goon advised him against taking up a career in drag. How wrong could he have been?

He toured for a few months with the show, and met his future manager and life partner, Jack Hanson. Then he left to do a West End drag revue. He arrived at rehearsals to discover that the promoter had billed him as Danny La Rue. Danny never looked back (unless he was being chased by someone, of course). He became the Queen of Drag, although he preferred to be described as a 'comic in a frock'. He was brilliant, and used to do Elizabeth Taylor, Zsa Zsa Gabor, Marlene Dietrich, and my old mate Judy Garland.

He was unique as a female impersonator. The rule of thumb was that, to be funny, every drag act needed to have a hint of Y-fronts beneath her sequinned frock. The public should know that it was a man playing a woman. Danny went an entirely different route. He was beautiful on stage, totally feminine and believable as a woman. Bob Hope even said that he was the most glamorous woman in the world. During his act you never thought of him as a man in drag, even though he was over six feet tall and used his masculine name. The only time you knew he was a bloke was when he came on at the end of his show in civvies and cried, in a gruff voice, 'Wotcher, mates!'

'Vulgar, yes, but there is nothing crude about me,' he used to say. He was a huge star—the biggest in the West End—and in the 1970s he was earning the equivalent of £2 million a year. He needed a big income as his frocks cost up to £5,000 each, and he had four homes and a nightclub (in Hanover Square) to run. He also had an entourage of about sixty people.

Like me, Danny was never a gay icon. We were both entertainers, not activists. His audience was, in the main, the blue-rinsed ladies of Middle England. They loved him. Danny told me that he got away with telling risqué jokes because everyone knew it was all just an act: he always saw himself as an actor. So did some other fine thespians. Paul Scofield wanted him to go legit, and Laurence Olivier asked him to play Lady Macbeth. Danny knew his limitations, though.

That said, he did some movies and TV: *Our Miss Fred* and *Mr Bean* spring to mind. He also had a top 40 hit with 'On Mother Kelly's Doorstep', and remains the only man to take over a woman's role in the West End when he replaced Avis Bunnage in *Oh! What a Lovely War.*

I can't overstate his popularity or originality. He was named as the Variety Club's Show Business Personality of the Year in 1969, Theatre Personality of the Year in 1970, and was given the Twenty-Five Years in Show Business Award in 1976. In 1979 he was named Entertainer of the Decade. Our Danny could do no wrong.

Wrong could be done to him, though. In 1976 he invested over £500,000 in Walton Hall, a country house hotel. It was to be his pension, and he ploughed another £500,000 into its restoration, which met with the approval of his good friend Liberace— something about which he, understandably, liked to boast. His stage life kept him away from the hotel, and he decided to sell up in 1983. Unfortunately, two con men offered him a bogus deal that would make him the majority shareholder in the hotel. They said that they were planning to invest £3 million in a venture that would see them flying rich Yanks over to stay there. He discovered six months later that they were being investigated by the police and that he had lost over £1 million.

Lesser men would have crumpled. Danny hitched up his sequinned frock and worked harder than ever to recover his losses. He put together *Danny La Rue's Dazzling Roadshow*, and toured his way out of financial trouble. I've always been inspired by the way he handled himself during that setback. I've always been inspired by him, full stop.

I first saw Danny perform in 1965 at the Whitehall Theatre in *Come Spy with Me*, which also featured Richard 'Moanyhole' Watters and Barbara Windsor. I went with two hairdresser friends, Neville and David, who did Babs's hair. I got to say hello to Dan as he jumped into his car and sped off to do another show. I hadn't started my own drag career at that stage, but seeing Danny La Rue fuelled my ambition to be a female impersonator.

Our paths crossed again at the Toucan Club. He was holding court, dripping in jewels and wearing a mink-lined suede overcoat. I had started doing my double act with Bow, and Ian Davy was our manager. Ian was also my biggest fan. He had a few jars on board, and approached Danny.

'That's Alan Amsby over there,' he said. 'He's going to be bigger than you.'

Danny went mad.

'How impertinent of you,' he growled. I was mortified, and years later finally plucked up the courage to apologise to him when I saw him at the Escort Club. He was very gracious about it. Extremely gracious. He followed me into the loo and we snogged. He was a good kisser, but that's where it ended. We laughed about it afterwards. I think he was marking his territory in an I-could-have-you kind of way. Or maybe he was just welcoming me home to London. I loved Danny, but I wasn't interested in him romantically or physically.

He was one of the kindest men you could ever hope to meet. He hated injustice and always looked out for the underdog. I remember being told how he stood up for Judy Garland at the end of her career. She was a very bad drinker, and collapsed on stage at the Talk of the Town Club. She had arrived late, and the punters were as pissed off as she was pissed. They started booing. Danny was furious and shouted the audience down, telling them to leave her alone. He carried her off the stage. That was our Dan.

Several years went by, and Danny came to the Opera House in Cork. I went to see him with David Gordon, and we had drinks in the green room afterwards. Although we were friendly, Danny was still the star and I was the acolyte. I saw him again at the Olympia in the late 1980s, and we decided to make a night of it. Dan had an Australian boyfriend at the time, who was also his piano player. His name was Wayne King. I'm not making that up. Say it out loud very fast: *Wayne King pianist*. What a monicker. Anyway, they had a terrible row and we all ended up in the Trocadero, at separate tables. Wayne was with the manager of a well-known gay bar. Danny was fuming, and said, 'I'm not leaving here until they leave.' There was a standoff, and we ended up staying into the small hours until Wayne finally buggered off.

Their relationship didn't last. They stayed friendly, though. Tragically, Wayne contracted HIV, and in 2000 Danny flew out to visit him in an Australian hospice. He discovered, to his horror, that Wayne's weight had fallen to just over two stone. 'He had to be buried in a child's coffin,' Danny later said. Typically, he threw himself into working for Aids charities, for which he was awarded an OBE in 2002. I used to joke that OBE stood for Old Bent Entertainer.

Speaking of charity: we're back to the evening in 1991 that I mentioned at the start. I was in Brighton, where Danny was due to do a one-night charity show. I arrived the evening before and headed to the hotel bar for a snifter of brandy. Danny was in the corner, unusually, on his own. He stood up when he saw me and called me over to his table. We had a magical evening, talking about the old days around London and the love of his life, Jack Hanson. Jack died in 1984, leaving Danny 'hysterical with grief'. He never recovered from the loss, and is buried with him. That night, for the first time, I felt I had arrived. We talked and talked and talked. He placed me on level pegging with him, asking about all the stuff I had been doing and really listening to my answers. I was no longer the starlet in his eyes. My hero saw me as his equal. It had only taken twenty-five years....

After that, we were the firmest of friends, and I used to travel over to see him, and we spoke regularly on the phone.

'How's Kitty Cat today?'

'Piss off, you old bitch.'

And he used to come and see me too. One time, in the 2000s, he flew over to open a hotel in Aungier Street. It turned out that old friends of mine, Lady Edith Foxwell and Barry the Butler, were coming over to visit me on the same flight. Lady Edith was the daughter of the Earl of Cavan, and was a famous socialite. I met her at the dancer Wayne Sleep's birthday party, and we became great buddies. She phoned my mum's house looking for me once, and the old dear took the mickey out of her accent, not realising she was a genuine toff.

'Barry the Butler' was Barry Greenwood Smith. He was ex-Merchant Navy, and possibly the number one butler in the world—if there is a top ten for butlers. He knew a lot of other butlers, and would take us to parties in some very salubrious houses. One mansion in which we spent the evening dated from the 1690s. It was all panels and oak beams. Wayne Sleep remarked that they could have done with some lino and wallpaper.

I called Danny, and he joined Edith, Barry, David Gordon and me for champagne and salmon sandwiches at my place in Drumcondra. We had a wonderful little soirée, with Barry telling yarns about the Royal Household staff.

Lady Edith lapped up the royal yarns, and we lapped up the champagne. I went through four bottles, then I had to nip down to the off-licence for more.

The following day, Edith, David, Barry and I went to see her old chum, Lady Dunsany, in Meath. We rang the bell on the old castle door. It took ages to open, and when it did, there was Lady Dunsany herself.

'I hope you don't have any cameras,' she said. 'We've been robbed, you know.' I didn't have a camera, and I still don't know why she asked that. Maybe she thought I was going to case the place for my crack team of cat burglars. She brought us upstairs, past the suits of armour and priceless paintings. I'd brought her a bottle of scotch, which she really appreciated. Lady Mountcharles came over, and we all had afternoon tea. It was a surreal afternoon.

I threw a party in Danny's honour later that week. Dublin society turned out in force: diarist Terry Keane was there, TV presenter Alan Hughes, Dermot Morgan and Peter O'Toole's daughter, among others.

Danny returned the favour with an impromptu evening at his home in Southampton. Barry and he were neighbours, and the three of us went for lunch. Danny looked magnificent in his grey silk paisley toreador jacket and leather trousers. I suggested going to the pub for some drinkies.

'Wearing this? Are you mad?' he said. So I swapped jackets with him. It felt extremely odd to be wearing the Queen of Drag's civvies. Odd, but good. We went back to Danny's place afterwards. It was stunning, with its antique furniture, three-seater Moroccan leather settees and grand piano.

'See that piano?' Danny said. 'Judy Garland, Liberace and Betty Grable all stood around that singing one night.'

'Could you not get the CD player to work?'

'Very funny. That was the best night of my life.'

He then showed me a beautiful set of crockery that Liberace had bought him. I had had quite a few glasses of pink champagne and was terrified of knocking the plates onto the floor. Danny loved his pink champagne—there were bottles of it everywhere bearing the label: 'Danny La Rue'. Or was it 'Danny La Cru'? Never mind. Out on the landing, I spotted a huge bouquet of artificial flowers. They were a memento of the night he did *This is Your Life*. Eamonn Andrews had hidden behind them before springing out with the Red Book.

In the run-up to that, Jack Hanson had told the show that he would only let Danny do it if the programme was an hour-long special. They agreed. Danny could hear him whispering on the phone to the producer and thought he was having an affair. Poor Jack got an earful over that, but had to keep mum until the big night arrived.

Danny's last major appearance was in *Hello Danny*, which was a biographical show staged at the Benidorm Palace in 2007. Not long before that, Paul O'Grady and I went to watch him perform at the Brick Lane Music Hall. We were both saddened to see this once huge star playing in such modest surroundings. We didn't tell him that, of course.

The last time I saw him was in 2008 at RTÉ after a *Late Late Show* appearance. He was with his long-time friend and dressmaker, Annie Galbraith. His health had deteriorated, and he had moved into Annie's house. He suffered a stroke, and developed cancer. Being Danny, he tried to remain in good spirits. Barbara Windsor went to see him in hospital not long before the end.

'You're not looking too bad, Dan,' she lied.

'Would you fancy a bit?' he replied.

Annie looked after him until his death in 2009. She was devastated when he left us. I still phone her, especially at Christmas, to see how she is and to talk about our old friend.

I was inconsolable too, and still find it hard to believe that he has gone. It still chokes me up not to hear his sequinned voice at the other end of the phone.

'How's Kitty Cat?'

He's doing fine, Danny. But he misses you terribly.

Wotcha, old mate.

Chapter Fourteen

Cat Burglar and Savage Do Time

Danny La Rue was the undisputed Queen of Drag. He always will be. Nobody could ever fill his glittering slippers, but there are those who come very, very close. Naturally, I'm one. The other Senior Drag Princess is Paul O'Grady, otherwise known as Lily Savage.

Paul and I have been mates for several hundred years. I first clapped eyes on him at the Vauxhall Tavern in 1986, where he was part of a double act called The Playgirls. I knew immediately that he 'had it'. He was going to be huge. Actually, he was huge. He was doing a striptease wearing a fat suit. He was also side-achingly funny. Pat and Breda McConnon were running the place then, and kept me on for a lock-in with the up-and-coming starlet. We hit it off immediately and shared details of our lives over a few sherberts.

Paul was born in Birkenhead in 1955, and his background is not a million miles removed from our hero, Danny La Rue's. Like Danny, Paul's folks were Irish immigrants. His dad, Paddy, had grown up on a farm in Co. Roscommon and moved to the UK in 1936 looking for work. His name was changed from Grady to O'Grady in a paperwork cock-up when he joined the RAF, but he decided to keep it. He married Mary Savage, who was born in England to a couple from Louth.

Mary was thirty-nine when she conceived Paul. There was a gap of ten years between him and his siblings, so naturally he was spoiled rotten. Just like Danny, Paul was raised a devout Catholic—Danny never lost his faith, by the way. It's odd to think of gay icons like Danny being loyal to a Church that rejected them for so long. David Norris is a devout Anglican too. I always admire that level of commitment to your beliefs, especially as it's not fashionable to say you believe in God. Personally I'm not religious, but I respect the faith of others. I sometimes envy it.

Paul, by the way, was turfed out of the altar boys after laughing during a funeral. He literally corpsed laughing. He may be the only altar boy anywhere ever to get the sack—something he is probably very proud of. Despite his devout upbringing, Paul was never going to be a priest, although he could have been whatever he put his mind to. He was bright from an early age, often showing a ferocious intelligence. Instead, though, he drifted, leaving school at sixteen and getting a job in the civil service. Paul was as good a civil servant as he was an altar boy, so that didn't last either. He also worked part-time as a barman in the Royal Air Forces Association (RAFA) club, and got the bullet from that for being 'incompetent and tardy'. As a youngster, Paul was fired more times than Nelson's cannon.

He worked briefly as an assistant clerk at Liverpool Magistrates' Court, but needed more money (he had a daughter after all), so he moved to London, where he made friends with the 'Harlequeens' and got his first taste of the drag set. But he got homesick: Paul is as Liverpool as scouse stew. He headed back, and ended up working for three years at a school for disabled and abused children. Later, in Camden Town, he would get a job as a care worker, living in with old folk and dysfunctional families.

I'm mentioning the above because it illustrates the kind of man Paul is. He's a multi-faceted performer who is, at heart, a carer. He really loves and respects people. This always comes across in his TV shows. You can see that he's just a nice man. It's written all over him. Or should be.

Eventually, Paul made his way back to London and started to create Lily Savage, part of whom is based on his aunt Chrissy. Lily made her debut in October 1978 at the Black Cap gay pub in Camden, miming to Barbara Streisand's 'Nobody Makes a Pass at Me'. Eventually, he formed a double act, The Playgirls, with a performer called Hush. It was as part of this act that I first encountered him in 1986.

Shortly after that Vauxhall gig, Paul came over here to perform at Shafts nightclub, and we went out on the town. He was building up a following on both sides of the Irish Sea. The audiences here loved him—especially the Dublin ones, as Liverpool and Dub humour is almost identical. Besides, Liverpool is really Ireland's capital in exile.

In 1993 I travelled over to London to see him share the bill with Victoria Wood in a benefit concert at the Palladium. He demolished the house. The audience adored him. Victoria brought him on at the end of the show, and the crowd went mental again. He had to hide behind the piano to give her a chance to perform. The punters only wanted him. That's the unique thing about Paul: he can upstage anyone without appearing to make the slightest effort. It's not just that Lily is a brilliant character who everyone can identify with; it's that he just oozes comic charisma.

We did a lot of ping-ponging over the years. He'd come over and visit me, and I would go over to him. I stayed at his first home in Vauxhall (which was tiny, and so old it was like a time machine), and then at his place in Tower Bridge. The profession was becoming very profitable for our Paul, and O'Grady Towers was gorgeous, all zhooshed up like a yacht, with rope bannisters and portholes, etc.

I went over to one of his birthday parties when he lived there. His old chum Ian McKellen (Gandalf the Gay), Babs Windsor, and anybody who was anybody was invited. I particularly liked chatting to Janet Street Porter. She's a real character.

Paul had a water cooler in the corner, and kept going over to refill his, and his guests', glasses from it.

'Have you got a kidney infection?' I asked.

'Try it,' he replied, offering me a glass. The cooler was full of vodka. Classy. There were a few hairs of the dog needed the following day.

Speaking of dogs, Paul's love for pooches is well known. I love doggies too. I even named one 'Lily' after him (and another, 'Danny', after La Rue). While I was staying with him, he asked me to take his pug, Buster, out for a trot. I wandered the streets with the little cutie, and was surprised at how friendly Londoners had become. People were smiling at me and saying hello. Eventually it dawned on me that it was Buster they were saying hello to. It was the first time a Pussy had ever been upstaged by a dog.

Paul loves animals so much that he bought a farm in Kent. Being Paul, it's not your typical farm. It has cows and goats and chickens and geese (the Geestapo, as he calls them) … and a heated swimming pool. It's built like a Swiss chalet, and has its own woodland too. It's a heavenly place. I spent a lovely Christmas there with him a few years ago, when he presented me with one of the best gifts I've ever received.

'Here,' he said, 'try this on.' He handed me a parcel. It was a beautiful overcoat.

'You know who owned that, don't you?' he asked me as I was pulling it on. It fitted perfectly.

'No.'

'Only Cary bloody Grant.'

I was stunned: it was beyond thoughtful. That's Paul all over though. He chose a gift he knew I would adore. A lot of thought went into that present.

I turn to Paul in times of crisis. He's always on the end of the phone if I ever need to unburden. He's a true friend and a beautiful man. I'll always be grateful to him for coming to my mum's funeral. I saw his face across the room, giving me strength.

I'll always be grateful to him for travelling over to top the bill at a tribute night that was held for me in the Tivoli Theatre in 1998. It had been organised by the Venetties, John and Paul Brady, to mark my thirty-five years in the business. Paul flew over with Jennifer Scott for the occasion. Also on the bill were Brendan O'Carroll, Gavin Friday, Gerry Brown, Helen Jordan, and my old partner in mirth, Sil Fox. One of the show's more surprising moments came via a phone call from Bono, who was in Canada. He sang 'Happy Birthday', Marilyn Monroe-style. It was great fun, but as always the personal highlight was to spend time with Paul.

He has had his own heartaches to deal with. In 2005, Paul lost his partner, Brendan Murphy. One day Brendan was sitting at the table and pointed at a cup. 'What's that?' he asked. Paul knew there was a problem, and they arranged an MRI. Brendan had an inoperable brain tumour. He lost his best friend, who had shared his life for twenty-five years, as a partner in life and manager. Brendan had helped Paul through the early days when he was earning £50 for standing on a beer crate in the corner of a pub telling jokes. They were mad about each other—a double act, forever play-fighting, getting each other in headlocks, and generally acting the arse.

Brendan was a wonderful, handsome man, intelligent and eloquent. He was forty-nine. It should never have happened to someone so young.

Apart from giving me strength, Paul also influenced my domestic situation. He made me buy my current house. I spotted it one day and remarked to him on the phone that I would love to buy it. I was dithering about money.

'Oh just go ahead and do it, you silly cow,' he said. 'You only live once.' So I did, and I love it. I will live here until I die. I've often said I'll be carried feet first out of it—God knows I've been carried feet first into it plenty of times. Pussy's Drumcondra Demesne has hosted some wild and fabulous parties over the years that Paul has attended, and made extra wonderful. He's impish and mischievous is our Mr O'Grady. I first got to see this side of him when we shared a jail cell in 1993.

Paul has always had some association with the law—breaking it, pretending to break it, or upholding it. He got into some trouble as a kid for a break-in, then he later worked as an assistant at a Magistrates' Court, and got his TV break as a transvestite tart in *The Bill*. He also starred in a musical version of *Prisoner Cell Block H*. He's a wannabe crim.

Our jail term began when I met the director Jim Sheridan in the bar of the Gresham Hotel in Dublin. I'd known Jim for years, having worked with him at the Project Arts Theatre in the 1970s. He had just finished a meeting with Sinéad O'Connor (whom I absolutely adore).

'What are you up to now?' I asked him over a brandy.

'I'm doing a movie about the Guildford Four called *In the Name of the Father*,' he replied. I have to be honest: while I had heard of the Four, I didn't know a huge amount about their backstory.

'Give us a part,' I said cheekily.

'Okay,' he replied, much to my amazement. 'You're going to play a tranny. I've already auditioned another English guy called Paul Savage. You'll be great together.'

I had no idea who 'Paul Savage' was, but I was delighted to be in a movie. The next thing I knew I was at a read-through in Kilmainham Hospital, which was the film's HQ. All the stars were there: Pete Postlethwaite, Daniel Day Lewis … and Mr Pussy, of course. We sat and waited for Paul and the gang from London to arrive. There was no sign of them. What we didn't know was that their plane had had to make an emergency landing, doing all that frightening stuff like adopting the brace position. (There were plenty of jokes about that afterwards.) Eventually, the door opened and in came Paul Savage. Do I really need to tell you it was O'Grady? He had taken his mother's family name for the screen credits.

'You should have told me we were going to act together,' I said.

'I wanted to surprise you.'

Well he did, and we shared a caravan on the set for nearly a month. I loved my three weeks working in the movies. (Paul did four. I only needed three to be fabulous.) I was picked up at my house at 7 a.m. every day and deposited at Kilmainham in a black limo, to be greeted with coffee and a croissant. The caravan was small but beautiful. It had a bench and a bed, and our denim prison costumes were hanging up behind the door. Make-up was right across from us. Presumably, being drag queens, they thought we'd take longer getting our slap on. Pete Postlethwaite was next to us, and Daniel Day Lewis was farther down the line.

It turned out that Pete lived in Peckham for a while, so we had some lovely chats about the old manor. He was a diamond bloke: very sweet and courteous, never 'The Great Actor', and always a good laugh. We celebrated his fiftieth birthday in the Dockers pub. I arrived in drag with his cake. He loved it.

Daniel was the same. He was very friendly, although I'm still not sure if it was him or the man he was playing, Gerry Conlon, that I chatted to on set. He was never out of character, even when he was having a tea break. He even stayed in Kilmainham Prison overnight just to feel what it was like to be locked up. It wouldn't have been me. I did a guided tour of the place and it spooked the bejaysus out of me. This was where the leaders of the 1916 Rising were executed. While I admire their bravery, I wouldn't want to meet one of their ghosts.

I wasn't the only one who admired their bravery. We were filming through Easter and, on Holy Thursday, the Breakers Yard, where the men were shot, was cleared of all cameras and props as a mark of respect. Paul laid some lilies at the spot where James Connolly was executed tied to a chair. It was very moving.

As was Daniel's performance as Gerry Conlon. He gave it everything he had, even insisting on having buckets of freezing water thrown over him. The beautiful madman.

Despite his obsession with getting roles perfect, Dan is very down to earth. In 2002 I was at the Dublin premiere of *Gangs of New York* when he spotted me in the crowd. I had been watching Leonardo DiCaprio poncing about like the huge star he is, being followed around by a cameraman who was filming his every move. Dan was with his family, having his picture taken, and called me over to give me a huge hug. Everyone who knew me was impressed with this—it was a generous gesture.

'You know Daniel Day Lewis?' gasped a journalist mate.

'Oh, we were in a movie once together,' I said as nonchalantly as I could.

Paul and I were constantly up to mischief. We nearly, accidentally, wrecked the set one day during a break in filming. We were hung-over, and went to lean against the jail's brick wall. It wobbled, and nearly toppled over. The bricks were made of rubber. I think Jim roared at us. I love Jim, by the way. He's a real Dub, and could easily be mistaken for a bus driver. And I say that in the nicest possible way. I know loads of bus drivers.

Paul and I had parties in my house almost every night, but we always turned up for work at 7 a.m. We used to take turns of the bed in the caravan, sleeping off our hangovers whenever we got a chance. I brought in cushions, candles, rosary beads and a picture of Danny La Rue, and made a shrine to the great queen. Before our shoots, we would kneel before him and intone: 'Oh Danny of the 1,000 years in the business, make us fabulous. Hahahahaha.'

Pete would sometimes shout at us from his trailer, 'Would you cows ever shut the fuck up? I'm trying to learn my lines.' This, naturally enough, made us pray even louder.

Our little trailer became a bit of a hub for mischief-makers between shooting, and there was an almost constant bubble of laughter. I was playing a character who had been involved in sweepstakes fraud. Paul was a murderer or a drug dealer. Or both. We christened ourselves Stella Crippin and Rita Hindley. Rita still calls me Stella to this day.

Our time 'inside' was great fun, but unfortunately didn't win us any Oscars. Most of it ended up on the cutting room floor. Jim still owes me another role. If you're reading this, Mr Sheridan....

My weeks at Kilmainham filming *In the Name of the Father* weren't the first time I've performed behind bars. Seven years earlier I had played to an appreciative audience at Ireland's most notorious prison. My manager, George, got me the gig.

'You're booked to do Mountjoy,' he said one morning in November 1986.

'Mountjoy, darling? Is there any other way to mount, other than joyfully?'

'Shut up, Alan.'

George was in a grump.

'The governor wants you on the bill for the Christmas show. There's a nice little handbag in it for you. And the opportunity to flirt with a few guards.'

I have to admit, the novelty of being the first drag act to play Ireland's most notorious prison was hard to resist. Here was a chance for me to sample jail life from the right side of the bars.

'I'll do it,' I declared.

'I know you will,' said George.

I don't live far from Mountjoy. There was no dressing room available for the gig (prisons aren't renowned for their privacy), so I got zhooshed up at home and was driven there in all my sluttiest gear. I wore a tiny mini, kinky boots … I looked fabulous. A lot more fabulous than Mountjoy. It reminded me of the opening scene in Ronnie Barker's *Porridge*. The same grim Victorian facade with its huge iron gate, which had a smaller door at its centre. George knocked gently upon it, as if he were worried the screws might be offended by someone banging to get in. Nothing happened. I rolled my (heavily made-up) eyes heavenwards and told him to stand aside. I had an expensive see-through wrap-around umbrella from Switzer's with a deadly metal tip. I rammed it against the door and crooned, 'Coo-eee, coo-ee! Let us in, we have a little Pussy for the guv'nor!'

There was the sound of metal rasping on metal, and a pair of eyes peered at us through the peephole.

'Howya, Pussy, come on in.' The door clanged open, and a group of prison guards crowded around the prison entrance to greet me. It must have been the first time they were actually happy to see someone arriving.

We stepped inside, and the second thing to 'greet' us was the smell. I had been told that prisons have a distinctive smell—I had expected something like a disinfected hospital. It was nothing like that. The air was tainted with the bang of stale breath and cheesy feet. A lot like a showband's dressing room.

'Okay, boys,' I said, handing a screw my umbrella. 'Where do we do the strip search?'

'That won't be necessary,' replied the chief guard. 'We trust you.'

'That's a shame,' I said, trying to sound crestfallen. 'Maybe *I* could strip search *you* instead?'

Everyone laughed. The proverbial ice was broken. We passed through the security area and were brought up to the governor's office, where the rest of the ensemble was gathered. Paddy Reilly, the legendary singer of 'The Fields of Athenry', was there drinking a cup of tea. He put it down and gave me a hug.

'You're looking good, Puss-in-Boots,' he joked, referring to my patent leather legwear. I was given a can of beer by a trustee, and settled in for some pre-show banter. The lag, whose name was Mick, explained what it was like to be a trustee. He had kept his head down and refrained from troublemaking. The guards trusted him, and he was allowed to do things like wash the floor when everyone else was locked up. He also did jobs for the guards. It seemed like an okay way to serve time, although it came with its own problems. Some of the harder heads called him a rat.

All the trustees seemed to get on well with the guards when I was there, and there was a lot of banter back and forth.

'Most of us get on okay with the screws,' said Mick. 'If you show them some respect they will generally return it. They're not the worst.' I gave him a few ciggies and slipped a couple to the other trustees (admittedly, the good-looking ones).

I got a tour of the prison. I don't remember a huge amount of detail, but I do recall that there were four main wings, each of which had three landings. My guide—a very nice young screw— told me that the prison had been built in 1850 and was used as a stopping-off point for prisoners being shipped to Van Diemen's Land. Originally, there were 500 cells, each designed to hold a single prisoner. By the 1980s they were holding more than that, which must have been fairly hard on the 'guests', especially as they had to sleep, live and crap with each other for most of the day in the cramped conditions.

Some people think that prisoners deserve to poo in a basin in front of their cellmates. They've committed crimes and deserve what they get. Ray Burke—that horrible man who used to be the justice minister—once referred to the Mountjoy inmates as 'thugs and scumbags'. Maybe some of them are, but most of them are from deprived backgrounds and didn't have the same opportunities that the likes of Burke had. They're not all monsters, and might not have ended up 'doing porridge' if they had good parents or had received a decent education. That said, Burke ended up doing porridge himself, so it takes all sorts. Personally, I'd rather watch an old lag crap in a bucket than be stuck in a cell with Burke.

It was just after Christmas (the show was on in early January), and it made me feel very sad to see the cells decorated with little bits of tinsel and tiny Christmas trees alongside pictures of the prisoners' families. Even if you didn't feel sympathy for the crims, you had to feel sorry for their kids, without their dads on Christmas morning. I knew that some of them would be let out for the day, but even so…

I didn't let that affect me, and was determined to be fabulous. Curtain up was at 6 p.m. I didn't have much to do except freshen up my slap as I had come in Pussy mode. It's funny—I think that if I had gone as Alan Amsby my nerves would have been all over the place. Not from fear of the audience of hardened criminals, but because, really, who likes the idea of being in prison, even if you can go home in the evening?

I was well used to knocking about with tea leaves and gangsters. South London and the East End was full of Del Boys and scary types like the Krays. I once had a fling with a lag. I know what they can be like. In the late 1960s, the Wimpy Bar in Earl's Court used to be a great post-show gathering spot for the drag queens of

London. One night I noticed a fellow giving me the eye. We got chatting, and he told me he was just out of prison. One thing led to another....

The next night I was supposed to meet him, but went to a party at Blossom's instead. He called there, and I could hear him shouting: 'Where is she? I fucking know she's here.' I hid, somewhat ironically, in a closet, while he stormed about searching for me. Eventually, I could hear him closing in. The door of the cupboard was ripped open, and there he stood, all red-faced and angry. I've always been a cool cat, so I just purred and said: 'Darling, thank God you've found me. The bastards have had me locked me in here for hours!'

When I arrived in Dublin, the criminal fraternity took me to their bosom—or I took them to my bosom. The screws got a taste of my criminal credentials when we were walking back from the tour of Mountjoy. A tall, distinguished-looking man, flanked by two guards, was being escorted back to his cell, and stopped dead in his tracks when he saw me.

'Howya, Pussy? Looking forward to the show.'

'You're looking well, Floyd,' I purred. 'They've told me if I do a good job they'll extend my run. That's a first, isn't it? Normally gits like you get time *off* for good behaviour!'

Floyd laughed, and was led off to his accommodation. I meant it when I said he looked well. He always did. On the outside he was the best-dressed crim in Dublin. Clothes were his speciality. Floyd would rob suits to order from Switzer's, Brown Thomas, Arnotts, Best's.... He would then take them into the dry cleaners to get the ticket and the tag. That way he could flog them as second-hand. The cleaners also provided a way of making money on the double. Floyd had contacts in dry cleaners across town, and would pay his moles a fiver to make the suit 'disappear'. He would then arrive, call out the manager and read them the riot act about losing his best suit. His rant would be peppered with references to a funeral or a wedding he was due to attend the following day. About 90 per cent of the time, the manager would offer to pay money towards a replacement, just to get him out of the shop. Floyd would then head out and around the back to pick up the 'disappeared' suit from his mate and slip him some readies. When he got too well known among the dry cleaner fraternity, he employed friends from the pub to work the scam. It made him a few bob, although he was seldom out of prison to spend it.

When he wasn't doing time, Floyd could be found taking orders and measurements around the north city pubs. He always looked like the most respectable of businessmen. One thing gave him away though: his teeth. The few he had remaining in his mouth were black and stumpy. They looked like the aftermath of a forest fire. You can generally tell a person's health and lifestyle from their teeth. Heroin attacks the hell out of them. Floyd was not a drug user though. He had a terrible fondness for sweets, especially Toffos. He got his nickname from a popular TV ad at the time, where the sheriff foils some outlaws, pops a Toffo in his gob and drawls, 'Go git 'em, Floyd' to his deputy. If you're under ninety-six you won't remember that ad. Mind you, if you're under ninety-six you won't remember much anyway, and you've probably forgotten what this chapter is about.

What I *do* remember is that the gig went brilliantly. I sashayed out to whoops and whistles: I was the closest thing to a woman they had seen in ages. I told them to shut up and be quiet or I'd have them all thrown out onto the street.

'You're only making noise to drown out the sound of tunnelling.'

Paddy Reilly pissed himself in the wings. Or more specifically, in his Y-fronts. Paddy was well used to the incarceration theme. He had a huge a hit with a song about a bloke on a prison ship, whingeing about some fields in Galway. Even the warden laughed, as did two guards who were leaning up against the wall.

'Oh, I love a nice screw up against the wall,' I said.

They were mortified, so I continued.

'How long are you together now, boys?'

I winked at the audience, and they went insane.

'They're a lovely couple, aren't they? I met them in Bartley Dunne's before they started dating....'

The concert was a great success with staff and inmates, and I promised to come back and do another. In fact, I was on a roll. Not long afterwards I was booked to do St Patrick's Institution for Young Offenders. That was a non-starter. My music had started and I was about to go on when the governor saw me for the first time as Pussy. His jaw dropped and he shook his head (not at the same time). He walked up and pulled the plug on me. It's the first time I've ever been thrown out of jail.

I've broken into jail too, which probably cancels out the shame of being booted out of Pat's. It was down the country. I won't say exactly where it was, for obvious reasons. We were driving back from a gig when our car broke down. The driver got out and started tinkering under the bonnet. It was a lonely country road, and the motor was full of our equipment. Just then, a garda car came around the bend and stopped. The guard, like most country guards I've met at that time of night, was keen for a chat. When he saw me, he got all nervous and self conscious.

'God, it's Mr Pussy, isn't it? The wife loves your show. She's seen you three times.'

Whenever I hear 'the wife' being mentioned as a fan, I know it generally means that the husband is a fan too, but maybe too shy to say so, especially if he's in a macho profession.

'You're very late on the road,' he continued. 'Why don't you leave the car there and I'll bring you back to Mrs ___'s B&B She won't mind putting you up this late if I have a word with her. We can stash your gear in the barracks. It'll be safe there.'

We knew it would be safe *anywhere* as no thief in their right mind would have bothered stalking those country roads in search of things to steal. It was the arsehole end of nowhere. We agreed, locked up the gear and retired to the lodgings recommended by this friendly public servant.

The following morning I ate the most incredible breakfast (Mrs ___ was a fan too), and sent the driver off to sort out the car. He eventually returned, and we headed off to the cop shop to pick up our stuff. What the guard had forgotten to tell us was that his country barracks didn't open for business until late that afternoon. He was one of only two guards stationed there. We cursed our bad luck. We had a gig in Dublin that night.

'We'll have to break in,' I decided. My driver looked at me as if I was insane.

'Break in? To a garda barracks?'

'Yes,' I said.

'Okay,' he replied, picking up a rock. 'Here you go. Fire that through the window.'

I took the rock and chose a window. It was the oddest thing: I had seen kids throwing stones at RUC cars and stations up north. I never thought I'd end up doing it myself. I decided I had to make a political statement to justify my act of vandalism. I thought of the Birmingham Six.

'Free the Pussy Two!' I shouted, flinging the rock as hard as I could at a window to the right of the door. The driver ducked down on his hunkers, prepared to leg it if the alarm went off. There was no alarm, which is hardly surprising as this was the late 1970s and nobody would dream of breaking into a police station in rural Ireland. In terms of disrespect and general morality, it would be like peeing against a statue of the Blessed Virgin.

I picked the loose shards of glass out of the frame and climbed through the window. I have to say, at this point, that the gear I was wearing was not ideal for burglary. My pants were too tight, and I had too many dangly bits: amber beads, a tassled top, and my favourite fringed waistcoat. The beads and the fringe got snagged in the frame, and I was stuck.

'Get me the fuck out of here!' I roared, panicking as I was now face down with my legs in the air. My driver came to the rescue, once he had stopped laughing.

'It's all right, I have you.' He placed both hands on the cheeks of my arse and started to push and shove me through the window. The sound of him panting and me groaning would have woken the dead (or just the deaf). It was at that moment when we heard the sound of a vehicle coming up the road.

'Fucking push harder!' I roared.

Mick put his shoulder against my backside and shoved as hard as he could. The sound of the car grew louder, and then suddenly stopped.

'By Jaysus, I've seen it all.' An ageing (and exceptionally dirty) farmer leaned out of the cab of his tractor and peered over at us. He was in no way shocked at seeing a middle-aged man fondling a drag queen's arse through a police station window.

'Do youse need a hand?' he asked.

'No, thank you,' I said as politely as I could, considering that my head was nearly on the floor of the station's front office. 'I've quite enough hands here, thank you.'

'Fair enough so, Mr Pussy. Have fun,' he said, starting up the engine again.

Mick was astounded, as I was, by the recognition.

'How do you know it's Mr Pussy?' he challenged the farmer. 'This could be anybody.' I wiggled my Cuban heels in agreement.

'Yerrr, shure I'd know that arse anywhere.' With that, he up and fucked off down the road and around the bend.

I laughed so much I fell through the window frame. I opened the door, gathered up our gear and left a note with a tenner attached for the broken window. I never heard anything more about it. Pussy the Cat Burglar had escaped.

It's heartening to know, however, that somewhere down in the lonely bog there is a farmer who had his deepest—and presumably weirdest—sexual fantasy fulfilled that day. Who needs porn when you have Pussy power?

Enough about crime. The year was 1993, and I was about to go into the café business … with Bono.

Mum and me.

Me and Bono.

Joe Dolan, Twink, Dickie Rock and me at Ronan
Keating's twenty-first birthday party.

Me and my mate Andy Bell.

Daniel O'Donnell with some tart.

Brother Patrick, the Grim Reaper.

Dermot Morgan, me, Jean Swift and Alan Hughes
at a party in my house.

Danny La Rue at the same party.
(And it was *some* party, I can tell you.)

Me with George Logan – known as Dr Evadne
Hinge (of Hinge and Bracket fame). Here he is
out of character on our way to a drag ball.

Me, Danny La Rue and John Traville
(aka Crystal Clear) in Blackpool.

Me with Paul O'Grady in prison.
We are in costume for the film
In the Name of the Father.

Paul O'Grady and me on the set of
In the Name of the Father.

Colin Farrell and a loose woman.

In bed with Brendan O'Carroll on a television show.

The Diceman (Tom McGinty) and me.
(Photo © Marc O'Sullivan)

I hate these stretch limos.

My favourite pic.
(Photo © Ross Waldron)

At home with Lily, up to her tricks.

Me on the tiles
– one of my favourites by Marc O'Sullivan.

Twink and me.

Me and Panti Bliss at Electric Picnic. (Photo © Fiona Morgan)

A selfie with Al Porter,
my favourite funny man.

Me, now.

Chapter Fifteen

Thank God it's Friday ... Opening a Café with Bono

If I had to pick one year as a turning point for my adopted motherland, it would be 1994. Everything that has happened in Ireland in the past two decades can be traced back to that year. The seeds of Ireland's self-confidence were sown in 1988 when Jack and the Boys lifted the country's spirits to their highest point ever. I'm not exaggerating about 1988. Ireland was ruled by England, then run by the Church, and was weighed down with centuries of post-colonial baggage and Catholic guilt. Irish people felt they were viewed as an inferior race—and this was certainly true in the minds of my former countrymen. Ray Houghton's goal against the Old Enemy in the 1988 European Championships was seen as a David versus Goliath moment. Payback for the shameful way England had treated Ireland over the centuries.

By 1994, the country was ready to exploit that buzz. People were starting to believe that Ireland could achieve on a world-class level, and on a regular basis. I say 'regular' because we already had U2, Sinéad O'Connor, Jim Sheridan, Neil Jordan and Terry Wogan, among others, flying the flag for Irish arts.

In 1994, Ireland won the Eurovision Song Contest at the Point Theatre for the third year in a row with 'Rock 'n' Roll Kids', performed by Paul Harrington and Charlie McGettigan. That was phenomenal in its own right, but what really made the contest special was the interval act. The world's jaw dropped and crashed through the floor when Michael Flatley blazed across the stage in a flash of silk and huge blond hair. *Riverdance*—with gorgeous Jean Butler and music by Bill Whelan—flicked a switch in the minds of young Irish people. Ireland was the envy of Europe and beyond.

Now you may sneer at that mention of *Riverdance*, but no country can really call itself a nation unless it has a sense of self-belief. The reception of *Riverdance* was one of the biggest confidence boosts this country has ever received. It was sexy, athletic, graceful, and based entirely on Irish culture. I'm getting a swell of pride, as an adopted Irishman, just writing about it.

On top of that, you had Jack Charlton being awarded the Freedom of Dublin City. In June his team qualified for the last sixteen stage of the World Cup. This was head-melting inspiration for a country as small as Ireland. Then, in August, the IRA—a source of shame for most Irish people—announced a complete ceasefire. Loyalists followed suit in October.

There was a lot to be proud of. That said, the most momentous event of 1994 took place on Suffolk Street, Dublin in March. Drum roll, please ... it was opening of Mr Pussy's Café De Luxe. Oh shut up, it *was* the most momentous event of that year.

In 1991, I was having a late-night glass of milk in Lillie's Bordello when I looked up and saw a face I recognised from around town. It belonged to Gavin Friday: fantastic and uncompromising artist and painter, and frontman of the famously avant-garde Virgin Prunes. He sat down with me and we began chatting.

He told me that his mum and dad were big fans, and used to go down to the Drake to see me perform. I told him they had fantastic taste. I also told him that I was twenty-five years here, and suggested he write a song about me. 'Write a song, write a sad song, make it twenty-five years long.' He did, and included it on his album *Shag Tobacco*. When he sang it at Carnegie Hall, he adopted my persona ('Ireland's most misleading lady'), and told the story of how we met. Yes, I did say 'Carnegie Hall'. He's a talented boy, that Mr Friday.

In Neil Jordan's film version of *Breakfast on Pluto*, Gavin plays a character called Billy Hatchett, who—although it may seem immodest to say so—is based on yours truly. Don't believe me? Cillian Murphy plays 'Kitten' Braden. Coincidence? No.

Gavin came to a few of my parties, and in 1992 he asked me to MC at his wedding reception in the cellars of the Clarence Hotel. It was a very cool evening. I met Naomi Campbell and Adam Clayton for the first time, and another young man from the northside of Dublin got up and did a number with me. I think his name was Paul Hewson. You probably know him as Bono. I sang 'Kiss me Honey, Honey Kiss me'... and I half stripped him. We had a drink afterwards and a good old natter. I thought he was lovely—very courteous and very, very funny, with a dry sense of humour. People think Bono takes himself seriously. He absolutely does NOT.

Neither does his best friend, Gavin. He's one of the most wonderfully talented, kind and decent men I've ever met. He's also got buckets of integrity. If Gavin says he'll do something, he'll do it. You may not hear anything for a while, but he'll suddenly turn up and say, 'You remember that thing we were talking about? It's done.' And that's how my entry into the café/nightclub business came about.

I went to a function in town one night, I can't remember the venue, and Gavin was there with the U2 boys. I joined them for a chat, and I still don't know how the subject came up, but I said I'd love to open a café in town.

'Are you serious?' Bono suddenly perked up. (Not that he wasn't already perky. If he were a dog, his ears would have been pinned back and his tail would have been wagging.)

'Honey, I'm always serious. Even when I'm not being serious.' By pure fluke, it turned out that Bono and Gavin had always wanted to open a greasy spoon café. It was a childhood dream, and they had been talking about it shortly before I met them. We went to a club on Dame Lane and chatted a little bit more. That was it. Just a bit of banter … or so I thought.

A few months later, Gavin came to a party in my house and asked to see me in the hall.

'I've got news for you. We're opening a café.'

'Oh, that's nice,' I said. He rolled his eyes to heaven in mock exasperation.

'It's for *you*, you dozy cow.'

My head almost exploded with delight.

'Keep it quiet,' he ordered, and I spent the rest of the night trying not to tell my guests that I was going into business with the world's biggest rock star, Gavin, and moviemaker Jim Sheridan.

A meeting was arranged at the accountant's, where we discussed our plans. Edge had come up with a name: 'Mr Pussy's Café De Luxe'. I was giddy with excitement, but did my best to disguise it. Afterwards, Bono drove Gavin and me to the venue on Suffolk Street in his Jaguar. There were kids' toys on the back seat. How lovely, I thought.

The café would open on the site of Norman Hewson's old Dillon's restaurant. Norman is Bono's brother. He had a new place next door called Tosca, which was one of the most popular eateries in town, and was tasked with keeping an eye on us.

Mr Pussy's café was like nothing ever seen before in Ireland—or anywhere else for that matter. It was the Liberace of greasy spoons, with more camping going on than you'd see at a boy scouts' jamboree. Gavin did most of the decor, with a designer and me. Our 'emblem' was a cat in the window (as opposed to a doggy in the window), backed by frilly pink curtains. The first thing punters saw when they entered were the Rules of the House.

'No drugs, no dogs, and drags by approval'.

The cash desk sold cat food—and yes, people did buy it. To the left of the till was the most extraordinary display cabinet in town. It was full of U2 memorabilia and celebrity gifts. There were Bono's 'MacPhisto' horns and gold boots, Paul McGuinness's monogrammed slippers, Jim Sheridan's T-shirt (emblazoned with 'Oscar nominee'), and loads of other goodies. The cabinet became a tourist attraction—as did I—and we kept adding to it.

One evening Naomi Campbell came in and handed me a pair of her knickers. They were signed 'From one pussy to another'. A few days later, Christy Turlington walked in with a bra hanging out of her pocket.

'You dirty cow,' I said. 'Just out of bed and no time to dress.' Christy laughed, and the bra went straight into the cabinet, where she had intended it to go. Before you ask … no, I wasn't tempted to perform in Naomi's knickers and Christy's bra.

I mentioned Paul McGuinness there. He's an incredible man: the fifth member of U2, who built them up and helped them dominate the world of rock music. I met him first back in the 1970s when he came to the Baggot and asked me to address Trinity College's Historical Society on the subject of women's liberation.

Me? Address the oldest undergraduate student society in the world? Against women's lib? In drag? Of course I would. It was a very funny evening, fuelled by Paul's sense of mischief. I was asked back to 'do the Hist' years later as guest of honour. I just sat there looking gorgeous.

I'm rambling again. Where was I? Back to the café....

After customers had their fill of gawking at all that memorabilia, their senses were further assaulted by the kitschy decor of the dining area. Mirrors everywhere were covered in sequins and feather boas. The walls were lovingly adorned with paintings of Gavin's 'Flying Mickeys' (cocks with wings, dear). We also had a mannequin with the uniform Charlie Chaplin wore in *The Great Dictator*. Bono bought it somewhere. It must have cost a fortune.

The toilets were outrageous. The men's had a plaster cast of a pair of boxers on the door. Boxer shorts. Obviously not a pair of boxers. That would have been just too weird. The ladies' had a bra. Both WCs had toys and water features and all kinds of camp nonsense.

Then there was the Royal Box. This was a balcony at the end of the room, which was draped like the box at Covent Garden. It was for VIPs, but as the place was full of VIPs milling about anyway, we let ordinary mortals use it too.

Our staff were beautiful. They were all carefully picked for their appearance, and had to look very 'with it', to use an old expression. One of my favourites was young Drag Princess 'Veda' (Enda McGrattan). Veda used to serve punters on rollerblades. She went on to win the 1999 Alternative Miss Ireland competition, and supported the Scissor Sisters with her band in 2004. My dressing room was downstairs, and Veda was always dying to have a look at my wardrobe. The bar staff used to send her down with my drink before each show.

I would open my door four inches, stretch out my beautifully manicured hand, and take my vodka with the words, 'Thank you, dear.' Then I would shut the door in her face. Veda, sweetie, I was only teasing you.

We served really good food ... on mismatched crockery. I insisted on this as nothing—including the cutlery—ever matched in authentic greasy spoons. We also had bottles of sauce on the tables too. When someone ordered a 'Pint of Pussy', a milk bottle would be delivered to their table. I got that idea from the Manhattan.

Customers could eat 'Pussy Pies' (steak and kidney), 'Gavin Fry-days', and everything you could expect to eat in a café … with the exception of the most expensive item on the menu: caviar and chips. It cost a fortune. Edge had it one night; I could never afford it.

We offered cocktails, vodka milkshakes, vodka jelly, champagne, and red or white 'tea' served in teapots. People still think we didn't have a licence and sold booze illegally. We let that rumour seep out to give the place an extra edge. As opposed to The Edge. We already had The Edge.

The night we opened, there were queues down Suffolk Street and up into Grafton Street. Although we didn't have an official 'opening', word had got out about us. People queued for hours just to have a look inside. And those queues didn't die off after the first night. There was always a steady stream of punters, from office workers to VIPs and clubbers, eager to come in for a nosebag and a shufti. We heard that Dublin's bus drivers were complaining that every time they passed the place people would get out of their seats on the upper deck to have a look at the café and nearly tilted the bus over.

At first we were open twenty-four hours, and I was there at night and during the day too. People complained if I wasn't around: they came in to see me. But it was too much, so we scaled it back. The place didn't really get going until around 3 a.m., when I would do my routine. This 'morphed' into bingo nights. Like my mum, I loved bingo. Long before the George started doing it, I had the bright idea of getting customers to play the OAPs' favourite game—with a camp twist. They loved it. We used a huge goldfish bowl as the tombola, and the prize would be a lift in the café's trademark gold Rolls-Royce and lunch for two.

Some patrons took the bingo very seriously. I came back to the café one night after my break and spotted Ronnie Wood of the Rolling Stones eating a bacon sarnie. I did a double take, and then composed myself.

'Do you like bingo?' I purred.

'I love it.'

Ron didn't say another word for the rest of the night, except to tell a few drunks to shut up and be quiet. And all he was going to win was a dessert. He's very thin, is Ron. He really needed that dessert.

Ronnie is a real scamp. I've drunk with him lots of times, and went to a party in his house in Kildare. Don't ask me what went on at it. It was a Stones party, so it must have been good—I can't remember.

Anything could happen at the café—and we encouraged as much organised anarchy as the place could handle. We would regularly go down to Grafton Street to bring buskers back to gig for a few bob and a meal. We also had our own house magicians, the Vennetties. One of the tricks they did involved placing a guillotine around someone's neck. One night they put Norman in it and lost the key. He had to walk around in it for an hour. They hadn't lost the key, of course. I told them to pretend they had. Hahahaha.

Another time, I was talking to a friend from a well-known circus family. I said I'd love to have a tiger cub in the place. The following evening they turned up with a cub on a chain. I say 'cub', but I mean GIANT TIGER. It was almost an adult, and up to my waist.

'Is it a man-eating tiger?' I asked.

'No,' came the reply.

'Good,' I sighed.

'It only eats women and drag queens.'

They walked it through the restaurant, and it was hilarious to see how people reacted. Most punters tried their best to look cool and not fling themselves under the table screaming.

'Get it a steak before it eats someone,' ordered Norman. So we took some fillet from the fridge and it sat on stage chewing raw meat and eyeing up the patrons. Then it got overexcited and had to be taken out.

I don't mean 'taken out' as in shot; I mean taken out of the place. Try and keep up, you silly cows.

There were so many famous people coming in and out that it's hard to namecheck them all without sounding a bit naff. I'll do it anyway. It wasn't that surprising though: the café was owned by Bono after all, and was internationally famous. MTV even did a piece on us. I was interviewed, in civvies, showing the crew around.

One evening, Gavin said that he and Bono would be coming in with Mel Gibson, who was shooting *Braveheart* here. I nearly danced with excitement. When I calmed down, I rang my mate Niall O'Farrell, who owned Black Tie suit hire. He sorted me out with a long slinky black velvet number with a train. I pulled on my best blonde wig, which I topped off with a femme fatale style hat and veil. I was festooned in false diamonds—or what was left of them after Bono's kids had rooted through my bling box.

I hovered until Bono, Gavin and Mel were seated comfortably in a booth. His Bononess nodded, and I came over and said, 'Hello, Mr Gibson, you're very welcome.' I was absolutely shaking with excitement. He was such a heart-throb.

Later, Bono and Mel went on to the Pod nightclub, followed by Gavin and me. Still in drag, I walked through the crowds into the VIP lounge and sat down next to Mel. We chatted all night, just about general stuff. He was gorgeous. I have no idea what happened to him over the years to cause his well-reported right-wing meltdowns. He was sweetness personified to me—and I was a gay man in a dress.

Afterwards, we strolled down the street together to his car. I don't know if anyone took a photo, but we must have looked like the oddest couple on the planet—Mad Max and Ireland's Most Misleading Lady.

People think they get a fully rounded picture of stars' personalities from what they read in the papers. That's rubbish, of course. Mel wasn't the lunatic he's been painted as. Van Morrison gets a hard time, too, for appearing to be grumpy. Maybe he is sometimes, but I've never seen that side of him. I knew him from the café and from around town. I recall one lovely evening when he invited me back with his friends to the hotel he was staying in. He played the guitar and serenaded us all into the small hours. He was very sweet. I had my dog, Lily, with me. She loved the singing nearly as much as I did.

Van has a great sense of humour—that dry Belfast wit that I really enjoy. One evening, I was on my way to the wrap party for a big Hollywood movie that had been shot here. Van spotted me on the road and suggested that we go in together. I was in full drag. That was typical of Van: he loved the mischievousness of turning up at a big bash with a drag queen.

Louis Walsh was another café devotee. I've known him for decades, since he started out in the showband business with Chips. He arrived in one night with a group of young guys and introduced them as his new band. They were Boyzone, and they were very sweet. Ronan is an absolute dote. He invited me to his twenty-first birthday, and I've always had a lot of time for him. Keith Duffy too. He is a hoot.

Not long after that first meeting in the café with 'The Boyz', I was judging a competition with Louis and started humming a tune I love. He said, 'That's "Words" by the Bee Gees.' The next thing I knew, Boyzone were at number one with it. I'm not saying I subliminally put the song into Louis' mind … to hell with it, yes I am.

Stephen Gately was a lovely boy. People on the scene knew he was gay, but it was never mentioned. I've always thought it's unfair to out people, especially youngsters on their way up in the business. It was heartbreaking to hear of his death in 2009. What a terrible waste. I can still see him and 'The Boyz' dancing their little hearts out on *The Late Late Show* with Gay Byrne … all that fame, and in Stephen's case, tragedy, ahead of them.

Speaking of Gabriel Byrnes, the other Gabriel Byrne dropped by whenever he was in town. Like Jim Sheridan, I've known him since the Project days, and would meet him for a drink now and then. He always loved my fur coats and said they were my trademark.

'Oh yes, love, I've got plenty of 'trade' with this,' I replied.

One time I was doing a play called *Up All Night* by Lee Dunne, which was directed by Vincent Smith. I had to do a cabaret scene where I went around the audience, slagging them—as I like to do.

'We have a great star in with us tonight,' I told the punters. 'He's huge in Hollywood, and one of the screen's biggest heart-throbs.' I looked down at Gabriel, who was redder than a well-spanked arse.

'What's your name again, dear?' I asked him, and the audience cheered.

Later, over a drink, I asked if he minded me singling him out. Of course he didn't. He's like that: very down to earth. Some celebs can be a bit snotty when you single them out. They see it as using their presence as an endorsement. Not Gabriel.

'No problem, Alan. If it helps you, I'm fine with it.'

Liam Neeson is another decent megastar. He emerged at the same time as Gabriel in John Boorman's *Excalibur*. Virginia Cole introduced me to him when he was playing the Indian in Noel Pearson's production of *One Flew Over the Cuckoo's Nest*. We met in the bar next door. He was sitting cross-legged on the floor like a student, and was friendliness personified.

I always looked forward to Shane MacGowan and The Pogues coming in. Shane is hilarious, and very good-natured. The first night he arrived I gave him some paper and crayons as a joke. He drew a wonderful picture of an enormous mickey. He hissed with pleasure through his trademark teeth-stumps as he handed it to me. It went into the cabinet.

If there could be such a thing as the 'Anti-Pogues', then it would be REM. They were such a well-behaved, quiet, softly spoken group. Not in the least rock and roll. Michael Stipe was quite shy. He was very fond of our veggie burger, and I got on well with him. His assistant had a headache, so I brought her down to the staff area and gave her an aspirin and a place to lie down.

Days later, a card arrived at the café. It was an invitation to attend a party the band was hosting at a castle they were staying in. They remembered my 'kindness', as they put it. I had only given the poor girl an aspirin. I went along and spent the evening hobnobbing with Lady Iona. I remember thinking: *if my mum could see me now....*

Whatever about Lady Iona, Mum wouldn't have believed that I would someday be rubbing shoulders with a member of the Kennedy family. I knew Kim Kennedy Smith, daughter of US ambassador Jean. She brought her mum in one day, and I gave her the tour. I remember, with horror, her looking at the wall and spotting Gavin's mickeys. She didn't flinch. Perhaps she had seen flying mickeys before. Who knows?

'It's a strange place,' she said, vaguely, afterwards.

I waved her off as Norman was walking out of Tosca.

'You're seeing off the customers now? Nice, personal touch.'

I shrugged.

'It's only the US ambassador,' I said, and flounced back inside.

The night of the Eurovision victory in May was absolutely bonkers. Everyone came back, and I danced a jig with Michael Flatley. It was a career highlight ... for him. Pussy doesn't dance with just anybody. I love the way Michael dresses. He's always immaculate, with every little detail perfect. He's a nice chap too.

Prior to *Riverdance*, the hottest Eurovision act in town had been The Hot House Flowers. They captivated Europe with 'Don't Go' in 1988. I always had a great laugh with the Flowers. There was a celebrity auction on at the Mansion House. One of the prizes was a night out with Fiachna from the group. It included a lift in a limo, front-row tickets at the Diana Ross gig in the Point, and the chance to tuck the handsome guitarist up in bed afterwards.

I thought: *I'll teach these little fuckers a lesson.* I asked the woman who was doling out the paddles to give me number sixty-nine. She did, and I won the bid. Sixty-nine must be my lucky number.

We were picked up at the café and brought to the Point. Diana Ross was right in front of us. I noticed that when she walked around on stage there was a tiny woman on all fours crawling behind her. I presume it was for security. Or maybe she had lost her contact lens. I didn't—and still don't—care.

I wasn't in drag. I was in the next best thing, though: a tartan jacket so loud you could hear it in Glasgow, and leather trousers. Madame Ross spotted me, or the jacket, and swanned over, smiling down at us. I just glared at her. Her dress wasn't as nice up close. The sequins were cheap. She'd never have made it on stage at the Vauxhall. Or the Drake Inn.

Fiachna had a blast. At the end of the show, we were asked by management if we wanted to go backstage. I said, 'Not particularly.' I think Fiachna was relieved. We went our separate ways, and I didn't hold him to the 'tucking in' part of the deal.

Diana Ross didn't come to the café. Who needs her anyway when you have Paul O'Grady coming over all the time and glamming up the place? Savage was always over and back with Brendan Murphy. He loved the place, and the fact that anyone could turn up there. I looked down from the stage one evening and saw a Hollywood legend in the audience. It was Sean Connery. He turned to one of the waitresses and said, in his lovely Scots voice:

'Verrrrry interesting.'

Other star noshers included Barry Manilow, Lord Henry Mountcharles, Brendan Gleeson, Barbara Walters, John Hurt, Minnie Driver, Colin Farrell…. Colin has told me he was a regular at the café, but he must have had false ID with him. He's only a child, God bless him.

Of course, the VIP everybody wanted to see was Bono. He never disappointed his fans, remaining polite no matter how jarred they were. He loved the 3 a.m. cabaret, where I would come on dressed in a black sequinned dress and huge blonde bouffant wig to introduce the likes of Chutney Houston (a Whitney impersonator).

Bono would stand in the Royal Box, smiling and clapping along with the rest of the crowd and entering the spirit of the place. I really, really like that man. I can't praise him enough, and get very angry when I hear the begrudgers at work. One Irish trait I've never admired is begrudgery. It's normally disguised as keeping someone grounded. Bono doesn't need me to defend him, but I know that his non-band work is done out of love and decency, not ego. He loves his country and yet he's treasured abroad.

As opposed to me, who loves his new country and is treasured as a broad.

Bono and Ali used to bring the kids in on Saturday afternoons and have tea like any ordinary family. People left them alone. I used to take their two girls—who were very young—down to the dressing room and dress them up in beads. Another time, Bono and Norman celebrated their dad's seventieth birthday there, changing the sign on the door to read 'Happy Birthday, Bob'. It was a real family affair, with Bono singing Frank Sinatra songs with Ali and me on backing vocals.

Edge is very cool too (as if you didn't know that already), and plays down his superstar status. A friend of mine, Penny Arcade, was doing her show *Bitch! Dyke! Faghag! Whore!* in town, and I invited Edge and a friend along as my guests. The show involves a lot of audience interaction, which might have been a bit annoying for Edge, given that he was on a night off. Or so I thought. He turned down the offer of a box, and sat in with the punters. He even went for a scoop in the bar afterwards and then on for a bop in Lillie's.

The next afternoon I arrived in work to an enormous bouquet of flowers, with a thank you note from him. What a gent.

Sadly, the café fizzled out after about two years. I just couldn't commit to being there all the time. We did it for the fun of it—I had no idea it was going to turn into a twenty-four-hour-a-day full-time job. Being part of something so special was the highlight of my life and career. We achieved what we had set out to do: open the world's coolest, campest greasy spoon. It's now part of the fabric of Irish history and urban lore. It's a shame it didn't last, but it was of its time, to use a cliché. Dublin was growing. It was a massively exciting time. It's a shame the place didn't last longer. Mr Pussy's Café De Luxe would thrive in post-gay-marriage Ireland.

All of that said, I would trade all of those celeb memories for the one of my mum looking over the sauce bottle and a plate of chips on the night of the unofficial official opening. It meant a huge amount to me to be able to show her how well I'd done. How I was accepted and befriended by some of the biggest stars in the world—for being me. We celebrated her eightieth birthday at the café in July 1994. It was strictly invitation only and was covered by RTÉ.

I can still see Mum being filmed in the back of the gold Roller as we arrived, saying, 'Oh noooo, I don't like thiiiiisss…'

And me replying, 'Oh, shut up you silly old moo.'

Thank you, Gavin Friday, for helping me to create such wonderful memories.

You're a very special man.

Chapter Sixteen

It was a Bumpy Flight, Mum ... But I Wouldn't Change a Thing

It's 3.42 p.m. on 3 October 2016. I'm sitting in my living room in Drumcondra surrounded by faces. The room is full of photographs from the fireplace to the piano. Thirty pictures ... and not one person in them is still alive.

Which is, to put it mildly, terrifying, dear.

I sometimes wonder why I was chosen out of all my friends to have had such a long and eventful life. Only sometimes. I don't sit around navel-gazing about it or pining for the old days. I miss the Ireland of twenty years ago and beyond. I miss Swinging London, but New Ireland is a pretty good place to live in. It's a bit too PC for my liking at times, but there is a sense that it's no longer sufficient to pay lip service to civil rights. Change must come—and it has come in terms of equality for gay people.

In 2015, Ireland became the first country in the world to legalise gay marriage. It's extraordinary to think that twenty-three years ago you could be jailed for being homosexual, but now you can walk down the street holding hands with your husband. Of course, it depends on the street. I wouldn't wear a patent leather basque and mince down Sean MacDermott Street or parts of Darndale. On second thoughts, maybe I would.

So Ireland has changed. Soon, there will be no gay bars left. The current generation of teenagers and twenty-year-olds have grown up with equality. The lines between gay and straight have blurred. That's how it should be. We're all human beings. In my heyday, if the coppers raided a pub, you'd grab the nearest lesbian and say she was your girlfriend. Now, gay pubs are mixed, so PC Plod would have his work cut out trying to separate the homos from the heteros. Not that the gardaí have anything to raid for now. In fact, there are 'out' policemen and women in Ireland. Even the GAA is slowly changing to GAY-friendly. In 2009, Cork's Donal Óg Cusack became the first GAA player to come out. It was a very brave thing to do, and inspired countless gay men and women—and straight people too. Everyone loves a hero, and Donal's revelation was heroic.

There have been countless other changes too. Too many to mention all of them. Playwright Mannix Flynn is now a member of the 'ruling classes'. I didn't see that coming. The Dublin City councillor was a well-known character about town. As I write this, he is staging a protest on a window ledge at City Hall. I don't want to get into that here. It's his crusade, and whether he's right or wrong, Mannix is a man of conviction (no pun intended), and I applaud him for that.

Mannix is a gifted writer and thespian. I acted with him at the Project Arts in Jim and Peter Sheridan's 1979 production of *The Ha'penny Place*, which was based on *The Beggar's Opera*. It starred Jeananne Crowley, Ciaran Hinds, Virginia Cole and the lovely Agnes Bernelle. Agnes and I were great mates. Her family had fled Nazi Germany, and she had a warehouse full of gripping stories. She was a lovely woman.

Mannix's character was married to Jeananne, and I was 'Lucy', his mistress. There was a scene when I had to visit him in prison and kiss him. One night he was annoying the hell out of me. I can't remember why. He might have eaten a garlic bulb or was just slagging me. It doesn't matter. I said to myself, fuck him, I'll put manners on the little pup. I stretched across the table, grabbed him and stuck my tongue down his throat. His eyes grew wider than the hubcaps on an articulated lorry. The audience gasped.

It was the first gay kiss ever seen on an Irish stage, although I was, strictly speaking, playing a woman, and Mannix is straight. Despite the shock, he laughed about it afterwards. Another night, when I was due to be shot, the gun didn't go off. I think I shouted 'bang' and did a dying swan routine. God, I love legit theatre.

Mannix turning to politics, the liberalising of Ireland, the economic crash, Brendan O'Carroll becoming an international megastar … the 2000s have been, generally, a bit mad. This is a memoir, not a history book, and I've decided to take the café days with Bono and Gavin as my cut-off point. It was my apotheosis. That's a word I've borrowed from the dictionary. Look it up if you don't know what it means.

I didn't just pack up my make-up and dresses and retire after the café. I hit the new millennium running, with a tour of Spain, gigs in the US and down the sticks, and reinvented myself as a TV personality. I was a regular on *The Afternoon Show* with Marty Whelan and Mary Kennedy, *Don't Feed The Gondolas*, *The Panel*, *The End*, *The Lyrics Board* and *Podge and Rodge*. The latter two are scabrous—and hilarious—puppets. I did their 'Ballydung' show in drag, and decided to give them something to remember.

The puppeteers would lie prone on the floor, working off a monitor. I stood over them, forcing them to look up my dress. I think it was the only time they've been speechless.

I also did reviews for TV3's morning show, including the MTV Awards (although that was November 1999, on the cusp of the millennium). I was out all night at the Clarence after-show party with Bono, Whitney Houston, Mariah Carey, Eminem and scores of megastars. I had a brief exchange with Mick Jagger. He admired my suit, which looked like it was made of fur.

'Oh, that's a nice bit of rabbit,' he joked.

'It's untouched pussy. Something that's rare in London … thanks to you.' He guffawed at that, and I swept out of the place, rushing home to get changed for TV. It was 4 a.m., and the show started in a few hours.

I arrived at TV3 in drag, swigging from a bottle of Dom Pérignon I had brought from the Clarence. I was at my most mischievous—and still half-cut—and determined to make Alan Hughes, Amanda Byram and Mark Cagney corpse. I achieved this, and I think we were nearly put off the air. Even going into the ad break, all you could hear was helpless laughter. I love that sound. It's why I'm in the comedy business. By the way, if you saw that show, it wasn't real champagne: I had filled it with 7UP.

I love working on TV. I love watching it too. The set goes on in the morning, and I'm not ready to roll unless I've seen *Bargain Hunt* and had my cup of green tea. (It's great for the skin.)

One of my favourite shows is *Mrs Brown's Boys*. It's been a sincere pleasure to watch Brendan O'Carroll's rise to international megastardom. I've known him forever. He's funny, warm, smart and generous. Once, when he was on Paul O'Grady's show, he mentioned me. He didn't have to, but it's the mark of a real pro never to forget your friends. Paul, typically, said that Mr Pussy did the cabaret at the last supper.

I texted Brendan to thank him, and he replied, saying, 'You're welcome. You paved the way for all of us.'

If you had told me thirty years ago that Brendan would now be the best-known drag artist on the planet, I'd have punched you in the spleen. Mrs Brown isn't classic drag, but he/she is the most plausible man/woman in the business. Brendan understands women. I think that's his secret.

Despite his fame, he's still a cheeky little Dub git, and likes to send himself up. He had a house-warming party, and I was there with Andy Bell from Erasure and Rory Cowan. We were leaving, and I said, 'Give us a shout.' He said, 'Ring the office.'

'Ring the office? Ring the *office*?! You cheeky little fucker. If you're not careful I'll buy the house next door and turn it into a kip.'

Andy reminded me of this recently, laughing at the slagging we Irish (I'm Irish now) give each other, and how it keeps our feet on the ground. Andy and I have been friends since we met in Lillie's Library in 1994. I was heading back to the café and spotted him alone in the corner.

'Come over to the café with us.'

'I've already been there tonight.'

'Well, come over again.'

He did—and he always goes wherever I want to go. I love that about him, and the way he makes me laugh. I call him 'Baby Jane', and we text all the time and meet up when he's over. I brought him to the George after an Erasure gig at the Olympia. The place filled up with queens, buzzing from the show and wearing his trademark angel wings.

'Is that *him* over there?' one excited young man asked me.

'Yes, but don't pester him.'

Naturally, EVERYBODY pestered him, but he took it all in his stride. He's a fans' man, is Andy. And the sort of guy you want to mother. Yes, I do have a maternal/paternal instinct, although I don't have kids. There are people I want to mother. One of them burst onto the pop scene at the same as Andy. Her name is Sinéad O'Connor, and we met through a wonderful friend of mine, Marianne Faithful.

Like Sinéad, Marianne had to deal with a hostile press at the height of her fame in the 1960s. She gained notoriety for her association with the Rolling Stones and all that old nonsense about Mars Bars, etc. None of that sex stuff was true; it was a tabloid fabrication.

Marianne is now best known for her cabaret work, interpreting Berthold Brecht. I went to see her at the Gate when she was in Dublin for a Brecht evening. Rory Cowan, of *Mrs Brown's Boys* fame, brought me. He used to work for a major record label, and knows many of the top stars. Of all of them, he reckons that she is the most special. He is in awe of her, as I am.

Rory, by the way, brought Elton John to a club I was involved with in the 1970s. I probably should have mentioned that earlier, but it's easy to forget Elton John. (Okay, my memory has the occasional wobble. It really did slip my mind.) I wasn't there that night. Years ago I was watching a documentary about him, and he was talking about the various aliases he uses when booking into hotels. He used to book his mum in as 'Mrs Pussy'. Since then I've wondered if it was anything to do with yours truly. I've met Elton a few times. Maybe his mum looked like me. Or maybe not. Anyway, if ever I see him again, I'll ask.

Back to Marianne. We had drinks in the Gate's green room, and instantly liked each other. She's wise and funny and very sweet. We exchanged numbers, and I sent her flowers the following day. She gave me a bell, and we arranged to go to the pictures. Not very rock and roll, I know, but we both love the cinema.

I was to meet her in Wynne's Hotel off O'Connell Street. This is a well-known haunt of nuns and priests. I liked the mischief of meeting one of the 1960s' Wild Children under the noses of the clergy. I was late, which for me is unforgivable. I'm a stickler for punctuality. She was standing at the bar wearing a raincoat and smiling. We had a drink, and went to see *All That Jazz* with Liza Minnelli, then on to the Trocadero, where I showed her the pictures of me on the wall. There was one from every decade I've been here. They were taken down during a redecoration. There's just one now.

Marianne never spoke about her days with the Stones. We just nattered away like two old girlfriends, reminiscing about London in the 1960s. She lives in Paris these days, and we've lost touch. My mate Penny Arcade was over recently, and met her. She was asking after me. If I ever want to get plastered in Paris, I know who to call. (Sorry, I couldn't resist that.)

As I said, ages ago, it was through Marianne that I became friendly with Sinéad O'Connor at a party in her home, Shell Cottage on the Carton Estate in Kildare, in the early 2000s. Sinéad was there when I arrived. I thought she looked a bit lost. I went over and started chatting, and we had a good laugh. Sinéad has the most wonderful dry, understated sense of humour. She is great for a chuckle. We became friends, and she used to come to my shows, heading out on the town with me afterwards, with her then-boyfriend, Dermott Hayes. Dermott, by the way, is a wonderful buddy. I've known him for twenty-five years, first as a journo, then as a chum. We've had millions of funny nights in Bruxelles with its lovely, kind, sweet owner, Dave Egan, and his wonderful family.

I recall spending a fabulous Christmas with Graham Murray at Sinéad's home. Graham is my best friend. I've known him from my café days, when he bribed the doorman to let him jump the queue. (Hello, Graham. See you for a sherbet later, dear.)

'What would you like to drink?' Sinéad asked us.

'Vodka,' I said.

'Tia Maria,' said Graham.

She went off to the kitchen and returned with a bottle of vodka and a bottle of Tia Maria.

'Here you go,' she said. 'That will save me running in and out.' That's the Sinéad I know: homely and laid back, contrary to the way she is portrayed in the media. She is very misunderstood. She's a hugely intelligent woman and a great mum. It really breaks my heart when I see her getting a hard time. She can handle it though. Never underestimate her.

I don't want to bash the press over the way they cover Sinéad's life. Journalists have always been very good to me. I've had a charmed career as an entertainer in that regard. Dermott Hayes, Tom Myler, Bairbre Power, Ken Sweeney, Eddie Rowley, Barry Hartigan, Amanda Brunker, Joe Jackson, Barry Egan … and all the 'diarists' have shown me kindness and respect. I'm sorry if I've forgotten any names. The *Examiner*, the *Echo*, the *Herald*, *Limerick Leader*, the *Press*, the *Sunday Independent*, *Indo*, *Mail* and the *Sunday World* all gave me oxygen throughout my career. Journos have a tough job, especially these days when they're competing with social media. I'm not kissing arses here—I genuinely mean it.

I have to mention one particular journalist. He's been a close friend for many years. I got to know him after doing a show in Renards. Eugene Masterson and I have had tonnes of adventures, from the US to Morocco, and the bars of Dublin. Thank you, Eugene.

The 2000s saw the untimely deaths of some other notable journos who helped me, directly and indirectly: Paul Drury, Peter Carvosso and George Byrne.

George, whose full name was John George Paul Byrne, was the son of a devout Beatles fan. His mates knew him as Ringo. He was one of the great characters of the Irish newspaper industry. George was hilariously curmudgeonly and opinionated, and knew everything there was to know about movies and music. He was widely loved, loyal to his friends and sought after for his company.

George told a story I only heard about in recent times through one of his colleagues. He had spent the night pissing it up about town after a gig, probably Something Happens (he was their biggest fan), and landed in Suesey Street nightclub. The place was crowded, and he got disoriented, putting his glass down on a table and forgetting where it was. He spent twenty minutes scouring the place for it.

He finally spotted it again, and with raised eyebrows and a theatrical 'Ah-haaaaa,' reached out and grabbed it. The next thing George saw was a large ring approaching his face at great speed. He woke up on his couch the following morning nursing a horrible hangover and a black eye.

Later, while having a cure, the hole in his evening was gleefully filled in by his *Herald* colleagues.

'You were trying to steal Mr Pussy's glass of champagne. He decked you.'

George loved to tell this story. It was a point of pride with him to be clocked by a drag queen, and it's one of the yarns his colleagues still recount, with boozed-up embellishment.

So did it really happen?

Yes, it did. But it was more of a slap than a punch.

Let's move on….

I continued to make new friends, and lose others through illness and old age in the early 2000s. The most significant loss was that of my mother in 2001. I still haven't recovered from her death, and never will. Mum's nagging was one of the chief reasons why I chose to become a female impersonator. Her constant haranguing in the morning used to drive me mad, forcing me to look at my life. When I was a wigmaker, I had to get the bus and the tube to work. I hated getting up in the morning. My dawn chorus wasn't twittering birds, it was a twattering old bird, Mum, yelling at me to get up and out of bed.

'Alan, get up out of bed. I'm not calling you again…. Alan, get up out of bed. I'm not calling you again…. Alan, get up out of bed. I'm not calling you again…. Alan, get up out of bed. I'm not calling you again….' Over and over and over again. I loved my bed, and sometimes Bobo the dog would snuggle up beside me and make it even more comfortable and harder to leave. I'd stick my foot out from under the covers and stamp on the floor, pretending I was up.

'I'm uuuuuuup, Mum.' Then I'd fall back asleep.

Eventually, I said to myself, fuck this, I'm not wasting my life getting out of bed for a poxy job. I want glamour and mischief. That's why I was determined to go into show business. The artistic temperament was there, anyway. Mum took me to the cinema at least twice a week, and I would come home and play out the roles I had seen on screen. I loved Old Mother Riley, played by Arthur Towle until his death in 1954. Arthur met and married Kitty McShane in Ireland in 1913, and they formed one of the most popular double acts of their day. He changed his name to Lucan, and Mother Riley was born in Dublin. He influenced everybody, including a young Danny La Rue. Isn't it extraordinary that all the great drag acts were either born here or of Irish descent? Danny, Paul O'Grady, Jimmy O'Dea, Jack Cruise, Panti … it's no wonder I ended up in Ireland.

I didn't go so far as to dress up as Old Mother Riley when I was a boy, but Arthur's performances made an impact. I did dress up as Tony Curtis though, first as a prince, then as a male/female musician. I vividly remember seeing Curtis playing the Black Shield of Falworth, and spending the next two days buckling swashes all over the house. Curtis's role as Josephine in *Some Like it Hot* had a profound effect on me. He was believable, gorgeous and hilarious as a woman, opposite Jack Lemmon and Marilyn Monroe. I wanted to be like him.

I met him once when I was flying from Dublin to London to go to Paul O'Grady's show. Tony was with his wife in the seat in front of me. They were all over each other like lovebirds. He was very old, completely bald and overweight at this stage, but still had that Curtis twinkle. I spent half the journey looking behind his ears for surgery scars. I didn't find any, by the way. Eventually we got talking, and I thanked him for all the lovely memories he had given me.

He was very sweet. I helped his wife with the bags, and left him waiting for his wheelchair and feeling grateful for having had the chance to shake his hand, and also a bit sad that time had caught up with my once-beautiful hero.

I did the famous Marilyn walk/wiggle as my friend and I headed to the baggage carousel. He didn't get it—he was in his late twenties. I couldn't believe that someone hadn't heard of *Some Like it Hot*, or of Tony Curtis. Times move on, and great stars are forgotten and grow old, fat and bald. That's the sad reality.

So how do I still look so good? I sleep well, eat well and walk a lot. (Not at the same time.) I make a lot of stews and love steak and salads. I don't go in for macrobiotic diets or any of that crap. Moderation is the key, and drinking lots of water to keep the skin supple. I drink green tea and take vitamin tablets too. That said, if anybody in my business tells you that they look young because of water and green tea, they're lying.

My secret is Dr Patrick Treacy of the Ailesbury Clinic. St Patrick banished the snakes from Ireland; Dr Patrick banished my wrinkles. He is the best in the business, and has done some of the world's top names, including Michael Jackson. His botox and fillers keep me looking young. That's not vanity, by the way. It's my job to look feminine, and younger than I am. Who wants to watch a drag queen with a face like an old saddlebag?

You'll have gleaned from that last sentence that I haven't retired yet. I don't think I could. I'm in 'semi-retirement', doing the odd charity gig here and there. I have osteoarthritis in my neck and the base of my spine. I can't bounce about on stage like I used to, and now wear kitten heels instead of Pussy Boots. My eyesight is dodgy too. Graham has to read menus for me. I hate wearing contact lenses, and often forget to put them in.

I've been playing Pussy for almost fifty years. I sometimes wonder how much of me is Mr Pussy, and how much of her is

Alan Amsby. If I were to put a percentage on it, I would say 35 per cent Pussy, 65 per cent Alan. I can do and say things as Pussy that I wouldn't dare do as myself. I'm actually quite shy and reserved. She is most definitely not. I put on the eyelashes, and she appears. I don't talk to her and see her as an actual person. I'm not mental. It's an act, albeit it one I love. I wouldn't still be doing it if I didn't.

It's a bit like being a barrister. You pull on your wig and gown, and say the most inflammatory things to people while 'in character'. Then you disrobe and go for a cup of tea. That's the best analogy I can come up with.

I remember I was once booked to do a show in Sides nightclub. I wasn't in great form, and didn't really want to do it. You have nights like that. For some reason there was a motorbike in the reception area. I can't remember why. It was probably just on display for the night. Someone dared me to enter the auditorium on it. I perked up. Or rather, Pussy did. I entered on the back of the Harley, and the crowd went wild. I played a blinder that night. I would never dream of doing that, but Mr Pussy would.

Still, it's nice to know that if I finally do retire, I'll be leaving the drag scene in exceptionally capable—and beautiful—hands. I've watched Ireland's drag princesses grow over the years. They call me Auntie Pussy, and I like to think of them as my nephews. They are wonderful to me, and it makes me proud to see their resilience, building up a thriving circuit since Shirley Temple Bar first started doing bingo in the George. There's Davina, Dolly Grip, Veda, and the lovely Bunny. I'm not going to namecheck everybody here—I'm too afraid I'll miss someone.

The queen of my drag babies is superstar Panti Bliss. Rory O'Neill became a symbol for the changes that modern Ireland has gone through, and was the Yes campaign's icon. That's not intended to place David Norris in the backseat. It's just that Rory became synonymous with the marriage debate. Ireland can be very proud of him. I certainly am, and am delighted to call him a friend.

When I started my career in 1969/1970, I was ground-breaking and daring. It may seem immodest to say that, but it's true. Ireland had never seen an act like mine before. I was a pioneer, and I like to think that Mr Pussy softened Irish attitudes to gay men. The audience was laughing with me, while my character laughed at them. We were all in on the joke.

Today, acts like mine are commonplace—although people tell me there's still only one Mr Pussy. Most major towns have their own drag acts. It's wonderful to think that I played my little part in creating a more tolerant society.

I'm not relinquishing my crown to the younger generation yet, though. I'm still full of energy, and would love to do more charity shows if the arthritis allows me. I'm still a kitten at heart, and love a good night out until the wee hours or dawn. I never go home before I visit Lillie's Bordello to chat with my mate Jean. The owner, Oliver Hughes, died very young this year. He was a lovely man.

Which brings me back to subject of mortality, and the friends who have now left me.

I'm surrounded by ghosts as I sit here in Drumcondra. Real ghosts as well as memories. My house dates from 1830, and is haunted. There's an area at the top of the stairs where it is always cold. I can hear voices whispering behind the door of one of the bedrooms. I'm not making that up! Some people might not like the idea of living in an old house, alone, with spooks, but I'm used to it.

Sometimes I feel sorry for them. I've probably scared the crap out of them, coming in pissed and shouting, 'Shut the fuck up with that whispering, you silly cows!' They leave me be, and I ignore them. The whispering has quietened down a lot since I got my priest friend from New York, David Byrne, to bless the house.

The other David Byrne has Talking Heads. My David has Talking Ghosts. There's a gag in there somewhere.

When I moved into the house, I found a picture in the attic of a priest. It was taken sometime in the 1920s. He's a very good-looking chap. Paul O'Grady fell in love with the snap when I showed it to him. I had to send him a copy. I have the mysterious Father X up on the wall by my front door so I can look at him every time I go out. I don't think it's him haunting the place, but I wouldn't mind if it was. He has a kind face.

I've lost many friends since the millennium, including my beloved David Gordon and Paul's Brendan Murphy. I also lost my best friend since childhood, Derek Banks. I knew him from the age of fifteen, and we used to go to go to the Cricketer's pub together. He was eighteen, and determined to be a hairdresser. He did his apprenticeship and became one of the top stylists in England, doing Fergie's mum's barnet, among other notable heads.

He used to look after my wigs and help me before shows. Despite living abroad, we kept in touch and used to visit each other. Like all true old friends, we could always pick up the conversation where we had left it months before. Derek shared my teenage years: all the pain, laughter, heartaches and hormones.

He was planning to come over and see me in Dublin, just at the start of the millennium. He bought his ticket and headed off to spend the morning in work. He was waiting for the bus when he suddenly took ill. He was persuaded to go to hospital, and they ran the usual checks, but missed a blood clot.

Derek died that evening.

He didn't know what hit him. I still think of all the fun we could have had as two old lads, and all the memories we could have shared in our dotage. His mum, Violet, was devastated, as was I. His sister sent me over pictures, and he now adorns my piano, one of the Missing Thirty I mentioned at the start of this chapter.

He's up there with my lovely dogs, Lily and Danny. Their ashes are in a box beside him. I hope he's not allergic to dogs. I don't want ghostly sneezing added to the ghostly whispers I already have to contend with.

I live in a haunted house, so I'd be foolish to think there was no heaven. How can anyone prove there isn't? I wish my ghosts would bugger off up to it. I doubt that it's all harps and halos. I'd get bored with that quite quickly. And all the white robes. I like a splash of midnight blue, and pinks and reds. I prefer to think of heaven as London in the 1960s with all my mates around me. Mind you, a lot of my friends died young, so they might ask, 'Who's this old queen joining us now?' I think I'll take Doctor Patrick Treacy when I croak. I'll have him bumped off and shoved into the coffin with me. I'll need someone to do my botox.

My mum will be there of course. She really was a saintly woman. Not in a Holy Josephine kind of way. She'd read me the riot act if I painted her as saintly. She was just incredibly kind to everyone she met—and most of all to me. Between the upbringing, cinema trips, nagging, and watching her getting made up, I have a lot to thank my mum for in terms of my life and career. I always craved her love and pride, which was forthcoming by the lorryload.

That lorry broke down in 2001. I had been over to see her as she wasn't feeling well: she had a chest infection. She was eighty-six, but still full of vim and vinegar. I brought her to the doctor's, and he gave her penicillin for what seemed like mild pneumonia. She had everybody around at her home, so I thought everything was fine. I kissed her and told her I'd phone her when I got home to Dublin.

I kept my word and called her as soon as I got in the door. My last words to her were, 'It was a bumpy flight, Mum.'

The next morning my phone rang. It was her neighbours. They hadn't been able to get into the house. They called the police, who broke the door down. Mum was sitting in her chair. She had passed away in her sleep.

My cousins said it was a good way to go. It could have been worse: she could have got Alzheimer's. I know they meant well, but there was no consoling me. I adored my mum. I can't describe the feeling of loneliness I now feel as I'm telling you this. I had no brothers or sisters. There was just Mum and me.

My mate Bernie travelled over to London with me. I went into the living room, and there was a photo on the table of me, aged three, holding Mum's hand. It hadn't been there the previous day when I left her. It was her favourite picture. She had obviously rooted it out and was looking at me right up to the end.

The funeral was a blur. I can't remember everybody who attended it. David Byrne officiated. Derek was there, as was George Logan's sister, Jennifer Scott. George was the Hinge in Hinge and Bracket, and an old friend since the 1960s. Jennifer came with Paul O'Grady, who was my backbone that day.

Danny La Rue sent flowers with a lovely note … which one of my relations took as a souvenir.

I placed the photo she left on the table in her coffin. I wanted her to know I was still with her. She is still with me. I have a photo of her on my piano, and every time I go out I give it a kiss.

I hear her talking to me, saying, 'Keep that chest warm. I don't want you getting pneumonia again,' and, 'He looks well, my son, doesn't he?'

I'm going to curl up and take a snooze by the fire now, in front of that photograph. Just a short one. I'm going to dream of Mum and Dad, and Swinging London. Later, I'll put on my best suit and head out on the tiles.

This pussy cat has several lives left.

Afterword

by *David Kenny*

It's mid November, and I am in Bruxelles pub on Harry Street. Jon Kenny is standing on the bar, gurning and singing a ferocious, aggressively camp version of 'We are the Champions'. His D'Unbelievables co-star, Pat Shortt, is giggling beside me, his magnificent gnashers neater than a row of your granny's best crockery. (Shortt definitely has the best teeth in the business.) Dermott Hayes, doyen of all Dublin Diarists, has pushed his trilby to the back of his crown and is making mental notes—his *Herald* deadline is only hours away. It's the eve of the MTV Awards in Dublin, and the city is buzzing with sightings of Bono, Mariah Carey, Iggy Pop, Mick Jagger, Whitney Houston…. It's 1999, and Dublin is partying like it's, well, 1999.

In the middle of this buffoonery is a man in a beautifully cut three-piece suit. He stands out like a kitten at a greyhound track. Alan Amsby is the fulcrum around which the evening rotates. We are surrounded by celebrities and wannabes, stars and comets (and a black hole: me). Of all the famous people in that bar, Mr Pussy is the person everyone wants to talk to. He is one of those rare show business creatures who have been afforded legendary status long before their time. Even by 1999, Alan had seen and done things that few could achieve in a lifetime, let alone in half a lifetime. He won't reveal his true age, but let's say he was in the early flush of middle age when I met him. I liked him immediately.

I am rummaging through my synapses here to recall that night in 1999, because, for me, it's an important bookmark in Ireland's social history. We had been a nation with a National Inferiority Complex. Younger readers won't have a clue what this means. To those of us over forty, that phrase is a reminder of how we were seen as a second-class country, looked down upon by Britain, while holding our caps out to Europe. The MTV Awards gave our capital the international 'hip' factor we had been craving. Euro '88 and Italia '90 did the spadework, as did our success in the Eurovision. We were always competitive, but we were becoming winners. In a few years we would lose the run of ourselves with the Celtic Tiger, but in 1999 we were full of hope. *Fin de siècle* Dublin was the coolest place on the planet.

Some more earnest readers will point out greater achievements in this period. Of course, having the MTV Awards here isn't on a par with the efforts to secure an IRA ceasefire, but I am referring to our national feel-good factor. We were feeling confident about ourselves—and morale is critical when it comes to nation building. That said, if you're earnest, why the hell did you buy this book?

Mr Pussy was one of my childhood comedy heroes. It may seem odd for a heterosexual, middle-aged man to have had a drag queen as one of his comedy heroes, but that's the way it is. Mr Pussy's appearance on *The Late Late Show* sometime in the late 1970s was the first occasion I can recall laughing out loud with my parents at someone on the TV. I was about eleven, but the shared laughter at Alan's mischievous antics made me feel like a grown-up. I hadn't a clue what the double entendres meant, but it was the delivery that made me belly laugh, along with seeing Mum and Dad chortling helplessly. I was laughing at them laughing. My sisters were in hysterics too. The cheeky, irreverent man/woman who was torturing Gay Byrne was an alien from another planet. He looked like a woman, and yet we knew he was a man. He was no panto dame with a hint of stubble or workman's boots beneath the hem of his dress. He was utterly believable—and more importantly, very funny.

He was different to anyone who had gone before. Old Mother Riley was slapstick gold; Danny La Rue made me giggle, but Amsby made me guffaw. He was shockingly funny: you never knew what was going to come out of his/her mouth.

That was a different country. Ireland is generally unshockable now. There are fewer boundaries to be pushed. It's a coarser country too. A week before I wrote these paragraphs *The Late Late Show* featured 1970s soft-rockers Smokey performing 'Living Next Door to Alice'. The audience sang 'Who the fuck is Alice?' during the chorus. It's a far cry from singing their greetings to relatives under the Gay Byrne regime: 'I'd like to "hello"/to Maisie from Raphoe" ', etc.

While comedy tastes change, Alan's act is still fresh. He was never just about being shocking. His gags were deftly delivered. He sent up his audience, while at the same time being in league with them. And this was at a time when homophobia was rife and being gay was an offence for which you could be imprisoned in Ireland. Yet here was a man stripping other men on stage. If he hadn't been dressed as a woman, he might have been lynched. Irishmen were not tactile in the 1970s. You barely hugged your dad, let alone allowed a bloke in a dress to strip you. It's testament to Alan's personality and great skill as a performer that he managed to walk this tightrope and thrive.

Where John Inman and Larry Grayson were gay stereotypes, Alan never traded on or exaggerated his sexuality. He didn't speak about it—not out of fear, but because he didn't think it was worth talking about. This book is the first time he's 'officially' come out.

Today, drag is mainstream and woven into the city's general entertainment scene. It may not have been so if Alan hadn't decided to make Ireland his home. He has influenced a generation of talented comedians like Panti Bliss. He's too modest to say that, so I'm saying it for him. I attempted, over and over again, to get Alan to take credit for the role, small or big, he has played in chipping away at homophobia. He fought me. Sometimes I felt like banging my head against the wall. At other times I felt like banging HIS head off the wall. He relented, and I've squeezed a few paragraphs out of him in which he highlights his contribution.

So what is he like? On stage as Mr Pussy, Alan loudly bubbles and fizzes like a bottle of Bollinger in a washing machine. When not in Pussy mode, he is shy, reserved, modest, funny-laconic, and very loveable. He is surprisingly homespun and traditional and courteous. He is also quite guarded and at pains not to hurt anyone's feelings. There is no score-settling here, and the only kiss-and-tell involves a quick snog with Danny La Rue. He is generous too, and goes out of his way to show gratitude for the breaks he has received.

There was a short period of trust-building at the start of this project. What seemed to be caution could have been frustrating for a biographer looking for juicy revelations and catty asides, but it wasn't. Alan is just a very, very nice man, and likes people. This is why he is still so universally loved himself. He is at home with lords and ladies, comic nobility, punters from Tallaght, Bono, Judy Garland....

When I met him in 1999 I was features editor at the *Herald*, and could smell a yarn. Over pints, I suggested committing his life story to paper. It took fifteen years finally to get him in the right frame of mind to do his book. I floated the idea with New Island, who I've worked with several times over the past two decades. Edwin Higel 'got it' straight away. His enthusiasm for the project made the collaboration seem like the perfect fit, which it was.

'It can't just be a series of anecdotes. It must reflect the changes Ireland has gone through in terms of homosexuality too,' he said with his trademark mixture of mischief and Teutonic efficiency. This, thankfully, is what Alan and I wanted too. We never wanted the social history to overshadow the man's story. Alan is not an activist; he's an entertainer. Like many straight people, I knew little about the struggle that community endured just to be treated as equal members of society. Writing this book was an education for me, and I felt both shame and anger when I researched the violent homophobia of the early 1980s. I think we have struck the right balance between light and dark here.

We agreed to do this memoir as a double act. He would supply the material, and I would write a book in his voice, fleshing out details and researching as I went along. I'm pulling the ghostwriting curtain aside with this afterword to say that while there are two names on the title page, this is Alan's voice.

Mr Pussy was written over seven months from March to October 2016. I met Alan twice a week in The Front Door bistro on Dame Street (thank you, Shane and Kelly, for the coffee). It was one long interview, not necessarily all done in chronological order. Alan has a phenomenal memory for people, dates and places, but understandably we wandered off all over the shop most of the time. My job was to piece together the jigsaw of his life. The challenge, as ghostwriter, was to keep asking myself: *what would Alan say here?* Over the course of doing this book, I have learned to second-guess him. For example, we were discussing a name change for his old headmistress, and both said 'Mrs McGregor' together. I haven't a clue where the name came from. I have also, correctly, predicted his dinner menu on at least one occasion. There are other, equally banal, examples too.

It's been a hugely enjoyable experience for me. I never thought, at forty-something (if he can lie about his age, so can I) I'd end up inhabiting the head of an Empress of Drag. I have started to call people 'darling', which is causing some discomfort among my mates. Lads, I'm not considering a career change. Please let me back into the pub.

Although Alan is in semi-retirement, I hope this book places him back in the limelight where he belongs. He's an extraordinary man, and I'm very proud to call him my friend.

I would like to thank the following for all their assistance, vision and forbearance. Firstly, my wife, Gillian Carroll, who gets angry with me calling her 'long-suffering', although she is. Thank you for putting up with me not getting a real job. You're wonderful, kind and generous, and I love you. Thank you also to Dan Bolger (you're a star, Dan!), Edwin Higel, Hannah Shorten, Michael Darcy and Aisling Glynn at New Island. Most of all, thank you to Justin Corfield for your preternatural patience and editorial skills. And for pointing out that there are a lot of gay Bond villains. We'll do a book on that some day.

I'd like to namecheck my sisters, Niamh and Deirdre, and their other halves, Rory and Martin; my in-laws, Paul and Carmel Carroll and Sophy, Dominick, Ben and Amelie Lewis; also Joe Garde. Well done, buddy, for your inspirational positivity. We're all very proud of you. You're looking great, as are Clio, Anna and Ruby. And to Gareth O'Connor and Daragh Redmond, keep bobbing along, old friends. Also, Tony, Sarah and Tim O'Donoghue. See you soon. And let's not forget Minnie and Noddy.

Finally, I'd like to dedicate my part in this book to my mum, Gráinne Kenny. You're a remarkable woman, Gráinne. Pass-remarkable too. And I love you.

Acknowledgements

Thank you to a special group of people. You didn't think we'd forget you, did you? Dan, Edwin, Justin, Hannah, Michael and the gang at New Island; Graham Murray, my constant companion and friend since the café days. Tony McCann, who doesn't look any different now to the way he looked forty-five years ago, and is still one of my closest friends. James Brown, for many a good night at his karaoke show and holidays together. Brendan and Eileen Grace, who I've known and loved since they got engaged several hundred years ago. Jim Harkins and Ian Fox, who have been together for fifty years. Helen Jordan for directing some great shows I've been in. Dr Patrick Treacy, for keeping me young. Wayne Sleep (for the trip home in a dustcart—you know what I'm talking about, Wayne). Noel Magner, for bringing me to Cork. Gerry Robinson, mates for years. Shay Healy (you were always a gentleman and a great help to me in my early days). Dave Morrissey, Jean and all the gang at Lillie's Bordello (where would I be without you?). The late Oliver Hughes (RIP).

Al Porter; Jim and Patricia McGettigan and family; John Traville, aka Crystal Clear; George Logan (of Hinge and Bracket); Jennifer Scott; Bil Keating; Alan McQuillan (Gaiety Theatre); Maureen and Jimmy Grant (Olympia); Robert and Rhona at the Trocadero. All the lovely staff at the wonderful 66 Restaurant; Dave Egan and family; Liam Carey, Shane Hughes, Kelly O'Keeffe and co at the

Front Door Bistro; Shirley Temple Bar, Veda, Davina, Dolly Grip, Bunny and all the Baby Drags; Yvonne Costelloe; Aidan Doyle; Larry Masterson; Richard Kavanagh; PJ Gibbons; *GCN Magazine*; Graham Staunton; Samantha and Barbara Mumba; Tina Courtney; Daniel and Majella O'Donnell; Gay and Kathleen Byrne; Pat Kenny; Aonghus McAnally; Mike Murphy; Gerry Ryan (RIP); the staff at the George, Panti Bar and the Front Lounge; Brady's Butchers; Boyle's Chemist; Tops for Pops; Gary Kavanagh; Miriam and Cecelia Ahern and family; Fr Brian D'Arcy; Baz; Anne Doyle and Dan McGrattan.

And finally, a very special thank you to Sean Mullen, my personal manager for the last number of years. Cheers, Sean.